Must Love
Fashion

By Deborah Garland

For my Mom, who set an example of strength and independence.

And my Husband, who didn't care about any of that.

And for my brother, Peter who left this world too soon. Your battles are over. You are now safe and forever in our hearts.

36°49.764 N
075°54.794 W

CHAPTER ONE

October
Prada U.S. Corporate Offices, New York City

Gwendolyn Foley tapped the toe of her left shoe...discretely, since it wasn't Prada.

Enrico Petrillo, Director of Operations, scanned her résumé and handed it to Salvatore Corella. The designer took her life's work in his hands, acting as if he had some place better to be at the moment.

Gwen's official job title at Starlight Elegance — a small fashion house specializing in exotic lingerie — had been Promotions Manager. She handled publicity and marketing, and scheduled pop up sales events all over the city. The company's dwindling resources slashed her PR budgets, forcing her to improvise for models. She quit when the owner suggested she attend an event wearing only a layer of black sheer fabric between customers' eyes and the skin she'd been born with.

But she didn't want this interview to be about hiring a colleague who desperately needed a job. She was tired of swimming in a small murky pond with big fish ideas that wouldn't have translated in the lingerie world. A prestigious fashion house like Prada would have been the next logical step for her career anyway.

She'd met Enrico last year during Fashion Week when Starlight had been given a tiny time slot to feature its spring line. Upon reading his *Must Love Fashion* ad, she felt comfortable emailing him directly. He had been eager to meet with her to discuss the Publicity and Marketing Executive position at Prada because he needed someone, fast.

"So Gwendolyn, what could you do for Prada that we have not already thought of?" Enrico asked leaning back in his chair.

Gwen confidently pitched her ideas. "I want to make sure *every* girl has at least one Prada label in her arsenal. I can see a campaign saying something like: 'Think about the one thing in

1

your closet you love the most.'" She flashed her hand like a banner in the air. "That *one* thing should be Prada."

Enrico's smile was charming. "Our Brand Manager will be pleased with your ideas. Andrew wouldn't mind if our brands were more...accessible."

Oh yes, Andrew Morgan. Tall, with hair the color of ink and expressive eyebrows to match. He was classically unforgettable, though quite *in*accessible at Fashion Week. But she'd been ecstatic to catch a glimpse of *the most handsome man behind the scenes at Prada.*

And boy did he live up to the hype. What Gwen remembered the most, however was how lost he'd looked.

She cleared her throat, and the thought of Andrew Morgan from her brain, to concentrate on this interview or she'd never get a chance to meet him. "And considering many Manhattan closets are no bigger than pantries, valuable real estate shouldn't be wasted on rayon and polyester, am I right?"

"What is in *your* closet?" Salvatore's thick accent would take some getting used to. Both he and Enrico enunciated their English, didn't speak in slang or contract many of their verbs; making every simple sentence sound formal and important.

"Ann Taylor, mostly," she answered. When Enrico pursed his lips, Gwen straightened her back and said, "Their wool trousers cost more than one hundred dollars." *Without a coupon.*

"What else?" Salvatore asked eyeing her cautiously.

"This and that." She was smart enough not to mention her favorite summer skirt from Target. People of average means were not expected to own Prada or its major competitors, Louis Vuitton and Gucci. That was what Gwen wanted to change. "The *one* thing in my closet right now is a Michael Kors dress."

"I hope you have a big enough closet for your new *Prada* clothing allowance." The director's accent was smooth and the words rolled off Enrico's tongue like Gwen was wading down a lazy river. He put his hand out to her and announced, "The job is yours if you want it, Gwendolyn."

It often took months to complete the hiring process with such high-profile companies. She was being fast tracked since Andrew had been in Milan for three months and a fashion show in L.A. was less than a month away. She signed her contract an hour later, and agreed to start the following Monday. A whole new life was waiting for her on the other side of the weekend.

As she gathered her portfolio and turned to leave, Enrico leaned in and asked her one final question. "But is it *Michael*, by Michael Kors?"

"Hey, Prada doesn't have a low cost line sold at Macy's," she said tugging at the *Simply Vera* blazer she'd bought at Kohl's.

It wasn't until she was back on the train going home that it all hit her. "I work at Prada!"

"Congratulations." The conductor was standing over her. "That'll be eighteen dollars."

The only downside was going to be the long daily commute to and from her house in Darling Cove, a hamlet on the North Fork of Long Island, where only a handful of people were stupid enough to live *and* work in Manhattan.

Starlight had allowed Gwen to telecommute. But even she knew it wasn't normal to go days without leaving the house or putting on makeup—or washing her hair. Everything about this new opportunity was going to make her life better. She could feel it.

With a smile, she handed over the cash to the conductor who quickly looked away. Her looks were often met with one of two reactions: complete salivation or frantic blinking followed by a head spinning around so fast it reminded her of the little possessed girl in *The Exorcist*.

An hour and forty minutes later Gwen hopped off the train. The air smelled of late harvesting grapes ready to burst off the branches in nearby vineyards. It's what she loved about living on the North Fork, a thin stretch of coast composed of unique glacial soil surrounded by the Long Island Sound and Atlantic Ocean. Darling Cove was one of the many small towns enriched by the wine industry, thanks to hot summer days and ocean breezes that float across the farms to keep the grapes cool and moist at night.

It was still warm enough to walk home. She was half-way there when a police car rolled up next to her. "Jaywalking is illegal ma'am," the officer said in a gruff voice.

"I'm on the sidewalk, Greg." She turned to her brother, covering her eyes from the sun's sharp angles. She loved this time of year for the long shadows and the trees in their full red and gold glory. "And who are you calling ma'am? You're five years older than me."

She got into his car and Greg handed her a package. "I caught the FedEx guy lurking around your house." Her brother thought everyone was either lurking or loitering or planning to lurk or thinking about loitering.

She'd suggest Greg get a girlfriend, but love was a taboo subject for him since his childhood sweetheart bolted out of town a few days before their wedding. It was Darling Cove's greatest scandal for a time. Until her dad, who was also a cop, bumped it off the top of the charts by shooting an illegal immigrant during a routine traffic stop.

"Thanks." Gwen was curious enough to tear into the sealed envelope right there in the cop car.

"Good news?" Greg asked.

"Depends." She shoved the stapled set of documents with a blue cover back into the envelope.

Looks like I'm getting a divorce.

* * * *

Same Day
Prada Group Headquarters, Milan, Italy

Andrew Morgan left his office carrying a purse discretely, since it wasn't Prada.

And it was *a purse*.

It was a Miu Miu prototype, and even though Prada was one big happy *famiglia*, the competing accessory lines operated like Interpol spies. He brought the white alligator bucket bag with braided saddle straps to the production floor with the Creative Director's notes and suggested alterations. The Production Manager cursed in Italian for several minutes and then looked at Andrew sheepishly. "*Scusa.*"

After being in Italy for three months training Marcello, the new Milan-based Brand Manager, Andrew was ready to go home to New York. His own job needed attention. The fashion show in Los Angeles would give him plenty to do and he was looking forward to long hours to keep his body busy and his mind occupied.

Ten steps from the production floor, a flurry of bodies rushed past him. *Must be five o'clock.* Andrew however left the building at a more measured pace, preferring to be unnoticed. At six-foot four-inches tall, that had always been a challenge.

A few blocks from his flat was the small plain church where he had lit dozens of candles, praying for his wife Cate's recovery. It seemed hypocritical to pass it by without stopping now she was gone.

Inside, the smell of perfumed smoke and varnished pews brought a rush of memories of the priest he met the day his wife had died. Andrew never expected to be a widower at thirty-eight. That only happened to older men. Those who sat on a park bench looking sullen and would say, *One day at a time,* when asked how they are.

Even after fifteen months, the memory of the young priest still sat in the back of Andrew's mind. For a man to dedicate his life to the service of religion at such an early age was a sacrifice that moved him. *'Soon Catherine will be with her king,'* Father Reilly had said, closing warm hands around Andrew's, which he knew were cold and clammy. They'd not warmed up very much since that day.

But it was time to move on…or so he'd been told. His mother had been the most vocal about it. She was such a force in his life that her opinions always resonated the loudest. Still, Andrew knew most people felt that way, and that he might be disappointing those closest to him.

After a final look around the small house of worship, he lit a candle, said a prayer and left.

His flat was moderately sized and simple. From the top floor, the view stretched out across the city to the River Ticino. After work, he'd pull up a chair and sit for hours; many nights skipping supper. The neighbor's black cat often sneaked in through his open window.

That night, the friendly feline rubbed his head beneath Andrew's chin, breaking him out of a trance. The purring sounded like a gentle humming engine.

Andrew tugged on soft ears. "I'm going home next week." His voice cracked; they were the first words he'd said in hours. Giving the cat a full body stroke, he asked, "Are you going to miss me?"

The cat sat back on his haunches and narrowed yellow eyes at him as if he'd understood perfectly. Which was impossible. Even if he had been taught to understand simple sentences, surely he'd been trained in Italian. Still, he looked put-off by the pending departure.

Andrew nodded off on the velvet sofa with his furry companion sprawled out on the rolled edge above him. Watching him. Watching over him.

Many hours later when Andrew awoke, the cat was gone. He was soaked in sweat, even though a cool breeze drifted in from the open window. The fresh air felt good in his lungs, but his body ached. He moved to close the window, and stopped. At two am the city had darkened enough to see the constellations above.

He'd spent many months wishing on Italian stars for Cate's recovery. There alone in the dark, he spotted one low hanging sparkle. The evening fog lit a halo around it. Andrew closed his eyes.

I'm ready to start my life over.

CHAPTER TWO

For her first day at Prada, Gwen chose the Michael Kors red coat dress with a shiny brass exposed zipper and sleeve adornments.

The dress was perfect for business executives to take her serious, while also reminding them she was a woman. She draped a coordinating scarf around her neck to hide the MK monikers, unsure if her new co-workers had a sense of humor. The elevator came to a shudder of a stop, she teemed with excitement, and gave the short skirt a tug. The doors opened, but all Gwen saw were empty desks.

She stepped into the open floor plan, alarmed. Walking to where she had signed her contract, she checked her phone and sat on a soft tufted bench. Patiently, she waited for the HR receptionist to show up.

Ninety minutes later, the clerk finally arrived. She sat, slurping at a Venti cup and pulled Gwen's file. "Yeah, we don't come in exactly at nine."

With several binders consisting of company policies, both New York and Milan's — she'd been told they were different — Gwen shuffled to Enrico's corner suite. He had streamed by earlier, encouraging her to meet him in his office when *'all of that administration stuff was taken care of'*. Thalia, his assistant, greeted Gwen with a pleasant smile. Long crystal blonde waves framed her pretty Northern Italian features.

"Gwendolyn!" Enrico stood behind an old-world walnut executive desk. Its intricately carved legs and patterned veneers suited someone of his European sophistication. "*Cara*, I'm so glad you are here. My Brand Manager is still in Milan. He will be back next week."

"You said in your email that Andrew had signed the endorsement contracts and that Salvatore has started interviewing models for the L.A. fashion show?"

"*Sì*. And now I need you to start working on the publicity for the show." Enrico led her out of his office while Thalia dutifully followed with Gwen's HR spoils. Several doors down, he stopped and fumbled with a set of keys.

"I'm getting my own office?" Gwen asked with a shiver of disbelief.

"Eh... In a way."

The door opened and a hint of musky cologne floated past her. Such an odd smell for an empty office. Except it wasn't empty at all. It was completely filled to the brim with binders, file folders and books. She turned to Enrico. "*This* is my office?"

"*Sì*. You will have to share with Andrew until we can find a better place for you."

"Um...Enrico, there's no place for me to sit." There was only one desk, and a messy one at that. Was she supposed to sit on Andrew's lap? His image in a frame drew her gaze. Ah yes, the beautiful man. *Oh all right.*

"I have a small writing desk on order for you. That should get you through until an office opens up."

Gwen eyed the large file cabinets she suspected weren't empty. The bookcases were filled with more binders, stacks of papers and small boxes. This wasn't the most ideal way to start a job. She'd already been told her position was sensitive, and that Andrew didn't even know she'd been hired to take over his PR responsibilities. Now he would be coming back to New York to find his job had changed *and* he had an office mate.

She stepped further inside and looked closer at the photo that had caught her eye. The man was so tall and striking she didn't even notice the frail blonde he was clutching on to. Holding up was more like it.

Enrico hovered at her shoulder and reached for the frame. "That is Andrew and his wife Cate. She passed away last year. Cancer. *Terribile.*

The word hit Gwen like a physical blow and the air in her lungs flew out so quickly she felt lightheaded. Cancer. *Just like her mother.*

"Andrew has not been the same. I'm ever hopeful that something or..." Enrico set his gaze on Gwen. "...someone will bring him back to us. The way he used to be."

It moved Gwen how much Enrico cared about this Andrew. Prada already felt like a family environment. Warm and caring. Those Italians and their *amore*.

"I will let you get started." Enrico placed the frame back in its original spot; his thumb brushing across Andrew. Her boss cleared his throat and said, "IT has a ticket to bring you a laptop computer and they will give you all of your log-ins."

"Thank you, Enrico." She closed the door and put her work bag down on Andrew's desk; assuming there *was* a desk under the pile of clutter.

She gingerly lifted a paper or two to see how many layers deep until there was an actual wood surface, but stopped when her scarf caught on her charm bracelets.

Needing more light to snap the frays free, she stepped to the window. It was as wide as the office and drenched the space with natural light. Past a few smaller buildings and structures in Riverside Park was the Hudson River. The sun sparkled off the calm current, filling her with the first sense of ease in several weeks.

"Not a bad view we have here, Andrew." Her grumbling stomach reminded her she'd missed breakfast. Activating her Yelp app, she hoped she could afford wherever it would lead her for lunch.

By Friday, Gwen had found publicity contacts and previous press releases from Andrew's confusing filing system for the L.A. fashion show.

He was due back on Monday, and now all these folders needed to be put away. Looking at the stack, Gwen panicked. She couldn't remember which cabinet drawer each had been plucked from. "Okay, okay, calm down. I'm not done with them, Andrew." She was practicing. He was already going to be pissed at this whole situation; a trashed office was only going to make him go postal. "And besides, I am in charge of publicity now, so I will put them away in my file cabinet. Whichever the hell that one was."

There was no point in leaving the office messier than she found it, however. She leaned across the desk to start organizing the folders. Pulling one out from under a tower of binders caused them all to slide down and crash into Andrew's framed photo. In horror, Gwen watched it shoot off the desk. The sound of shattering glass made her legs wobble. She crouched down to retrieve the frame and a sliver of glass nicked her finger.

"Ouch."

Thank goodness he wasn't back until next week. She tucked the mess under some papers on this desk. "Now I have to buy a frame."

Annoyed, she roughly draped her scarf around her neck and put on her coat. But those frayed edges once again caught on one of her charm bracelets and this time dragged the scarf through the arm hole.

"Son of a..." Her free hand reached up to loosen the scarf from her neck before it strangled her. But it snagged on the clasp of her necklace and twisted; trapping her as if she were in a straitjacket. "Are you *kidding* me?" she growled.

Furiously, she shrugged out of the coat, sending it flying across the office.

"Excuse me." A deep gravelly voice drifted in from the doorway.

Gwen swung around and locked eyes with the most devastatingly handsome man she'd ever seen. *Andrew!*

"Oh hi!" She held up her hand revealing the tangled mess she'd made of herself.

"Looks like you've gotten yourself tied up there." Andrew put his bag down and moved toward her with powerful long legs covered in what she knew had to be a pair of Prada dress slacks. In an instant, he was touching her hand and...her neck. "What's caught on what here?"

"I can do it." She backed away. It was startling to be so close to him. That photo did *not* do this man justice. He was even more stunning in person. He was so tall and broad. Heat radiated from his body; removing the chill that clung to her all week from the drafty window.

"I think you've done enough." Andrew snagged her wrist again. His commanding hold made her feel like Lois Lane when Superman rose up, caught her and said 'I've got you'.

To maintain her sanity, Gwen wiggled attempting to free her body from his grasp. "Really, I can fix this. I'll cut the scarf."

"That's just half your problem." He ran his large hands across both the scarf and the necklace. Lifting and twisting, he looked at her through dark carbon eyes with tiny flecks of silver that sparkled. "You may lose the necklace too."

"Why?" She struggled to breathe.

"It's hopelessly caught."

"Hopelessly…" she repeated softly. The power of his touch and the way he looked at her, she wanted to melt in a puddle at his feet.

He shook his head, like maybe he'd been caught in this moment too. "I…uh, have scissors in my desk." He leaned down to open the top drawer, but paused. "I did."

"Try that other drawer. I moved some things around." She pointed to the left pedestal.

Looking at her with curiosity, he squared his shoulders, lengthening a long torso. "*You* moved them." He bristled, but tugged her closer.

Men and their stuff.

"Yes. When I was looking for—"

"Who *are* you anyway?" His gaze swept over his desk. "And why are you even in my office?"

"Um…" *Huh, boy.* Enrico had had a week and apparently, still hadn't broken the news! This was going to be bad.

"Wait, are you one of my new interns?"

A thirty-five-year-old intern? "No. I'm your new PR Executive."

Andrew released her and stepped back. With his arms tight against his chest, he declared, "I don't need a PR person."

"Enrico hired me last week. We have a fashion show coming up." She made an attempt to fold her own arms and tone down her inability to tie a scarf around her neck, if she were to make him believe she could market a high-end fashion event.

"I know we have a show coming up."

"But there's been very little marketing, no events have been set up for that week, and the programs need… Where are you going?"

He rushed past her, only stopping to notice the broken frame sticking out from under a pile of papers. He slid it out. The photo of him and his wife was now under a spider web of cracks. Without looking at her, he stalked away and in the direction of Enrico's office.

"I was on my way out to replace that," she said and chased after him.

* * * *

"Andrew!" Enrico's eyes lit up with surprise and stood up at his desk. "We were not expecting you until Monday."

"I took an earlier flight back." Andrew glanced behind him. That woman had trailed along while trying to unravel herself. He grabbed a scissor from Enrico's desk caddy and thrust it at her. "Here."

"Who taught you how to hand someone a pair of scissors?" she challenged him with a disapproving frown. The tip and blade side was facing her.

"Gwendolyn, *cara* what have you done to yourself?" Enrico pointed.

"Just got a few things caught up." She grabbed the scissors from Andrew. Dangling them in her free hand, she attempted to slide her fingers through the handle.

"Oh, for goodness sake. Who taught you how to *use* scissors?" He took it from her and held her wrist, her pulse thundered beneath the surface. His thumb brushed against skin he wasn't expecting to be so soft, igniting a spark deep in his bones. It traveled through his body unravelling his thoughts.

With palms beginning to moisten, he picked through the row of charm bracelets to find the one that had snagged the scarf. The silver rings jingled softly, tickling a nerve inside him. He tucked the scissors under his arm and with his hands, ripped the scarf free. Her arm smacked forward into his chest. Long fingers lingered against his shirt. He swallowed nervously, watching her slide her hand away.

His gaze locked on her face, unable to let go. Who was this woman who could captivate him? So quickly, so easily, so fiercely. He'd not looked at another woman like this since...

The woman cleared her throat. "Thank you. I'll get it out of the necklace."

"Turn around," he said in a voice he hadn't used in years.

His command sent her blue eyes twitching, but she did what he asked, turning in a fluid and sexy swirl. There was so much hair, a sable waterfall. Her hands reached back, lifting the wild mane from her shoulders. Moving all that hair out of the way, released a scent he wasn't familiar with. In a bold move, he took the strands from her, grasping the bundle of silk and draped it across her right shoulder. With the back of her blouse fully exposed and the scissors in his hand, he had a wild desire to just slice the center seam to expose this creature. Only something unnatural could drive him to such a state in a short amount of time.

"Do you have it?" she whispered, twisting her neck so he could only see her pale lips.

"I see it." With the scissors back in his hand, he snipped a section of the scarf, and with his fingers, picked away the left over frays out of the necklace's clasp. Her neck was blazing hot. The skin was so fair, like this part of her body had been hidden from a man's view.

She slowly slid the scarf away and turned around. Her face was lost in confusion and he suspected his was as well. "Thank you." She looked at the scarf clenched tight in her fist, like the moment had struck her in the same way, and she couldn't bear to maintain eye contact.

Forcing away how she was making him feel—or he'd go insane—Andrew turned back to his boss. "So Enrico..." His voice was shaky. "What exactly is going on here?"

Enrico tilted his head, as if to say, *You tell me*. Instead he spoke to the woman.

"Gwendolyn, it's almost six. You should be going home. Enjoy your weekend, *cara*."

"Are you sure? I can...stay."

"No, we got it, *Gwendolyn*," Andrew interjected with a *let the men handle this* tone. He regretted it immediately when her soft smile faded and blue eyes narrowed at him.

"Thank you, *Enrico*," she said looking at his boss. "*You* have a good weekend as well."

She spun around and stalked away. The way she moved and the sway of her hips held his attention. But he was glad she was gone. Her hair smelled like a field of wild roses and it had been making his head fuzzy.

Clearing his mind, Andrew turned back to his boss; the man he worked with for ten years. The man who had said 'Anything you need, suono', in his time of despair. Enrico was a man with heart, often referring to him as 'son.' *Uh oh*. Enrico called her *cara*. Even Italian bosses don't call their female executives 'dear' anymore. Hopefully, he hadn't just insulted the man's niece.

"*Suono*, sit down." Enrico pointed to a guest chair in front of his desk.

"I was sitting on a plane for nine hours." Andrew folded his arms.

"You have been gone for three months—"

"I've been in Milan." He pointed to the two luggage cases sitting outside his office. "On an assignment you gave me."

"And while distributing your workload, it occurred to me that I had been drastically overworking you, *suono*." Enrico removed his glasses. "You can imagine how that made me feel, knowing those last few months before Cate…"

Andrew shook his head. He expected Enrico to assign his day to day tasks to others. But working with the Milan brands re-energized Andrew about his own work. "*Sì*, yes the position had gotten a little overwhelming. But being with Marcello forced me to hone a few of my processes that could help get our marketing campaigns out sooner." He opened a production binder sitting on Enrico's desk. "For example, even before the designers—"

Enrico reached across the desk and touched his shoulder. "I cannot wait to see what you have come up with. But it's late, you have been traveling." He straightened his spine, indicating he was about to be the boss. "Andrew, I hired Gwendolyn to run the PR side of your brands' strategies."

Press releases and dealing with the media gave him a stomach ache, but he'd still rejected every candidate's CV that Enrico had emailed him. Now that it was done however, a small sense of relief settled into Andrew's aching back from the long flight. "I'm sure someone else could do a better job at that than me. But you should have at least told me you went ahead and hired someone. I came here and found that…that woman in my office. What else—" Startled, he held his breath.

Every cubicle on the marketing floor was jammed with people and all the offices were occupied. *Oh God*, she'd have to work *in his office*. A woman who stung his pleasure sensors like a hornet. A woman he'd also just insulted.

"You are right." Enrico ran a hand through his silver hair. "I'm sorry I did not tell you beforehand."

"It's okay." He rested his hand on Enrico's shoulder. At least Prada didn't hire just anyone. This…Gwendolyn must have come from another prestigious design house.

"*Suono*, I know you and Gwendolyn will work well together. She is very smart and had a stellar résumé." Enrico pushed a few papers around on his desk. "Here. Salvatore approved of her as well."

I bet he did. Andrew looked over the CV. "Starlight Elegance?"

"Everyone has to start somewhere, *suono*." Enrico smirked.

Hmph. Andrew was surprised his own unorthodox *foot in the door* would be brought up after all this time. He handed the CV back to his boss. "Have a good weekend, Enrico."

"Get some rest Andrew. You and Gwendolyn have a lot of work to do."

He walked back to his office, frustrated. *Starlight Elegance.* Last year at Fashion Week, even he had blushed at the skimpy thongs and lace bras.

Andrew's heart raced wondering if any of that lace and satin was under Gwendolyn's clothes just now?

CHAPTER THREE

Andrew left Prada an hour later.

For Enrico's sake, he would try his best to make it work with Gwendolyn. Two porters were carrying a writing desk through the corridors headed for his office. But he'd already rearranged his desk to the way he had it before he left for Italy. Moving the mouse back to the right side of the monitor had given him pause. *She's a lefty.* That's why she couldn't manage the scissors.

Guilt crept through him. The email he sent to her before leaving the office probably came out harsher than it should have. He was tired, jet-lagged, hungry and annoyed. Annoyed at the situation. Annoyed that she'd been in his office all week, sitting in the chair where he took the call from Cate. 'It's bad, Drew. It's real bad', she had cried.

The two suitcases felt heavier with every flight of stairs he climbed to his apartment—a four-story walk up on Seventh Avenue South. He'd been living there for nearly a year, and it still didn't feel like home. The leave he'd taken from Prada in the last six months before Cate died had been unpaid. And mounting medical bills had almost crippled him financially. The precarious money situation, and being unable to look at the walls of the co-op he'd shared with her, had made the move to someplace new the right decision for him.

Initially, he set up the small one-bedroom apartment with just the bare essentials, using the only credit card that wasn't at its limit. But while he'd been away on various business trips, he'd returned home to find additional furniture—his mother's doing.

But the refrigerator looked like it belonged to someone who didn't spend a lot of time there, or someone who couldn't afford to eat. Andrew was somewhere in the middle. Even when he was home, it remained shockingly empty...aside from takeout boxes and plastic bowls. He'd never had to fill a refrigerator from scratch before. How much did a bottle of ketchup cost anyway? He'd gone from his parents' Fifth Avenue apartment to an NYU dormitory, to a series of rentals with roommates and finally,

Cate's fully furnished Upper East Side duplex. There had never been a need to purchase furniture or appliances.

He took a bottle of water out of his carry bag from the airport and sat at the small kitchen table. It was a little ugly, but at least it was his. So, this would be the furniture he would bring into his next relationship. He snorted. Was there a woman out there that would want or need any of this?

The idea of his *next relationship* startled him. Gwendolyn's piercing blue eyes hadn't left his mind. Sapphire blue…yes that was the color. Like the ocean, wide and deep. He'd spent the better part of the last hour trying to place the color of her eyes.

He wasn't planning to stay celibate for the rest of his life. Cate had even told him to move on. 'Drew, you're a good man. Please find someone when you're ready. I don't want to leave this world knowing you'll be alone'. But Gwendolyn's long raven hair, dangling down her back, thick and shiny as satin, had ignited a physical reaction he wasn't expecting.

He'd always had a thing for blondes. There were plenty of brunettes and redheads he'd found attractive but he'd rarely been attracted *to* them. This had been a first. Plus, his work in the fashion industry had consistently put intensely thin women in his path. Gwendolyn had curves and…ample cleavage. The slit in her short kick-pleat wool skirt revealed toned muscular thighs when she walked. Thighs he could imagine wrapped around his hips and…

Jesus. How was he going to work in the same office with that woman if he already couldn't stop thinking about her?

* * * *

Gwen bounded down a set of metal stairs; the whoosh of the departing train propelling a gust of chilly air against her bare legs.

"Dad!" she huffed at the handsome older man waiting for her next to a police car. "That's misuse of state property."

They had the same dark blue eyes, and even though Martin Mallory had two other children, she noticed an extra sparkle when he looked at her. "I was in the neighborhood."

In a town less than seven square miles, *in the neighborhood* was never more than a few blocks away. Every day this past week Gwen felt gloriously anonymous among the millions of people in Manhattan. In Darling Cove, she felt on display; like everyone was watching her.

She cinched her jacket closed, thankful for the ride. It was still the fall, but soon there would be snow. And ice! The six block walk home to the waterfront in the winter may force her to do as her mechanic suggested and put that insane amount of money into the car she'd been neglecting. Money she didn't have.

"So, how's the new job?" Martin asked, backing out of the spot marked *Fire Zone*.

"So far..." It had been going well. And then Andrew showed up... now she wasn't so sure. That intense moment they shared would linger between them for some time. No, she wouldn't let him or his gorgeous face get in the way of excelling at her dream job. "It's great," she answered finally. "The energy in that office is so amazing."

"Does everyone speak Italian?"

"Some do, not everyone." She'd heard the velvet romantic language here and there. The staff was a combination of New Yorkers, Italians and a few job-swappers from Paris. It was as if Prada had tossed all its employees' names in a large bingo cage and reorganized the company by pulling names from the bin and then placing people on planes.

Moving to Italy was not something she'd protest over.

"And have you made friends?"

It was like she was still in kindergarten. The hassle of being the youngest. "It's only been a week, Dad, but so far everyone has been nice."

Except Andrew. *Nice* didn't really cover how he'd acted around her. He was the person she needed to work the closest with and he made her sizzle and sweat. This already had *complicated* written all over it.

Since Dan had walked out, Martin fretted over her living alone. But Gwen loved her house and refused to give it up. Even if it meant the horrific commute and long grinding days that made her look like she stepped out of a swirling vortex, rubbing dry, tired eyes.

"I see your brother installed those lights I suggested." Martin squinted pulling into her long driveway.

The bright obnoxious spotlights always made her expect to see a helicopter circling overhead and to hear attack dogs closing in. "Yes, all the bugs in the neighborhood are dead." She opened the car door. "I assume since you're on duty, you can't come in for a glass of wine?"

Martin smiled. "I'd love to, pumpkin, but I've got a few more hours to go." He'd taken mostly nightshifts since her mother died.

And now the family of the man Martin had shot and killed had filed a wrongful death suit. The man had fit the description of a person wanted for assaulting a minor, so when Martin asked for identification and the man reached under his seat, Martin's police training prompted him to shoot.

He'd been cleared by several investigators and not charged, but a cloud had settled over him. He preferred to keep hidden from the residents he'd been protecting for more than thirty years. Their icy stares filled him with shame for bringing a national tragedy into their beautiful wine-country paradise.

"If you want some company when you get off…" Gwen pointed to the house she and Dan purchased a few months before their wedding. "I'll be right here."

"Deal." He leaned forward and kissed her forehead. "Lock up behind you."

"Yes, sir." She dragged herself out of the warm car, a mist already coming off her lips. Her dad backed out of the driveway. She waved and turned around to go inside. The house, originally a cottage on the Great Peconic Bay, was once her dream come true.

She had fallen in love with it as a child when she and Faith Copeland—Greg's ex-fiancé had ridden their bikes to the waterfront. The older couple who had lived in the house before were always holding hands. Gwen thought the home was magic and the key ingredient to a happy ever after. Now it was the main reason she was drowning in debt.

Before Dan confessed that he was no longer in love with her, they'd hired a contractor to add a second bathroom. Her tiny home had become the place Dan's out of town relatives chose to enjoy the rocky shore line and rich warm sunsets on the Long Island Sound. Gwen had been running a bed and breakfast with one damn toilet! And the only reason Dan agreed to the second bathroom was because visiting nephews had been gloriously missing their target. Her spa-like bathroom looked like a porta-potty at an outdoor summer concert by the time visitors had packed up and left.

The crafty contractor they hired, however had exploded the project into a full dormer renovation. Somewhere in the process, Dan, who had originally agreed to everything with enthusiasm, lost complete interest. All the design decisions fell on her shoulders. The end result was breathtaking, however. It was the most beautiful Goddamn thing she'd ever seen. She couldn't believe it was the same house. Even the burn of having to scrape together an extra seven thousand dollars to replace the vinyl siding on the entire house — thanks to Bill's patch-and-match disaster — had been soothed. The dark charcoal shakes and stark white window moldings gave her house that beachy look found on the south shore in Amagansett and the Hamptons.

The day Dan rolled up on the newly paved driveway from one of his many business trips still made Gwen ache and stew at the same time. His eyes should have been wide with wonder at the magnificent home she had designed for him. Walking toward the house however, he wore that same indignant blank stare she hadn't recalled him being without for several months.

"Look!" She had been bursting with excitement.

"Yeah, it's great," he'd said, dropping his cold gaze back to his phone.

She tugged him toward the house, saying, "Come take a look inside. They finished the kitchen today."

But Dan's fingers tightened around her elbow. "Gwen, we have to talk."

A month later he'd moved out.

That was a year ago. Now Gwen sat in that kitchen alone with a half-eaten pizza and a bottle of wine. Her dad texted that he needed to work through the night. She suspected he hated being alone in an empty house too.

Dan had taken most of the furniture when he left. Some bean-counter's way of making the assets balance since she insisted on keeping the house. After Dan's reckoning, her dad and Greg brought over the small shit-brown loveseat from Martin's basement. She'd been poised to refuse it, but didn't want to tell her father it was where she and Dan first had sex.

If that weren't embarrassing enough, she didn't have enough money to furnish the brand new master suite and was sleeping in the spare bedroom with a mattress on the floor, like she was a meth-head.

Living pay-check to pay-check wasn't part of her idyllic childhood dream.

"Pay-check!" Gwen perked up and moved through the dark to find her laptop. The display lit an arc of blue light around her. "Let's see what my new take home pay will be."

Clicking through various screens to find the ADP app to see her pay-stub, she noticed a Prada icon on the bottom tool-bar.

She opened her work email and saw that the message on top was from Andrew Morgan. There was nothing in the subject line.

Oh boy.

Gwen was going to need to open a second bottle of wine.

CHAPTER FOUR

By Monday Gwen still hadn't responded to Andrew's message.

Email made it too easy to fire off a response in anger, knowing the person on the other end would walk away and think *I'll deal with that bullshit later.* Instead, she printed it out and made notes. The practical side that sometimes overshadowed her creative nature would have to deal with Andrew Morgan. In person.

Which was going to prove challenging. The man dripped with such raw masculine intensity, it was going to be hard to complete a sentence around him.

In addition to saying that he would go through his files and decide what to hand over, he said he would do this in his own time. He'd obviously found the mess she left behind.

Furthermore, he had made it clear that it was *his* office. He notified her that the writing desk had been delivered and that was where Enrico said she was to work...temporarily. But Andrew made a point to remind her that as Brand Manager he had a staff. Employees would often come to him with personal issues and to maintain their privacy he would need to close and lock his door for these sensitive meetings.

Gwen understood this office situation was going to inconvenience *him*. But his complete lack of empathy toward how this would affect *her*, a fellow exec who also had responsibilities, was just downright rude.

The locked door that morning sent Gwen over the edge. Fuming, she hunkered down in a nearby conference room with her laptop resting on her thighs. It was currently doubling as an audition studio to conduct the last round of model auditions for the L.A. fashion show.

Gwen spent all morning tucked into the corner trying to write a press release while listening to Salvatore's thick accent.

"Walk, turn, come back. Now do it again, with feeling. Is that all your hair? Extensions, she will need extensions."

To the next model with wild tresses, "That is way too much hair for the delicate frock she will be wearing."

Salvatore had not only softened since her interview and turned gracious, he became a relentless flirt. Smoothing his Northern Italian blond hair, he had welcomed her to the pastries and paninis laid out on the other side of the room. The photographers, assistants and stage director munched on the sandwiches and sweets. Yet the models eyed the table like it had been festering with poison.

In a fresh email, Gwen addressed the locked door situation:

> *Good Morning Andrew. I'm in the west conference room if you need me. Please let me know when I can get into the office. I'm starting the press releases and will need to access the files from the last show.*
> *Thank you.*

On a small plate, Gwen packed half a mozzarella and pesto panini, an assortment of olives and a tasty looking scone. Balancing everything on her lap, she unwrapped the sandwich and dragged the napkin across her legs. It hadn't hit her how starved she'd been until her watering mouth opened to take a scrumptious bite.

"Gwendolyn?" Andrew was standing over her.

She put the panini back on the plate. Wiping her hands on the napkin, she smiled. "Yes?"

"Why don't you come in and we can go over the press releases." Something told her Andrew wasn't the type to embrace a working lunch. But when she left the untouched plate on the metal chair, he pointed and said, "You're allowed to eat in my office."

Fearing intense hunger and low blood sugar may make her dizzy, she picked up the plate. "*Our* office," she mumbled under her breath.

"What?" Andrew turned back sharply.

She exhaled. "I'm sorry. It is *my* office too, right?"

He pursed his lips together and then smiled, showing perfectly straight white teeth above a plump lower lip. "Yes, it is. Just bear with me. I have to get used to it, that's all."

Before she could say anything else, his long legs carried him down the central corridor and she had to scurry to keep up. On the walls, sharp black-and-white photographs showcased Prada's most celebrated designs.

In the guest chair on the opposite side of Andrew's desk, she made herself as comfortable as she could, balancing her plate of food in her lap, with the laptop and the notes on a tiny side-table. The meeting table tucked into the corner hiding under a mound of crap would be a better place to work, but she would be stay silent about that. She considered it a small blessing that his phone rang as soon as they sat down, giving her an opportunity to take a few discrete mouthfuls of her panini. He began speaking perfect, fluent Italian and her jaw dropped, nearly spilling the food right out of her mouth.

She spun away to hide the mess. *Get it together, woman.* After a final fortifying swallow, she smoothly turned back around. Andrew was standing, looking for something on his desk. The way he lifted folders open and slid loose papers inside with long fingers, absent of any wiry knuckle hair, Gwen released a sigh. Damn, this man-made *filing* look hot and steamy.

All his movements were slow and measured, like a panther stalking his prey. Her eyes continued to wander… Sitting on one finger was a braided silver band. *He still wears his wedding ring.* "Sorry about that." Andrew patted his long torso looking for something.

You know what'll look good on you? The old joke made Gwen start coughing. *Me.*

"Are you all right?"

She covered her mouth and nodded, although swooning over a man who was still in love with his deceased wife was ridiculous. "Before we get started, Andrew, I wanted to say I'm very sorry about your wife." That was how she was raised. A kind word of acknowledgement had significant meaning to people who had lost a loved one. Ignoring it, or pretending it didn't happen meant a person was empty and shallow.

24

But Andrew's body froze and his lips curled into a shape that would suggest he has tasted something bad. "Excuse me?"

Uh oh. "Enrico told me what happened. I'm just letting you know that I'm very sorry. Cancer is—"

"Okay. That's kinda my personal business." His fists were tight and a vein in his neck was ready to pop. "But thank you, I appreciate the sentiment."

"I didn't mean to upset you." She released a sharp breath. "I just thought it would be rude to sit here, look you in the eyes..." As gorgeous as they were. "And not say something. That's all." She leaned her body against the back of the chair.

"You're right. Sorry. It's just that I haven't met many new people since..." He rolled his lips in, like just saying the words were difficult. "She was everything to me."

"Everything," Gwen repeated softly, watching him.

Andrew looked back with dark questioning eyes, but said nothing. He filled a room with his presence. To say a woman was everything to him...

She cleared the emotion from her throat. "Anyway, I've written some preliminary press releases. Can I see the event planning that went on at other shows to make sure I'm not missing anything?"

"Yeah." Andrew stood. God, was he tall. Folders, binders, accordion files, large brown envelopes and plastic Trapper-Keeper like zipped billfolds were pulled from the file cabinets she hadn't even been able to get to. One by one, they were all piled in front of her, some almost toppling to the ground before she caught them. In a matter of minutes, the desk was covered in papers, loose sticky notes and photographs. "Here, this is everything you need to create the media kits, write the press releases, and set up the interviews."

"That's a lot of paper Andrew." She began to organize the pile. "Ever hear of this thing called the computer?"

He tilted his head to the side and flattened his smile. "So, your computer skills went to good use at Starlight Elegance?"

Her eyelashes fluttered. "Excuse me?"

"I'm sorry. I just don't understand how a promotions person at a lingerie company—"

"I was the Promotions *Manager*. And Starlight had a *lot* of competition. There's a company out there called Victoria Secret. Didn't your wife ever buy anything from them?"

The blood drained away from Andrew's face, leaving a startled ghostly expression. Damn it! Gwen pushed the pile aside and waved her hands. "Andrew, listen I'm sorry. I didn't mean for that to sound…"

His large hands covered his face. According to Enrico he'd done this job by himself all these years. He'd never had to open up…like this. The messy office was a symbol of what he'd become. *Lost.* Just as Enrico had said.

Andrew rubbed one thick eyebrow, like she'd given him a headache, and said, "Please have everything completed before we go to L.A."

It was best to let him cool off. She slipped a few brief looks in his direction to see if he was watching her, hoping for another chance to apologize. But his cell phone rang. Looking at the screen he said, "I need to take this and I need to be alone."

She nodded. "Right. Sure."

He turned around sharply and spoke into his phone. "Mira, what is it?"

With the bundle in her arms, Gwen stood and stepped toward the door. Once she was in the corridor, it slammed behind her, sending a burst of air across her shoulders. Her long hair flew forward and around her face. She spit out a piece of hair that lodged inside her mouth. *And who might* Mira *be?*

"Oh, my gosh!" Thalia had been walking by and must have heard the commotion. "Let me help you with these."

Gwen gently released the pile. She had a feeling Andrew didn't label or date his documentation. "Thank you, Thalia."

"Come on." She shook her head in Andrew's direction. "Enrico is at Flagship for the rest of the day. You can sit in his office."

Walking by desks of people, Gwen brushed off reactions that were a mixture of smirks and smug chin lifting. She suspected many of the women salivated over Andrew and were jealous as hell of how close she would be working with him.

Heh. I just make it look fun.

* * * *

Andrew was sitting in his office Tuesday morning, with a model across from him crying hysterically, when Gwendolyn whirled in like a tornado.

"Sorry. Trains. Delays." She plopped a slate blue trench coat and a creamy white leather tote on her desk. "Let me get my laptop and I'll get out of your way."

Before she could fly out of the office, he stood. "Gwendolyn, wait."

She stopped and slowly turned around, a look of mild panic on her face. "Yes?"

He'd been too harsh on her yesterday. It was a low blow to drag Starlight Elegance into the conversation. He had planned to apologize as soon as she came in, but then the tall blonde model showed up. "This is Mira, she's going to be in the L.A. show."

"Oh! Hello." Gwendolyn sounded like he was showing her a puppy.

Andrew huffed. It was one of the reasons Mira was so upset. Feeling like an object. The scrutiny gets to models more than the starvation sometimes. She attempted to compose herself with a weak smile.

"Mira, look at Gwendolyn." Andrew spun her chair in that direction. "She's what? A size four?"

"Four?" Gwendolyn smoothed her black pencil skirt.

He winked, knowing that was probably wrong. But it didn't matter what size she actually was. Her figure was phenomenal. Perfectly proportioned. A nice change from the stick figures walking around. Her cheeks glowed with fresh skin; she was healthy. Full of life.

"So?" Mira whined.

"*So*, if she looks so good as a size four—"

Gwendolyn blinked feverishly at the *so good* comment.

He shook his head and continued, "Anyway Mira, *you* are not fat."

"You think you're fat?" Gwendolyn asked, sinking into the chair next to her. Her face was full of questions, as if they were speaking to a beautiful peacock who looked in the mirror and only saw a dirty city pigeon.

Mira threw up her hands. "I've put on a few ounces."

"Ounces?" Gwendolyn dropped her chin.

"Mira, it's fine. I promise you." Andrew placed his hand across his heart. Beating. Rapidly.

"Tell that to the *master*," she challenged and stood.

Gwendolyn's eyes trailed upward taking in Mira's impressive six-foot height. "Who's the master?"

"Salvatore," Andrew answered letting spite slip into his tone. He looked at Mira and said, "If he gives you an issue at all for the show, you come to me. Okay? I'm in charge here. Not him."

Mira ran long thin fingers down her neck. "Okay Andrew." Her eyes flitted to Gwendolyn. "Can I speak to you in private for a moment, please?"

"Oh yes. I was leaving," Gwendolyn said and walked back to the door.

But Andrew stepped in to block her path. "Actually, Gwendolyn and I have a lot of work to do."

Just ticking his cheek sent the message that he didn't want to be alone with Mira. After a slight nod, Gwendolyn inched back toward her desk. "Right. For the show. I'm in charge of publicity now. You want people at your show, don't you?"

The way Mira sized Gwendolyn up bothered Andrew. The hawkish look of disapproval given to him said, *I know what you like Andrew, and she's not it.* Still, she grabbed her Fendi wristlet and draped her fur trimmed vest over her long forearm. "I will see you in L.A. then, Andrew." She held out her hand to him.

He clasped her cold fingers out of politeness, gave her hand a quick squeeze and dropped it even quicker. "Sure thing."

Mira made a practiced turn and sashayed out of the office. Her movements were precise and robotic…and she had about as much appeal to him as one of Salvatore's hollow dress forms. How could he have ever been attracted to that kind of woman?

Gwendolyn watched her leave, smoothing her hands over her pencil skirt again. His eyes tracked the motion until she picked up on his stare.

She raised an eyebrow. "Does that happen often?"

He wasn't sure how to answer the question. Sure, models fled to his office for either comfort or a job. And in the past for a date or a meaningless hook-up.

Then he married Cate. The aggressive ones didn't respect his marriage, though. The idea of *that* starting up again made him queasy. A generic answer for Gwendolyn right now was best since she was watching him and he was getting uncomfortable. He put his hands in his pockets. "Sometimes."

"Let's make sure our calendars are linked so I will know in the future when to avoid the office. I find them...creepy."

"Find what creepy?"

"Models. *Runway* models."

A rush of heat slammed against his neck. "Uh, what...what about *male* models?"

Her body turned in his direction, her eyes regarding him. "I don't know. I don't have experience working with any. It's not like Starlight hired men to model their thongs."

His chest tightened, his eyes grazing across her body. *Is she wearing a thong right now?* He pulled on his tie. "That would be something to see."

"It's like anything else, there's always a double standard. The male models I see in ads are usually tall and really good looking." She stopped, her eyes sweeping up the entire length of his frame. "The whole androgynous thing done to women on the runway, doesn't do it for me."

"*Do* it for you," he said quietly, listening and thinking. At that moment, he wanted to tell her that *he* modeled at one time. She would never figure it out. He used the name Drew Michaels, when he did. Michael being his middle name. No one at Prada knew...except Enrico.

"But these models for the women's collections..." She leaned against her writing desk and began emptying contents of the tote bag, starting with a laptop. "If there were aliens watching us, I'm pretty sure they would look at models and say, *Never mind boys, some other planetoid species beat us to it. Let's see what's happening on Mars.*"

Andrew roared with laughter, grateful for the break in his self-inflicted tension. A girl with a sense of humor. No, not a girl. She was a woman. Mature. Smart. Confident. Sexy and…silly. He didn't think he would find that quality endearing. Pouty and annoyed had turned him on for years. He took a breath and said, "It's a battle I've been fighting since I got here. Trying to work with models that look more like the average human being."

"Except the average human being can't afford our clothes. Try making them less expensive, first."

It was not the response he was expecting. But he enjoyed the idea of healthy banter with Gwendolyn. He liked the way she talked; expressive, full of emotion. He approached her, anxious to see how far he could take this and said, "I have a better shot at sending down a model with two percent body fat than lowering our prices."

"You both have zero shot," Salvatore said from the doorway. He walked in all swagger and ego. "Hello Gwendolyn, how are you today?"

"Good. You?" She leaned on her desk, smiling. Her right leg bent. Like she was…enjoying the attention.

"I am much better now."

Really? But Andrew stepped back. Salvatore rarely set his sights on someone from the office. What did he want with Gwendolyn?

The same thing *he* did apparently. Andrew sucked in his breath so harshly, he began choking in his own saliva.

"Are you okay Andrew?" She moved quickly in his direction and laid a hand on his arm.

"Yes." His skin tingled from the touch of her fingers. So warm and comforting.

Human contact… It was remarkable how it could seem foreign after so long without it. But was it more than that?

Women hadn't stopped looking at Andrew. But, it was how he looked back. At first through happy married eyes, then through despair from caring for a sick wife and then heartache of a widower. Who was he now?

What did he want? *Who* did he want?

Gwendolyn's large blue eyes searched his face to make sure he was all right. Salvatore forgotten.

It was clear who and what he wanted...but was that wise?

CHAPTER FIVE

Andrew had been too quiet for Gwen's taste the last two days.

The interaction after Mira left their office were the last full sentences he had spoken to her. Things had been going so well between them, he'd been warm and friendly. What had cooled his heels?

Gwen tapped the end of her pen against a folder on her desk, almost hoping he'd look up and tell her to stop. *Tap Tap Tap.* Nothing.

A faint ding made her look at her laptop. Another email from Salvatore caused a small smile to form. Since she'd sought refuge in that conference room, he'd been acting as if she had been there to send a message. It was hard to tell if any of this charm he'd been pouring on was real. Did he think he needed to seduce a good PR strategy out of her? For the time being she was polite, even while turning down invitations for coffee or a drink after work. He was certainly handsome enough, but she wasn't interested.

If a strange man like that, all charisma and talk, came up to her in a bar, she wasn't sure she would want him, either.

Now if *Andrew* came up to her in a bar...

He was still quietly working at his desk, typing away at his laptop. What did those fingers feel like on bare skin? Soft, *wet* skin... *Stop it.*

He sat hunched, completely unaware of the mountain of mess around him. What the hell was his apartment like? In her mind's eye, she wandered past what she thought a typical man's apartment would look like. Simple kitchen, probably dishes in the sink. A plain living room, maybe a pop of color. Andrew *did* work in fashion. But...she swallowed. What about his bedroom? Was he a man who left an unmade, crumpled bed? His scent lingering on the sheets. Was he a man who didn't change those sheets often, even after several women have been in it?

Gwen put a hand over her mouth. *That* thought ignited a twinge under her skirt. And a man that good looking must have had his share of women between the sheets. Maybe he'd had more than one at a time to prevent a line from forming at his door.

Her eyes wandered to the picture frame on his desk, which she replaced earlier in the week. Did he still live in the apartment he shared with his wife?

And had he brought a woman home in the time he'd been alone?

Gwen looked down and sighed. This was getting her nowhere. Except frustrated as hell. She twisted her fingers; her palms were damp and she ached from being turned on thinking about Andrew Morgan. Not good. She had to work closely with him. Even once she was out of that office. It was best to keep things professional.

He was still just sitting there, typing away. She had emailed him ideas for the press releases two days ago, but he had yet to respond. She was in a holding pattern until then. There was no point in going to the art department if Andrew hadn't approved the copy.

Bored and restless, she stood and stepped to the window. Through its reflection, she could see Andrew still in his own little world. Her movements hadn't made him budge. To the right of his desk, boxes were piled up against the wall. In between the stacks were folders. It looked very unsteady, like she shouldn't go near it. Cautiously, she approached the boxes, anyway. Being closer, she was able to get a better look. They were labeled with other shows' dates and cities.

On top, was the last fashion show Prada did in L.A. *Bingo!* That was sure to have a chock-full of info she could use. She considered asking Andrew to help her. Some men liked doing things for women. But his body language at the moment told her he didn't want to be disturbed.

She removed one of the chairs from the table in the opposite corner — which was still covered in a mess of papers — and carried it to the stack. She slipped off her shoes and stood on the vinyl seat.

"What are you doing?" Andrew's deep voice startled her.

She turned quickly, flailing for something to keep her steady and nearly toppled off the chair. Andrew jumped from his seat to reach her, his large hands settling firmly on her waist. The hold made her feel like falling even more.

She gazed down, but he looked…mad. *Catch flies with honey, not vinegar*, her mother would say. "Thank you," she said smiling to get a reaction. Nothing. *Oh well*. The release of his grip made her able to speak again. "Um, I see that box up there is labeled with info from the last show we did in L.A. I wanted to look inside."

"There's nothing in there for you." When she crinkled a brow at him, he backpedaled, "I mean, there's nothing in there, publicity-wise."

"Okay, but this is my first really big show. I would still like to see what you've felt was so important that you kept it in a box for six years."

He huffed. "Fine, let me get it."

"I'm right here. I can reach it." She leaned forward and hooked her fingers under the box, which slid easily from its place at the top of the stack…until it caught on the one below it. The entire heap began to wobble and with her hands full, the only thing she could use to stop it from toppling over was her body.

The quick movement made her lose her footing again and her stomach did a little flip as she started to fall. Andrew lunged to catch her, sending them both crashing into the wall of stacked files and folders. They landed in a tangled heap on the floor; paper and publicity paraphernalia spilling all around them. Binders, fabric, brochures, wristbands, access cards—Andrew's entire career at Prada dumped out onto the floor around them.

Andrew was utterly still, although his strong hands were still clutching her protectively against him. The solid heat of his body beneath her, and her own body's instant reaction to it, made Gwen sit up with a start.

She pushed her hair out of her face with shaking hands and looked around at the mess. *I'm in so much trouble*.

Andrew said nothing and stood.

Trembling, not just from the fall, but from being so close to Andrew, Gwen got to her feet as well. In a low and somber voice, she said, "Andrew, I am so, so sorry. I will clean all of this up. Just go back to…doing whatever you were doing. You won't even hear me."

He stomped in the middle of the mess, his face even. *It's when they don't yell that you have to worry.* He grabbed the box that fell the farthest — the one marked "L.A." He picked it up and the sound of broken glass from inside meant Gwen may have destroyed something important. Oh crap!

"Here." He roughly shoved the box at her. "Can you work in the conference room for the rest of the day, please?" The lack of emotion in his voice sent a chill through her.

"Please, let me clean this up." She grabbed onto to his arm.

He wrenched away. "Don't touch me!"

She staggered back, feeling like she'd been slapped. "You know I didn't want this to happen."

"Just go."

Gwen slinked away with her head down. Again. This was becoming their narrative. She'd get somewhere with the man. Then crash. Either she'd say something he didn't like. Or touch something he didn't want her to. *Or* make him touch her. The tangled scarf, the unsteady chair… Each time, he sprang to her rescue and then vaulted away, even further.

It didn't even matter what was in that damn box anymore. She was too afraid to go through it now — seeing whatever trinket he'd decided to keep shattered because of her would break her heart.

This was supposed to be her dream job, but from day one nothing had gone as planned. She was hired behind Andrew's back and shoved into his office. He was a proud man who preferred to do his job, his way. Alone. He was also recovering from a terrible loss. She'd become too close to him and now he acted like touching her made his skin crawl.

Perhaps after this show, Gwen would see if Gucci was hiring.

* * * *

Andrew had lined the fallen boxes in front of the window, full of regret.

35

Enrico walked in an hour later holding the box marked "L.A." When his boss closed the door, Andrew grew even more concerned. He had acted abominably toward Gwendolyn. It would have been dumb of her not to go to the boss, so he decided to strike first. "Look, I know Gwendolyn must have said something to you. I'm just out of sorts."

"*Suono*, I know." Enrico's voice was calm. "Do you need some time off?"

"No!" shot from his lips. The last thing he wanted was more time to himself to think and wander the streets where every corner held some kind of memory of Cate. "I'll apologize. I was wrong."

"There is an open office on the designer floor. Gwendolyn has asked me if she can have it. I will have her desk moved out of here tonight." Enrico set the box down; it was clear he was annoyed.

"The designer floor?" A small twinge of panic swelled in Andrew's chest. Salvatore's fawning had been irritating to watch. The idea of Gwendolyn sitting near that man every day, made his teeth grind together.

Andrew had been trying to make sense of his own feelings. Watching her when she didn't realize it. Listening to her talk to others just so he could figure out who she really was. Meanwhile, Salvatore just stomped around trying to lure her into having lunch and drinks after work. The invitations were crude and demanding. *Women don't want to be dragged around by the hair anymore, Salvatore.*

"Andrew?" Enrico prodded him out of his thoughts.

"Let me talk to her first. I'll straighten this out. It would be a waste of time to make her move twice, when an office opens up on this floor. Plus, I've wanted to get out and visit some of the newer local retail stores. So we won't be in each other's way so much."

"You must understand, if she comes to me again..."

"Understood." Andrew made a fist against his heart. "I'll make this right."

While he was afraid he'd mess up trying to explain why she couldn't have an office to herself right now, he also didn't want to spend all weekend thinking about what he would say. Unfortunately, after searching the entire marketing floor and stalking the ladies room, it was clear Gwendolyn must have left for the weekend. If she were still here, he would have spotted her immediately. Her lush curves and long silky hair stood out against the sea of bland assistants and interns. His fists curled in frustration. An apology would have to wait.

Stepping into the evening air cooled his ears, which had been raging all afternoon. He drew a breath, raggedly sucking in the fresh crisp hint of pine and sweet seasonal nuts. The holidays were approaching. Last year had been miserable. And he didn't want to feel that way anymore.

With no one to rush home to, he crossed Eighth Avenue to walk all the way downtown. Passing the bar he'd heard others at Prada talk about, he turned back and gave into the urge for a beer. The border around the sidelights was tinged in amber and the crackled glass made the faces and bodies inside a little blurry. The silhouette of Gwendolyn's body however was unmistakable; she'd imprinted on his psyche and he would soon know her anywhere. Even though he still wanted to speak to her, he'd find someplace else to have a drink.

Andrew released the handle, letting the door close. But a group of men at a table in the corner were watching her. Pointing. Andrew knew how men looked at women they wanted. His chest pounded at the thought of one of those men…having her.

Enrico should have picked up on the apparent attraction Andrew couldn't seem to shake disguised as kindergarten hair-pulling. Sitting across from her every day, he'd been struggling to tamp down the excitement he got from just looking at her. His darkest fear however, was that he was just so damn horny and he would do something very stupid. And if she landed beneath him again, he wasn't sure he could control himself to not yank up her skirt and screw her right in the office.

A man in a business suit from the corner table strolled across the bar and seated himself next to her. An immediate feeling of rage soared through Andrew's body, forcing his hand back on the wooden handle. He yanked the door open with unnecessary force. He still hadn't figured out what he was going to say; he just wanted man away from her. Now.

Ignoring the looks he was used to getting, he strode across the planked floor to where Gwendolyn was sitting, ready to put a hand on her shoulder. Her sparkling blue eyes widened as her stare collided with his in the long mirror behind the bar.

Gwendolyn twisted around and small creases formed above her nose. "Andrew?" She looked around like she didn't believe he was real. "What are you doing here?"

"Can I talk you?" He turned a stern expression to the suit. Cheap; not Prada. "Alone."

After a stare of contempt followed by the once-over Andrew had come to expect because of his height, the man took his drink and slinked away from the bar.

Gwendolyn released a ragged breath. "Okay."

Relieved, he slid into the open stool next to her. "I want to apologize. To start, I want to make sure you know, you've done nothing wrong. I've just—"

"Do you want a drink?"

He blinked several times, curious she didn't let him finish apologizing. Most women would pounce on the opportunity to make a man grovel. It became clear as crystal to him right there...Gwendolyn wasn't like most women. "Yes."

He ordered a pint of Blue Moon from a woman behind the bar who attempted to flirt with him. Gwendolyn smirked into her wine glass, watching the whole exchange. With the beer in his grasp, he took an anxious sip, causing an embarrassing gag. He put the glass down to wipe his mouth.

"You don't put the orange in the beer?" she asked, her voice light and friendly. Long fingers, which he'd noticed were absent of any rings, flicked the fruit slice into the amber liquid. The silver charm bracelets lined up along her wrist clanged softly. Ever since he'd helped her detangle herself from that damn scarf, that jingle-jangle had been making him salivate like Pavlov's dog. "Now take a sip."

He did and smiled. "Yes, it does taste better this way. What are you drinking?"

"A Malbec." She swirled the dark burgundy puddle around in her glass. "It's not the best, but not bad for ten bucks."

"The next one is on me. And that one if you haven't paid."

She clinked his glass. "The guy you kicked off that stool paid for it."

CHAPTER SIX

The way Andrew smiled at Gwen made her toes tingle.

If it was possible, he wasn't very attractive when his shoulders were up around his ears. She liked him better this way, relaxed, sitting with his spine softened. One sip of beer was what he needed. She opened her mouth to say something to that effect but her phone lit up with a call.

Andrew looked at the screen and wrinkled his nose.

Holding up a finger, she said, "Yeah Greg?" She rolled her eyes. "I'm fine. I know I was supposed to be on the earlier train. Well, who told you to wait at the station? I know it's dark when I get there, but it's seven thirty." *I'm sorry*, she mouthed to Andrew. "There's a martial arts class that gets out at eight. The street is filled with people. It's for kids, Greg. I have to go. I'll talk to you later. Love you. Bye." She tapped the screen and turned back to Andrew. "Sorry."

"If that was a boyfriend, he sounds very protective of you."

Gwen dribbled her sip. "That was my brother."

"Oh!" His eyebrows dipped; he was so hot when he did that. "Older?"

She nodded, squeezing her glass. "Greg's not married, so he stalks me and my sister Skye. He was engaged a while ago to his childhood sweetheart. But…"

"But…what happened?" Andrew asked with sincere interest.

"A few days before the wedding she took off."

"Ouch."

"Yes, another great Mallory family scandal."

"Why Mallory?" A puzzled look fell upon his face.

"Mallory is my maiden name."

"You're *married*?" His eyes flew to her bare left hand.

The startled reaction confused her about how to answer a very simple question. Was. She. Married. "*Technically*, yes. I'm in the middle of a divorce." When Andrew's eyes fluttered and it seemed he was searching for something to say next, she explained further. "My husband Dan moved out about a year ago. He filed divorce papers recently, but I still have to sign them."

"Oh." Andrew looked down. If she didn't know any better, she would say he looked even more confused. This conversation could spin in the wrong direction very quickly.

Gwen took another sip of her wine and made direct eye contact. "Andrew, I'm very sorry I brought up your wife the other day."

He tried to jump in, but her hand instinctively went to his lips to shush him. As pink and full as they were, she wasn't expecting them to feel so…soft and moist. She lowered her hand immediately. "We have to get to know each other professionally before we begin to discuss anything to do with our personal lives. However, to level the playing field I will tell you that my husband moved out and left me with a house to pay for." The courts didn't give a damn that he'd just left. "Anyway, I need this job. I need the pay-check. And I'll do whatever *you* need me to do to make this working relationship successful."

"Gwendolyn, you're doing a great job."

"Really? I'm so excited about this fashion show. I want to make…someone like you proud."

"Someone like me?"

"Yes." She looked down. "You were right about Starlight not being very—"

"No, Gwendolyn. I'm sorry. That was completely out of line." His hand rested on hers.

"I just need you to trust that I can do this." The feel of his hand was making her jittery. She edged it away so she could pick up her phone.

Andrew's expression settled into a contemplative stare. He inched closer. "As long as we're talking about former employers, I'll tell you something about me that only Enrico knows."

Gwen's mouth was open the entire time she listened to him reveal his secret past as a male model. It wasn't hard to imagine. He was the perfect specimen of a man. Tall, broad shoulders, prominent cheek bones and full lips. "Is that why you asked me what I thought about male models?"

And if Starlight had designed male thongs and Andrew was one of her models…

"Self-consciously, yes. It's something…I'm proud of but also ashamed of at times."

"Being rewarded because you're tall and beautiful is—" She quickly looked away. *I just called him beautiful.* Licking her dry lips, she finished. "I mean…having someone think you're good enough to show off their clothes is nothing to be ashamed of."

"Thank you." His head had lowered but his dark eyes were glued to her.

"Thank you for confiding in me," she responded humbly. Her head was spinning and not because of the wine.

"We're a team, right?" Andrew had become a different person. He was speaking to her like…a friend. An entirely different side of the man had emerged.

"Absolutely." She clinked his glass again.

Andrew smoothed his tie and sat up straight. "Speaking of being a team, Enrico said you asked to be moved to an office on the designer floor."

Her cheeks blazed with heat. She'd almost forgotten about the request. So this was business. *Not* pleasure. She took a breath. "It's hard to share an office. No matter what the circumstances."

"I'd really rather you not sit on the designer floor."

She leaned in. "Why?"

"That floor is chaotic. *I* can't think straight when I'm down there."

"I think it's kind of fun. Lots of energy. It'll be like watching *Project Runway* every day, all day." She wiggled her shoulders, letting her passion show through. "I love the creative process. Seeing them take a bolt of fabric and with a few clips of the scissors and stabs of the sewing machine needle…voila! A dress. It's really quite fascinating." She paused and sat back, staring into her wine to avoid eye contact. "Besides, you can't like me being in your office"

"Actually, I do."

She looked up, startled by the confession.

He pressed his fingers together. "I thought it would be annoying. But you're pleasant enough to be around."

Pleasant enough… *Oh yeah, Mr. Morgan, talk dirty to me.* "I have to be honest though, the mess and clutter that I have to look at every day, is kind of getting to me."

"I'll work on that. I promise." He finished his beer and took out his wallet. "You're not going to be happy listening to Salvatore yell all day, trust me."

"Yeah, but it's mostly in Italian." Her finger nails scraped the bottom of the pretzel bowl. It was empty again and she was too embarrassed to ask for another refill.

"Thank goodness…I'm sure if it was English, we'd have dozens of lawsuits on our hands."

He was keeping her away from Salvatore to protect the company from a lawsuit. How very…*corporate* of him. She shrugged her shoulders. "Okay. At least until the fashion show, deal?"

"Deal." His lips agreed but his eyes said *maybe*.

Her phone buzzed and vibrated. It was Greg again. She dumped it in her bag. She didn't want him or her father to worry, but she was an adult. An adult who was allowed to go out after work and come home late.

Or…not at all.

Her wary eyes sneaked a glance at Andrew paying for his beer. A knot of emotion settled in her throat. How could a man be that handsome? His round, deep-set eyes were tipped by jet black lashes. Thick and expressive eyebrows curved down toward his roman nose. His fair skin was holding on to a few shades of a left over Italian summer tan. When he smiled, his square jaw tapered down to a round edge. Underneath, she could see the gentle curve of his throat. Soft skin she wanted to bite. *Gasp.* No. No. No. Hooking up with a co-worker was a bad idea. Especially one who she would have to sit across from every day for the foreseeable future. "Well, this was…fun. But I should get going." She slid off the seat and her head felt lighter than she had expected.

"I didn't realize it was this late." It was the first time Andrew had looked at his phone. Its glossy screen had stayed dark and silent the entire time they had been talking. "Are you okay to get home?"

"Sure. Sure," she answered, not looking at him, but checking the area around her for all her bags.

"Gwendolyn, do you want to share a cab?" His gesture was inviting but his voice was nervous and tentative. Like his instinct as a gentleman knee-jerked the offer. But then he thought better of it.

"Nah. I want to walk for a little bit," she said pulling her laptop bag over her shoulder. "And please, call me Gwen. I have a secret to laud over you now."

The way he smiled made her wonder if getting this man to soften up was such a good idea. What if he *did* want her? Would she have the resolve to say no?

He followed her out the door and bent his body into a bow. "Have a good weekend, *Gwen*."

She'd made so much progress, anything but a smile now might push her back. But an uncontrollable urge overpowered her to lean in and hug him. *God*, he felt so good. His body was so powerful. However, while she was hugging him, reveling in how good it felt, Andrew's body stiffened like a piece of plywood. *Uh oh.* She stepped back and looked down at the sidewalk. "You have a good one too. Bye."

Gwen sprinted away from Andrew as fast as she could, her high Prada heels wobbled with every repentant step.

* * * *

Andrew didn't move.

The feel of a woman's body, strong and healthy against his rendered him...immobile. Speechless. He'd been cold and mean to her these past couple of days, yet it came so easily to her to forgive and embrace him. She wasn't a petty person or a grudge-holder, and it elevated her in his mind.

And in his desires for her.

A cutting wind woke him out of the trance he'd been in. If he spent any more time standing outside the bar with a catatonic look on his face someone was certain to call the cops. He walked a few feet in the direction of his subway, but stopped and turned back toward the office.

Prada's marketing floor was quiet. He unlocked his office, stepped inside and closed the door behind him. *How* did *this office get so out of control?* Of course, he never thought he would be under a microscope. Shows were the priority, not cleaning out his office.

Andrew dropped his bag on the messy desk and put his hands on his hips. Enrico had mentioned there was an unoccupied office on the designer floor. He stepped back to go look and smacked into a body.

"Sir?" The startled voice with a Latin ring asked, "Is everything all right?"

"Yes. Yes." Andrew got his breath back, the white patch on a blue shirt caught his interest. *Maintenance.* "Is there a way you can give me a hand with something?"

"Of course, sir."

Andrew brought him down to the designer floor. Ah! Just what Andrew was hoping, a large office and a small desk. "Okay." He turned to the maintenance man. "What are the chances we can move this desk upstairs and move my desk down here?"

The man nodded his head and seemed eager to help. Andrew guessed he probably spends every Friday night sitting on a chair with nothing to do. In two hours, a team of porters had Andrew's old desk emptied, dissembled, brought down to the designer floor and reassembled. At the same time, another team took the smaller desk and did the reverse. When he tried to help, he was cheerfully dismissed. "No, no sir, we got it," one of the porters said.

While the desks were being switched, Andrew went through his file cabinets. In the staff lounge, he grabbed a box of large garbage bags. He'd been in his position long enough to know fabric samples from a fashion show six seasons back could be tossed. Several drawers which weren't even full were emptied without any stress. Two whole cabinets could be given to Gwen.

In his bookcases, fancy binders lined the first few shelves but the rest were filled with crap. He tossed the crap, consolidated the binders to one bookcase and gave one to Gwen as well.

By three am, there were six large black trash bags in the hall and the office had been transformed to a comfortable neat space with two desks on opposite corners. The walls were neatly lined with a combination of bookshelves and file cabinets. He wanted it to look perfect and even wiped all the furniture down with polish. Andrew was also able to dig out his round conference table from under a blanket of old newspapers. It would be a place where he and Gwen could sit together to have meetings.

The new space excited him, made him feel like he could be more productive. He'd been accumulating junk. And each year in the time-span between lines being released, there was always this pipedream he would have time to clean. But that never happened. Enrico used that down time to whisk Andrew all over the world.

Exhaustion had finally taken hold of him. He'd intended to walk earlier but now he would definitely take a taxi. On his final scan of the room, he spotted loose papers peeking out from under Gwen's desk. One of the porters must have knocked over the trash can. Andrew picked up the papers and crumbled them in his hand. A stiff card, one that did not bend like the other discarded papers, caused him to open his hand.

It was a small envelope. He unfolded it. The loopy handwriting that Andrew didn't recognize read: *Gwendolyn*.

Inside was a card that he would expect to accompany a floral arrangement. However, there were no flowers, remnants of dead leaves or traces of wet muck that accumulates at the bottom of a vase anywhere in the office or the trash. Curiosity and the desire to glimpse into Gwen's life was too powerful to ignore. Andrew's immediate guess was the soon-to-be-ex-husband. Maybe asking her to take him back. What idiot would *leave* her in the first place?

Standing next to the elevator, Andrew stared at the sloppy script, his heart pounding with anticipation. In the closed space of the car, he opened the envelope feeling like he was about to sneak up on her.

Andrew's eyes filled with rage taking in the words scrolled across the card. Nope, not the ex.

Think about it, bella- SC.

CHAPTER SEVEN

The bright sun stung Gwen's eyes Saturday morning.

Her hand blocked its rays as she peeked through her fingers to find her way to the coffee machine but stopped. The rich aroma already filled her kitchen.

"Good morning, sunshine!"

Gwen whirled around. "Jesus! Skye, don't do that!"

Her sister's blonde hair sparkled in the sunlight and there was a tinge of moisture on her shoulders and legs. "Sleeping in so late?"

"It is a Saturday." Gwen breathed in the steaming black silk heaven coming from her coffee maker. "How long have you been here?"

Skye returned to the rectangular wood breakfast table Gwen classified as *reclaimed* since she'd found it at a garage sale. "This is my second cup."

Her sister's Golden Retriever padded over to Gwen. A large tongue splashed across her face. "Hello Casey." The dog who now sat and began to scratch was always welcome in her home, even if the clumps of strawberry blonde fur she left behind were not.

"Hey Gwen, who's Andrew?"

The carafe slipped from her fingers and hot coffee trickled down the cabinets. "What are you talking about?"

"You were murmuring the name *Andrew* while you were sleeping." Skye unraveled several paper towels to clean the spill.

"I…I was?" Gwen dabbed her forehead, still moist with sweat. She'd woken with raging nipples and a throbbing between her legs. Yeah. She knew she'd been dreaming about him, but she'd had no idea she'd been calling out his name!

In the dream, they were back in the bar. Their conversation had played out as it had before. It was as if it were a movie and she was watching it. Standing outside herself. But whereas Andrew hadn't reacted to her hug; in Gwen's dream his hands gripped her shoulders and he hungrily kissed her. Those full pink lips were on hers and a warm tongue teased her mouth.

In another flash, they were in his office, *their* office where he'd thrown her on his messy desk shoving papers and folders aside. His free hand rummaged under her skirt. How real it felt, was what Gwen remembered. And how good it was. She'd been thrashing around, absorbing the desire from his long fingers sliding inside her. But her flailing hands smacked into the picture of Andrew and his wife. The glass sliced into her fingers, just as it had done in real life. The pain had felt as real as the pleasure.

"Earth to Gwen."

Rubbing a fingernail against the healed cut now, she looked up at her sister. "He's a guy I work with."

"That hot, huh?"

"You have no idea." Gwen draped her body against the cool marble of her countertop in an attempt to lower her body temperature.

"Tall?" When Gwen pressed her eyes closed and nodded like she was agreeing to an ice cream cone, Skye hissed with delight. "You like 'em tall. Which is why I have no idea what you saw in Dan. What else?"

Ignoring the dig on Dan's short stature, Gwen said if only to remind herself, "Andrew is completely off limits, so the rest of his features are irrelevant."

"Is there a no-romance policy at Prada?"

"Just the opposite. It's like a meat-market there."

"What's the problem?"

"Skye, I'm an executive now. I can't go home with a co-worker and then show up the next day in the same clothes." Although technically she had plenty of opportunity to get more clothes, nice ones if she did ever dare to do something like that. "You know that's not me. Or did you just meet me?"

"Hmph." Skye pouted, clearly annoyed she'd been denied more juicy details about Andrew.

"Anyway, I like the job. Thanks for asking about that."

"You must love fashion for you to haul your cookies all the way to the city every day."

"We can't all have a nice little law practice here in town." The coffee she drank too quickly was still hot and burned her lower lip. "And we didn't all go to Columbia."

"Gwen, you went to FIT."

"Yes, but I can't break out mom's old sewing machine and make clothes in my garage." Even if that were a viable option to make money, she had none of her mother's sewing abilities. New York City's Fashion Institute of Technology, however taught her valuable merchandising skills. Gwen stood to take her coffee back to her bedroom. There had been a fire burning beneath the surface of her skin moments ago, but now her body had cooled. "Are you done with your run, or on your way?"

"Taking a break, want to join me for the second half?" Skye mindlessly thumbed through a stack of papers on the counter.

"Yeah. I'll put on something more appropriate for running." Gwen had wandered into the kitchen wearing an extra small thong and a *Love Pink* tank top. One benefit of living alone.

"Yes, a jogging bra at least." Skye pulled out an appointment card from the heap. "Gwen, what's this?"

She snatched the reminder from her sister. "Nothing."

"Gwendolyn Mallory, this is two months past due." Skye put her hands on her hips. "Don't play games with this."

"Everyone is just being super cautious. Okay. I'm fine." Gwen refused to believe that just because her mother died of breast cancer, her path had been predetermined.

"But you're at risk."

"And so are you."

"*My* mammograms don't come back abnormal, Gwen."

* * * *

"Andrew Morgan," he answered his cell phone, all groggy with sleep.

"That's very formal for a Saturday."

"Hi, Ma." He rolled his lips in, thinking he was still at the office. But he was face down on his bed, still fully clothed. He'd been too exhausted to remove anything except his shoes at four am when he'd finally made it home. "What time is it?"

"It's almost noon."

"I got in late."

"Were you on a date?"

The notion startled him. *A date*. But the woman's face, who came to mind as soon as his mother said the words, unsettled him. "No, and please stop posting those inspirational greeting cards to my Facebook page."

"Have you had a chance to get out and meet anyone, my handsome boy?" His mother had always been 'damn proud' of the man he'd become; polite, good natured, smart and considerate. And handsome, she liked to boast. But that would be more her accomplishment than his.

"Not really." And last he checked he was a *man*. But he didn't mind that she wanted him to move on. "I've only been back a week and I have a fashion show coming up. I'll be even busier." He wandered into his kitchen and cursed at the few scattered grains of coffee at the bottom of the Café Bustelo can.

"Maybe someone at work?"

The metal container slipped from his hands and clanged against the ceramic tile floor, spilling what could have been at least one small cup of coffee. He pinched the bridge of his nose. "Ma, Cate passed away—"

"Two years ago."

"Fifteen months." He considered counting the months a step in the right direction toward letting go. It started with hours, then it was days, and then weeks... Soon it would be years. "I'm still—"

"You're too good a man to be alone. You gave all you had to that woman,"

"Ma, please don't start. Okay, you won. You got your wish, Cate is gone."

"For Pete's sake, I didn't want the woman to die! I just never thought she was right for you. And that business about her not wanting to have children—"

"Can you *please* stop bringing that up," he said feeling his throat closing.

"Andrew, I'm sorry. But I promise you, one day when you're a father...and you *will* be a father someday Mr. Morgan, you will know that one ounce of your child's heartache will be like a grand sword slicing through your own heart."

"Ma, stop binge watching *Game of Thrones*." But he did release a small whisper of laughter.

"I'm onto *Outlander* now."

"Great. I'm getting a kilt for Christmas, I know it."

Mercifully, Sarah changed the subject to gossip in her Fifth Avenue building and he was happy to listen while he put on workout shorts and a tee-shirt. But before he was able to get a sock on, his mother interrupted herself and said, "Your father's calling me from the golf course. Bye, love you!"

"Love you too." It struck Andrew how good that felt to say out loud.

He sat on the edge of his bed, and took a few breaths.

On his nightstand was the large brown envelope he had recently received from Cate's sister. Apparently, his wife had tucked away some racy honeymoon photos in several of the books he let Julia take. His friends had been divided when he had announced he was marrying the woman he'd only known six months. All the photos from that trip to Paris were postcards from happy ever after. All Andrew was left with now was...after.

A hat box with other photos from their life and his past sat on the top shelf of his closet; he would slip these in the box and like the others not look back. Andrew thumbed through his junk mail inside the package until he got to his *GQ* magazine. No matter how many emails he sent, it was still being sent to Julia. The subscription had been a gift from Cate their last Christmas together. Behind the mag was another publication. "Great." Andrew gripped the Victoria Secret catalogue. It was in his name because he made the mistake of placing an order *once*. Gwen had asked if Cate had ever bought anything, but it was him!

Alone in his quiet kitchen, he pawed at the thick glossy catalogue. The cover model—a striking brunette, caught his eye. Her long wavy sable hair called out to him like a mountain begging to be climbed and conquered. He shifted in his seat while peeking at the pages. He found the model again and again but one image stuck in his mind. She was in a thong, covering her bare breasts and flashing a sneaky smile.

It reminded him so much of Gwen.

He stirred in his chair from the swelling in his groin that was starting to accompany thinking of her. It wasn't the first stimulation he'd felt since Cate passed, but his daily arousals were more mechanical than sexual. Until Gwen. Her smooth sensual glides through the office, blended with her quirkiness, had captured his attention and wouldn't let go. He let his mind wander a little further, imagining how she would feel writhing beneath him. He blew out his breath.

Getting involved with a co-worker had always been on Andrew's *to-don't* list.

CHAPTER EIGHT

An envelope was taped to Gwen's office door on Monday morning.

She shifted her workbag, her purse and a small lunch cooler to one arm. Balancing the pile, she tore the envelope down and lifted the flap. A jingling sound from inside intrigued her. Inside were two sparkling silver keys on a small, round wire fastener.

All her bags tipped to the side and began to fall. She managed to catch the laptop case by the strap, but the rest went flying. "Son of a—"

"Ciao, *bella.*" Salvatore's accented voice was as rocky as the shoreline behind her house.

"Oh, hi." Gwen let him pick up her bags.

The keys were cool in her hand, as she slid one into the keyway. With a slight turn of the handle, the door swung open. She froze for a moment. Holy crap!

On Friday, she had left an office that looked like a tornado had struck. There were still two desks, but now hers didn't look like the dinghy floating behind a crowded yacht. Behind her desk were two bookcases and to the right along the wall before the window sat a file cabinet.

"I see you redecorated," Salvatore said, dumping her bags on the desk.

The windowsill had been cleaned and dusted off. Before, it was a sloppy depository for old, fashion programs. Now, it was lined with Andrew's travel trinkets and in the center, the small violet plant she had brought with her. On her first day, she'd crammed it into the few inches of available space to catch a hint of sunlight. Now, it sat front and center, soaking up the rays streaming in from the clean windows. He had *cleaned* the windows!

She was fingering the plant's velvety leaf when the reflection changed from the city view to Andrew's hunky body in the open doorway. Gwen spun around to face him. "Did you do this?"

He was holding a tray with two coffees, his canvas workbag slung across his broad chest. "Yes," he replied coolly and put the coffees down. "Good morning, Salvatore. Can I help you with something?"

"No, no. I was helping Gwendolyn."

"Really? With what?"

"He just grabbed my bags for me." Gwen moved in Andrew's direction and his posture immediately relaxed. "I got the keys you left me."

"The porters did that actually. They must have made them up this morning."

"Andrew, this is so amazing. Thank you. But you didn't have to. Or at least, I could have helped."

He looked down at her, ready to respond but then he turned and glared at Salvatore instead. "Do you need me or Gwen for something? Because she and I have a lot of work to do. The show is this Friday."

The leather of Salvatore's jacket squeaked when he brushed his hand through his thick blond hair. "Gwendolyn, are you free for lunch? I'd like to talk about what I mentioned last week."

"What was that?" Andrew jumped in.

Stepping back, Gwen realized she was watching two elegant beasts sizing each other up. Salvatore had been needling to see her outside the office. She considered saying something to Enrico, but so far, it'd been harmless.

Andrew on the other hand; his acceptance of her, rearranging the office for her, and now the daggers he was throwing at Salvatore...*that* moved her. Andrew had been working there long enough to witness Salvatore woo and wine many women in that office and must be protecting *her*.

"Actually, Salvatore..." Gwen stepped in the middle of the men. "Andrew and I are going to plan a kick-off meeting where we can talk about your theme for the show. I've already reached out to the art department to get a few samples of a logo I have in mind."

"That is very proactive of you. Yes, I will look forward to your invite on the Outlook." Salvatore stepped away eyeing the reorganized office and the desks gleaming with fresh polish. His light eyes moved back to Andrew, and he gave a slight, formal nod. "Mr. Morgan."

"Signor Corella."

The designer moved slowly out of the office glancing back at Gwen. She blinked her eyes and gave a little wave, but Andrew closed the door before he could wave back. "So when is this meeting we're having?"

"I have no idea." She smiled at the cardboard tray he brought in earlier.

"Oh, I didn't know how you take your coffee." He pulled a Grande cup from the tray. "I just got you a latté."

"That's perfect." The cup was warm in her hands. "How much do I owe you?"

"Don't be silly. It's a coffee."

Right. Doesn't mean a thing. Cleaning out the office for me, also nothing. Probably just making amends for his bad behavior on Friday. After a sip, she scanned his side of the office. "Is this the same desk?" Either she grew a few inches wider or the desk was smaller.

"No, I downsized so we could fit in here more comfortably."

"Andrew!" She put the cup down. "I said I would move."

"*I* needed to declutter. It was a good thing for *me*."

Gwen looked around some more. Her map of the world had been pinned to the large cork board in the corner. She'd left it on Friday rolled up lying under her desk, feeling there would never be a place for it. And that Andrew wouldn't appreciate it. She pointed. "You hung my map."

"Yeah." He lifted his hand to acknowledge what he'd done. "It was very clever. I wouldn't have thought to hang something like that in here. But we *are* a global brand. Manhattan can be so confining and feel so closed in at times."

"It's easy to forget there's a whole world out there." She stepped to Andrew's side of the office, where it was hanging. Her fingers floated over the length of the Italian peninsula, starting at the base. "I've only been to south Italy." On a family vacation a few months after her mother died, the remaining Mallorys landed in Naples, drove to Sorrento, stopping in Pompeii. They took day trips to Capri and drove up the Amalfi coast. It'd been Elizabeth Mallory's dream holiday. The family took the trip in her honor. Milan, the landlocked city seemed a world away. "What's *Meelano* like?"

"You don't have to pronounce it that way around me." He smiled and stepped just close enough that, even from behind, she could sense the warmth he exuded. "*My* impression of Milan is, it's New York, London and Paris all wrapped up into one."

"Have you been to Paris?" She turned around and held her hands together, eager to talk about the city she loved.

He looked down and flattened his lips. "Uh, yeah." His head hung a little lower. "On my honeymoon."

Damn it! "Well I lived there for a summer."

He perked up. "Really?"

"Vacationing there is nice." She wanted to downplay being a tourist. "But living there, you feel as if you're a part of the city — you know, walking among people as neighbors. You've stayed in Milan for extended periods of time, right?"

"Yes." He sounded as if he'd run out of breath, like the conversation had exhausted him. But he smiled and added, "I'm sure you'll get to Milan eventually."

"You think so?" Their bodies were inches apart. There was a trace of coffee on his lips, and the hint of mocha was sexy as hell.

"Of course." At this proximity, she had to dip her head back to make eye contact. It made her feel vulnerable. He watched her eyes, darting his own from side to side as if he was searching for something to say next.

Damn, she liked being this close to him. A sizzle shot through her body and her senses came to life, along with her nipples. *Uh oh.*

"We have a lot of work to do," he said while she stared helplessly. It was a small relief when he stepped back.

But the way he made her body feel alive was on display. She crossed her arms and stumbled to her desk. *What was happening here?*

"Shall we?" He pointed to the meeting table he had cleared off.

"Sure." She grabbed a spiral notebook and sat.

Andrew had printed out the emails she had sent with her press release ideas. At first seeing the red ink splashed all over the page made her sink in her chair. Instinctively she reached out to take the pages back. "Wait, let me have another shot at this."

His hand covered her. "No, it's fine. I just added some teasers in Italian."

"Teasers?" she asked thinking about him as a model, sauntering down the runway; his eyes hooded and his lips parted. He may have been showing off the latest suit, but Gwen could bet every woman must have been wondering what was underneath.

"Yeah, Enrico likes it. Just plop them in, when you write the final draft."

"Okay." She tucked the papers in a folder and took out an image she wanted to use in the program. "What did you think of the cover art? I kind of like this visual of L.A."

The image was slanted, forcing their heads to tilt in the same direction. Her hair swept across his shoulder making his nostrils flare. "I think it's great, but I would cut the angle slightly. I get the effect you're going for." He took the paper from her hand, his fingers brushing against hers. "We have to be conscious that people will be viewing it on their phone."

"Right. Don't want to cause pile ups on a California freeway." Gwen swallowed, wondering if pictures of Andrew should be several pages deep into the website as well. Seeing him for the first time would make her swerve out of control.

He stood to get his laptop. *God, that man has such a great ass.* He had the file downloaded from her email. With a few swipes of his long fingers, he played with the embedded image to resituate it.

"Wait, that's too far. Now it looks like we just made it crooked." She leaned over and readjusted it herself. The keys were still warm. Her stretched arms crisscrossed over his, but he didn't move or adjust himself.

"Yes, that's perfect," he said quietly.

"It really is," she agreed in a breathy rush.

Andrew didn't move. Dark guarded eyes were watching her. Long arms tangled with hers, their heads dangerously close.

With one puff of his chest she would feel his lips. One delicate flick of the tongue, she'd taste its lush surface. A feather light wisp was all she wanted at the moment. *Oh God.* Her heart was ready to explode.

"Andrew…"

"Gwen?" he whispered, his shoulders tensing.

The ringtone on her phone, flickered both their eyes in that direction. *Dan.* The annoying clatter came between her and Andrew like an iron wall.

Gwen sucked in a breath and slid her hand away. "Dan?"

Andrew sat back and wiped his mouth.

"Hang on," she said into the phone and looked at Andrew. "I need to take this." She stood and stepped out of the office. It was weird that Dan was calling her now. His FedEx surprise a few weeks ago was his only contact in months. "What?"

"When are you going to sign those papers?"

"So now you're in a rush to get divorced? You left a year ago."

"I just want this all official, so we won't have to file joint taxes again."

She rolled her eyes in exasperation. He was concerned about his *tax bracket?*

With the whirlwind of the new job, the fashion show and…and Andrew, she'd almost forgotten to get back to Dan with the list of concerns Skye had with the decree. "I'm sorry to ruin your plans for the New Year, but I have some issues with that document."

"Your sister is not a divorce attorney. Give it to a professional. Now."

"Don't order me around." Her mind raced to remember Skye's objections. "You left me with that house to pay for. I'm barely able to eat."

"What? Prada doesn't pay well?"

She smacked her forehead. Figures. Dan had found out about her new job. "Since you know so much about my life, then you know I was out of work for weeks before I got this job."

"Get a lawyer Gwen. And sign the papers."

"Stop telling me what to do!" She looked up to find Andrew watching her. She moved to the elevator lobby. "I'll tell you what, I'll make this easy for you. I want this changed from a no-fault divorce, to Abandonment."

"That's not going to happen."

"That's what *did* happen, Dan." She spotted Andrew walking toward her with his coat on. "Hang on, Dan. Andrew, I'm sorry. I'll be back in the office in a few minutes."

"I need to get to Flagship. I sent that revised image to you. You should get that program finalized." He was all business. No hint of the man who'd been about the kiss her.

"Okay. Andrew, wait!" She held the elevator door before it closed. "I have to be somewhere tomorrow morning. I'll be a little late."

His eyes, pinched in irritation, lowered to her phone. "Fine." The doors closed while his gaze was laser focused on her. It made it difficult to stand. And made her hate the man on the phone even more. She may very well have been in that elevator with him, kissing him, going to Flagship with him. It would have been her first time, and she wanted it to be with Andrew. To see the store through his perspective.

"Gwen!" Dan shrieked.

"Okay! I'll sign the papers, but there's one thing I have to have or the deal is off and I'll get some shark to tear you apart."

"What's that?"

"I don't know if it was intentional but your lawyer forgot to include one important provision."

"I don't have all day, Gwen."

"To give me my damn name back. It's Mallory in case you've forgotten." Gwen clicked the phone off.

If it worked for Tina Turner…

CHAPTER NINE

On Tuesday morning, Gwen gasped for the air she'd been holding.

"Breathe Gwen."

The mammogram machine released her throbbing tender breast.

"One more, Gwen. You doing okay?"

What if I said no? She nodded, regardless, and placed her hands in the position she'd learned years ago. The whine of the machine was the prelude to crushing pain. It wouldn't be so terrible if it weren't for the ribbons of scar tissue banding the upper and lower quadrants of her right breast from past biopsies.

Because of her mother, she and Skye had been getting mammograms since they were in their late twenties. But the smallest calcification found during Gwen's first mammogram had put her on a vicious cycle of follow up mammograms that found more calcifications that were biopsied only to be followed up with another mammogram that…found more suspicious cells. And so on and so on.

All of Skye's tests had been clear. Putting the pressure on Gwen to keep up her testing. But she had drawn the line at genetic screening. She'd been coming to this hospital every six months, and the way these people hovered over every miniscule dot that appeared on her dark gray films, they would certainly catch anything early.

"Okay, wait here. I'll go show these to Dr. Sage."

Gwen stepped away from the machine and took a seat while Maya, the same woman who'd been taking her films for years, ran off to find the radiology doctor. Gwen suspected the results would tell the doctor nothing — as usual. *We'll need another biopsy just to be sure.*

Gwen's mind wandered to Andrew. *Back* to him really. She'd not heard from him the rest of the afternoon yesterday. And went to bed last night, wondering what if…what if Dan hadn't called. The jealous look in Andrew's eyes made her tingle, but the way he'd taken off hinted at a battle going on inside his mind.

Would it be easier if he were divorced as well? Sitting in a hospital gown, waiting for mammogram results made thinking about his deceased wife surreal.

Gwen typed 'Cate Morgan' into Google to pass the time.

A few blogs announced the news of her death. *Catherine Morgan, former Lanvin model. died on July 4 of last year,* one old blog post started. Ah ha! She was a model. That was obviously how she and Andrew had met. Gwen's eyes shot to the cold tile floor. It would make sense if Andrew didn't want to get involved with someone else in fashion. So many reminders.

Gwen read through some more reports of Cate's death. The website she found stopped her left index finger from flicking the screen down; catemorgan.com/blog.

It was a simple and clean WordPress theme. One post revealed that Cate had a rare tumor diagnosed when she was just out of college. She had survived the disease once. What that meant was, that like most women who'd beaten cancer, Cate had found herself back on the battlefield. But fighting an army of cells who had retreated to study their enemy to figure out a sure-fire way to win the war.

Cate's struggles while she'd been married to Andrew were more difficult than in her youth. In one post, she detailed how she'd started saying no. No to repeated tests. No to biopsies. No to surgeries. She'd been fed up and had enough. *Amen, Sister.*

Cate had also done something else Gwen thought was extremely brave. Each post included a mirror selfie, showing what the disease and those treatments had been doing to her magnificent appearance. By the last post, the poor woman was almost unrecognizable.

When the disease spreads, it chooses what organs to attack as if it's spinning a wheel at a summer fair, Cate had posted. For her, it was her intestines—which had subsequently been removed. And before the colostomy bag had been installed, she spoke frankly and painstakingly about the nights she'd woken up in a pool of her own urine. And how her wonderful husband would re-make the bed at all hours of the night. What a visual. Andrew Morgan certainly personified the ideal of *For Better or Worse.*

Gwen clicked a few links; she had a strange desire to see a picture of Andrew. In the picture on his desk, he looked different standing next to Cate. The shape of his smile was different from the way he smiled at Gwen. Holding Cate, it was more of a brave face. Around Gwen, and only when they were alone, Andrew appeared relaxed and sometimes relieved. Perhaps that was the man he used to be — the person Enrico had said he hoped would return.

Oddly, there weren't any pictures of Andrew on Cate's blog. "If he was my husband, I'd get tee-shirts made up," Gwen mumbled to herself.

"What was that?" Dr. Sage, a thin cheery blonde, was standing over her.

"Um, nothing. So?" Gwen let her phone slip into her bag.

"There's a batch in the corner I just can't get a clear picture of," she said through clenched teeth, clearly frustrated. It was one of the reasons Gwen kept coming back to this hospital. From her first irregular mammogram, she had the feeling her fight was also going to be their fight.

"But I thought the reason for inserting the clips was so we would know those areas were clean." Her right breast was filled with metal markers to show where cells have already been tested. Her X-rays were starting to look like the sky on a starry night.

"This spot is slightly higher."

Of course, it is.

A dark reality crept over Gwen; she'd no longer be covered under Dan's health insurance once her divorce was finalized. And Prada had a ninety-day probation period. Even then, her coverage may not be as good. Gwen may have been able to wiggle her way out of some of Dr. Sage's past biopsy recommendations, but with her health coverage in limbo, it was best to do this one as soon as possible.

"This one will be quick and there won't be much of a scar," Dr. Sage said, leading Gwen to the procedure room.

On her phone, Gwen opened her calendar to account for the additional time. She typed in the words *Emergency Biopsy*. Her schedule was shared with the entire marketing department, so everyone would know she was out for legitimate purposes.

Her eyes shot open. *Andrew!* After a nervous breath, Gwen backspaced and retyped: *Emergency Appointment.*

* * * *

"Andrew, I found this beautiful woman in the lobby," Enrico said smiling.

The doorway was filled with a woman in a stylish trench coat, with her dark mocha bob brushing against the collar. "Ma, what are you doing here?"

"I was in the neighborhood." She tucked a lock of hair behind her ear, revealing a firm jawline.

"You were wandering up and down the West Side Highway?" Andrew stood and folded his arms. "Enrico, thank you."

"My pleasure." In his suave Italian style, Enrico took his mother's hand and kissed her knuckles. "Until we meet again, my lady."

The look on Sarah's face was excitement with a hint of mischief. Andrew would have to remind his father to get off the damn golf course once in a while. His mother looked ready to run off with anyone who looked at her. She swung into the room. "What a gentleman."

"Can I get you an espresso, Ma?"

"No. Vile stuff. I prefer tea. But not until later." She stepped to the window and gazed at the view. "When did you get this office?"

"About four years ago. I've been inviting you, but you've been turning me down."

"Your father's job keeps me busy."

"You've stopped being his legal secretary decades ago."

"You think those little girls in that office know what they're doing?" She turned and ran her fingers along his desk, still smooth from his cleaning blitz. Her eyes settled on the framed picture of him and Cate. Sarah pursed her lips and turned away. Pointing to Gwen's work area, she asked, "What's this?"

"It's a desk, Ma."

She narrowed her eyes — the same color as his. "I see it's a *desk*. Whose is it? Did you get a new secretary?"

"No. She's not my secretary." He made sure to say that loudly. Rumors were swirling over Gwen and what her role was, since Enrico had kept hiring her on the down-low. Even from him! "She's a new PR exec."

"Public relations. So exciting." Sarah lifted a folder from Gwen's desk but put it down to pick up a bronze frame. "Is this her?"

The photograph in his mother's slender hand, which was adorned with a large diamond, perplexed Andrew. He hadn't noticed the personal items Gwen had added to her workspace. A younger version of his new co-worker sat cross-legged in the center of a group of people Andrew could only assume was her family. On her left was a cute blonde with similar shaped eyes. To her right was a young man. *Must be her brother, Greg.* Why had Andrew remembered the name so easily?

Standing above them was a man with salt and pepper hair and an older woman. Andrew should have noticed *her* first. He thought of the picture of him and Cate on his own desk. Gwen's mother must have been sick when the picture was taken. The woman was frail and thin. Hopefully she was better now.

On a tack board behind Gwen's desk were a few more photos. More recent he could tell. In the close-up someone had taken of Gwen, he could count the freckles on her nose. Her husband? A tinge of anger bubbled up inside him.

In a photo below she appeared again with the blonde from the other picture. In the backdrop were rows of vineyard vines, a bright blue sky and a halo of sunshine on the horizon. Yet, all Andrew could see in that picture was Gwen. "Uh yes, that's Gwendolyn."

"Gwendolyn?" His mother nodded with approval. "That's fancy. Where is she from?"

Andrew smiled. "No."

"She's from a place called 'No'?"

"It doesn't matter where she's from." He took the frame out of his mother's hand and put it back on Gwen's desk. Andrew had grown up listening to his mother make hypothetical matches for him. He was an only child, and his father lost a brother in the Korean War. Andrew was responsible for the entire Morgan name.

His mother never liked Cate. Sarah had 'put up with' his dating of model after model. Waiting for him to get it out of his system. When he married one, she had gone through the roof. It didn't matter that Cate had adored him. When Andrew had to make the painful confession that Cate didn't want to have children, it was like he took the knife in his own hands and sliced himself away from his parents for a while.

Andrew wouldn't have faulted Cate for her decision to remain childless, except she hadn't told him how she felt, until *after* they were married.

It was possible she would have come around to the idea of children, but shortly after their first anniversary she began to experience symptoms of relapsing. Andrew had gone into his marriage thinking he had a beautiful sophisticated wife who would give him plenty of sons to ensure the Morgan name.

Instead he ended up a widower. Heartbroken and alone.

"So let me buy you lunch," Sarah said, taking his arm and leading him out of his office. "There's a nice lawyer in your father's office I want you to meet."

Grunt.

* * * *

There was a trace of perfume in the office when Gwen returned.

Draping her coat on the task chair, she noticed the picture of her and her family had been moved. Gwen narrowed her eyes at the girls who had been slinking by her office, peeking and leering at Andrew; stalkers with astonishingly small waists and thighs. Everyone in that office was a size two and below. Gwen, a curvy size six felt like an elephant tromping through the narrow lanes of desks and equipment.

She popped a piece of gum in her mouth to cover the lingering taste of the pizza she wolfed down in the cab.

Andrew was frazzled and jittery when he walked in a few minutes later. "Oh, you're here."

"Yes, my appointment took a little longer than I had hoped, sorry."

"No problem." He looked at his phone.

She wanted to step closer to him and place a hand on top of his; return to the moment they shared yesterday. Instead, she stood frozen in the middle of the office.

He looked up at her. "Something wrong?"

"I'm sorry about yesterday." She searched for a reaction to know if he tossed and turned last night about it too.

All he tossed was his phone on the desk. "For what?"

*For...*almost kissing him. Taking Dan's call. What was she thinking? The moment was clearly gone. Or he was ignoring it. Two can play that game. "Nothing. Do you want to go over the schedule for tomorrow and the rest of the week?" She still needed to wrap up all the loose ends for the fashion show. It had crept up so fast and she was getting nervous.

"Sure." He patted his desk looking for something and brought his hand to his hair, which had a mussed-up quality about it.

A shock jolted her. Had he been with a woman?

In response to how she'd made *him* feel?

No, that was ridiculous.

Still, a harsh reality set in, making her shiver as if a hairy spider was crawling up her arm. If she continued to work there, she would eventually have to accept that Andrew was going to date *someone*. And those someone's were all over the place, lined up and waiting. *Ugh.* She was going to have to watch him be all gooey with another woman.

"What is it?" Andrew asked watching what must have been a strange look on her face.

"Um, nothing." She set her smile back to its even setting. "Are you all right? You seem a little...off."

"I just had lunch with my mother."

His mother. Oh, thank goodness. The idea that he had a little lunch date with his mom was endearing. "That's nice," she answered, simply to acknowledge what he'd said.

But he shook his head in frustration. "I love the woman, but she makes me crazy."

Having her own family butt into her life on a near constant basis, Gwen could empathize. "My dad makes me a little nuts too. At least you're a man." When Andrew stood up straight and abandoned his futzing and watched her with curious flat lips, she clarified, "I'm sure she doesn't hover over you always thinking something is going to happen to you."

"Oh, I would expect a father to be like that." He swiped a note pad and dragged his chair across the room to her desk. "And mothers hover too. In other ways, you know what that's like, I'm sure."

She cleared her throat, hating to have to correct him this way. "My mom passed away right after I graduated high school."

His eyes were full of regret, glancing at the photos on her desk. "Gwen, I'm so sorry. I didn't know."

She shrugged her shoulders. "How could you know?"

He released a sharp breath. "I still feel terrible. I feel like I bit your head off when you first mentioned Cate."

"Andrew, that's different." She took a seat at her desk. "My mom died a long time ago. Your wife passed recently. Plus, it was your *wife*. The person you're supposed to be the most...intimate with."

"Yes, but I think losing a parent is different. I mean; I'll eventually get another wife." He rolled his eyes in embarrassment. "Okay, *that* came out wrong. What I mean is—"

"Of course, you'll *eventually* find someone else. You're a young man." She sneaked another look out her office door to the sea of faces peeking at them above their monitors. "It's not like you won't have any takers."

He caught her looking that way. "I certainly couldn't date anyone out there."

"Out there?" Gwen jammed a thumb in the direction of the entire marketing floor.

He released a slow breath. "They all work for me."

"Yes. That would be messy. Right?"

"Yeah, and illegal...right?"

"Are you asking me or agreeing with me?"

He released a low chuckle. "I get that people at work hook up. But if I were to do it, it would have to be the...right person."

"Someone you can trust."

"Someone who isn't...married."

Gwen choked and her lips parted. "Or separated, *waiting to be divorced.*" Yes, surely that would be a problem. Divorces meant baggage and damage. Who would want that?

Andrew studied her for an extra minute.

She opened her laptop. "Anyway, I sent that image to the art department. They worked up a draft of the program. I'll print it out." She stood to go to the copy room, but Andrew's hand closed around her wrist. Freezing her in place.

"Gwen...is everything all right with you?"

"Yes of course," she choked out shivering at his touch.

"Your husband isn't *bothering* you or anything, is he?" Andrew's jaw was tight.

"No. And he won't be my husband for long. He just called asking for the signed divorce papers."

"Oh."

"The only reason I haven't signed them, is because I've been so caught up with the new job and...and with you." She absorbed the eyes fixed on her. "And the show, of course."

"Right."

Being so close to Andrew yesterday refreshed the longing to be kissed and held in a strong man's arms.

His gaze shifted to the doorway.

"Is this yours?" Thalia was there with the program Gwen had printed.

She shot out of her seat to take it. "Yes, thanks." Yesterday happened so organically, it would be futile to try to force it back to the surface. She handed the program to Andrew and leaned over his shoulder while he looked at it.

"This looks amazing, Gwen."

"I think we make a good team, right?"

He nodded and thumbed through the rest of the program.

Gwen amused herself watching him and thinking of playing *one-on-one* with Andrew — shirts or skins?

Skins, definitely.

CHAPTER TEN

Gwen stood in the Prada bathroom stall, her head against the partition, running the check list for L.A. in her head.

The limo was picking them up in an hour to bring everyone to the airport. She hadn't been paying attention to the two women having a conversation by the sinks. Working with twenty-somethings had been like watching reality television. She'd already learned to tune out their silliness.

"Don't do it Amber!" one of the voices warned.

"Why? He's single."

"That's only because his wife died."

Gwen's head lifted swiftly. They were talking about Andrew.

"She died more than two years ago," Amber whined.

Gwen shook her head wondering *when did facts become irrelevant?* It was the most astonishing thing, listening to her co-workers walk around lecturing others with inaccurate nonsense.

"Besides, I heard even before his wife, he only dated models. I'm sure that's who he'll end up with again. You know, once you go model you don't go back."

"I can pass for a model."

"You're barely five feet tall, Amber."

Ah ha! She was able to place Amber, who worked for Andrew—which meant that little troll could easily kick Gwen out of the office. She swallowed, imagining Amber trying to draw Andrew into some childish game.

"At least we know he won't go after that cow penned up in his office. Who did *she* kill to get that spot?"

Hey!

"She's not a cow."

Yeah, I'm not a cow! Gwen only wished she could see who this voice was. Someone deserved a nice souvenir from L.A.

"Amber, I think you need to go get a macchiato or something. You're out of control if you think Gwen is fat."

Hearing her name was unsettling enough, but the mention of Andrew's dating habits prior to Cate made Gwen stop listening for a moment. Was it true he had *only* dated models? And now, with all the fashion shows coming up…

"Anyway, *that* cow is not a threat." Amber sounded overly confident.

"I don't know. She is gorgeous, if you ask me."

Gwen sucked in a deep breath and in a bold wave of confidence flushed her bowl. The chatter by the sinks stopped immediately. Upon reaching the women Gwen focused her glare on Amber, who had turned white. The other woman, someone Gwen didn't recognize, cringed — probably in solidarity for her friend.

Gwen rinsed her hands, her eyes locked on Amber through the mirror. She wrung the loose droplets into the sink and stepped to the paper towel dispenser. She winked to the other girl before walking out of restroom, feeling victorious. Little Amber and her friend might be right about Andrew only wanting to date models.

Before.

The way he'd been looking at *her* lately hinted that he may actually want something different this time around.

And Gwen figured out the key ingredient to prod Andrew…*Jealousy.*

* * * *

"On behalf of myself and your Atlanta based Delta crew, welcome to Los Angeles."

Fucking finally! Andrew hadn't felt six hours take so long since he'd been a child waiting for the bell to ring on the last day of school.

Other planes were blurry visions in the distance, while his sat on the runway for a little longer. Time grinding by. The sizzling oil rose up from the tarmac, blending the departure line into a rainbow of colors. But his ire was smoldering hotter than the ninety plus degree temperature outside the little window to his left.

For the entire flight, all Andrew had heard was Gwen's laughter. From four Goddamn rows back. Even listening to music with his headphones on, or trying to concentrate on the movie he'd been dying to see, or reading the book he'd been so drawn to at home in New York, his attention couldn't be diverted.

All he heard was Gwen. Talking and laughing. How Salvatore managed to get a seat next to her was infuriating. Why had the company travel agent randomly paired *them* up? Enrico lounged in first class, while Thalia sat alone in the row behind him. Even her snoring couldn't distract him. Or the little kid next to her who kicked his seat most of the flight.

From the moment Gwen entered Andrew's airspace three weeks ago, he hadn't been able to get her out of his head. But he'd been playing it cool. That's where guys get into trouble and good women get away, though.

Still, it wasn't prudent for Gwen to become so attached to Salvatore. That was why Andrew had never become immersed in any one designer, one line, or one product. It was an evolving business. The most beautiful, praised and famous dress had a short shelf-life. There was always another beautiful and praise-worthy dress ready to be celebrated.

There would be other shows. And other designers. Gwen would be promoting not just clothing but also the accessory lines. Even shoes were a different animal. Showcases were not the same as fashion shows. They were more business oriented, less glamorous. Gwen might find herself sorely disappointed when the Miu Miu line released their spring handbags.

Okay, not really. He'd seen the sketches and some of the samples with his own eyes. Gwen was going to love them. He could imagine her face lighting up, handing her that white bucket bag. It brought a small smile to his own mouth. Until he heard that cackling laugh of hers. Again.

The plane finally parked at the jet way. Thank God! Hopefully Salvatore enjoyed these six free hours. Designers put in eighteen hour days before shows. "Soak her up, buddy. You won't have time to take a piss once you get off this plane," Andrew muttered.

Salvatore's phone had not stopped ringing, and messages started dinging as soon as he turned it back on. He and his team of design assistants would have to pick up trunks of clothes, shoes and bags for the show from the cargo area.

"Hey. Where were you all this time?" Gwen asked in a cheery voice getting off the plane.

"In my seat." He shook his head, not meaning for that to come out so gruff. But how could she have not noticed him? Salvatore probably had her engrossed in one of his outlandish stories. "Did you check a bag?"

"No." She removed her suit jacket, exposing toned arms in a sleeveless top. "Just this guy right here."

His gentlemanly upbringing kicked in and he took the handle from her, their fingers tangled for a moment. "I got it," he said softly.

"Thanks." She draped her jacket across her arm and followed closely as they made their way to the exit. At times, her hand rested on his back or tugged his suit jacket so they wouldn't become separated. Each touch was followed by a soft smile on her lips when he looked at her.

In the limo, Gwen huddled close and with every sharp turn, leaned against him. He could feel the moisture on her skin from the L.A. heat simmering beneath her blouse. It would have been cozy if Enrico and Thalia weren't there. Enrico's assistant drained her battery by taking pictures and posting to Facebook and Instagram, announcing all the *likes* she'd been getting.

Gwen snapped a few photos as well, but instead of sharing them with so-called 'friends', she showed each one to Andrew. "Look!" she said with excitement and intimacy. It was like he'd been the only person in the car. The only person who mattered. He'd not been aware of how he craved that type of attention. Getting it from Gwen felt…amazing.

The JW in Downtown L.A. was Andrew's favorite hotel of all the Marriott's. The side facing the Nokia Theater was sheathed in glass. Inside that wing, the ceilings were three stories high. And the roof deck beat the crap out of any chic Manhattan night spot. The rooms were large and while some spaces might be considered *dated*, Andrew appreciated the *Old-Hollywood* glamorous feel.

With their sleek charcoal Prada suits, sunglasses and rolling high end luggage, they could have been mistaken for FBI agents. Gwen stepped forward to get in line at the front desk, but Andrew held her arm back gently. "We have priority check-in."

"I feel like a celebrity." She squeezed her shoulders, as if hugging herself.

"The way you'll be swarmed at the show, you'll probably decide you don't like it very much."

Behind them, a raucous scene was taking shape. Someone had been leaving the lobby bar, but was now running away from a group of photographers who were yelling and snapping pictures. They asked questions that made no sense to Andrew. As the crowd rushed past them, he instinctively put himself in front of Gwen.

From over his shoulder, she rested her chin against his ear and said, "I think you're right."

* * * *

Gwen stepped into her hotel room, suppressing a delighted squeal.

OMG! It was a suite! She rushed to the full-length window and pressed her hands against the glass. The skyscrapers rose up around her like columns in a cluster while the rest of the city was mostly flat. Many of the taller buildings were branded by their company names: Bank of America, Wells Fargo and Citigroup. In the distance bronze mountains kissed the blue sky. White caps drizzled down the side like they'd been coated with vanilla ice cream.

The time on her phone had finally updated from New York to Los Angeles. The disparity wasn't just the distance and the temperature…she'd landed in a different world. Once her phone finished syncing, it vibrated telling her texts and emails were waiting.

"Great," she grumbled seeing how many messages had poured into her inbox while she'd been traveling. "It's five pm in New York. As far as I'm concerned, it's happy hour." Gwen tucked her laptop under her arm. With her new expensive shades, she sailed out of the suite in search of a glass of wine and Wi-Fi.

An hour later, her half carafe of sauvignon blanc was empty, and her cheese and cracker platter had been reduced to crumbs and red peels of gouda skin. She read email after email, but paused on one and cried out, "No. No. *No*. This isn't happening." She grabbed her phone and called List LA.

"Kirsten, it's Gwen Foley at Prada. I just—Yes, my flight was fine. I want to—Yes, it's much warmer here than in New York. Can we discuss—" *This is why I hate calling people*. All they want to do is *talk*.

"Kirsten!" She ducked her head, embarrassed that others on the patio had wrenched their necks in her direction. "*Please*. I got your email with the confirmed list of attendees. Is that number right?"

Her legs wobbled in the elevator and down the hall to Andrew's room. He hadn't answered his phone or responded to texts and emails. It was her tears and business card that coaxed his room number out of the manager.

After her frantic knocking, Andrew finally answered. He was in a tee-shirt that looked as if he had taken a shower in it. It was soaked, his pectoral muscles outlined deliciously. "Sorry, I just got back from a run." He wiped his hands on his shorts.

God damn! She wiped her own brow and got herself in check. "I need to speak with you. I've made a horrible mistake."

He stepped aside. "Come in."

"No."

"What?"

"I can't go into your hotel room. It's not appropriate. Can we speak downstairs?"

"Gwen, we have suites for this reason." He tugged her by the wrist, his large fingers wrapped around the base of her hand, easily. Commanding and powerful. "I assure you, it's fine."

She stepped inside, and from a short distance away, got a look at his legs. Covered in Prada trousers, they were a mystery. Now that he was exposed…he was as muscular as she had dared to imagine. And yikes. Those shorts were…short. She prayed he wouldn't start to stretch and expose something she didn't think she could handle. Instead, he took a bottle of water into his hands.

Oh, please dump it on your head.

She did a double take when she realized he was talking to her. "Huh? What?"

"I said, do you want some water?" Andrew held the bottle out to her.

Only if I can I lick it off your lips.

"No, thanks. Listen, Andrew." She held her stomach. She'd made so much progress with him and now it was all going to crumble. "I received the response count from List LA for the show."

"That bad?" He wrinkled his nose.

"No!" She held up her hands. "Just the opposite. I never...I never gave them the ballroom's capacity."

"And?"

"We're overbooked by more than double."

Andrew relaxed. "It's fine."

"How can it be fine? We have three hundred people coming and one hundred and twenty seats."

"This is L.A. They won't all show up. List LA knew that."

Yes, the local publicity firm had to have known the capacity. But Gwen approved the list. She just never counted. "Has this ever happened to you before?"

"I never stressed over the headcounts to be honest with you." He moved closer to her. "I relied on the people I hired to manage all that. But I'm glad you're going to be on top of that more. It *would* be a disaster if everyone showed up."

On top... Gwen shook her head. "Andrew, I'm sorry. I take full responsibility. This will never happen again."

A long stare was followed by, "That's certainly refreshing."

"What is?"

"To hear someone own up to a mistake." He lifted his arms over his head. "All I get are excuses and how it's someone else's fault."

Gwen was about to ask him how his workout went, hoping that would lead to him letting her feel his biceps, but the sound of a loud knock forced Andrew in the direction of his door.

"Morgan." Salvatore glided in, moving right to Andrew's windows as if he was checking to see if the view was better than the one in his suite. "Enrico wants to meet immediately. We've booked the private dining room."

"Signor Corella. Come in," Andrew said, clearly annoyed.

"Ah, *bella*. You are *here*." He cast a sideways glance at Andrew. "Saves me a trip to your suite."

"Let me get the rest of my papers," she said, noticing the scornful stare that had developed between the two men. Sitting with Salvatore on the plane was a genius move. Still, she didn't want to professionally come between them. Salvatore *was* a brilliant designer. The runway rehearsal and the media previews meant this collection was going to be spectacular. As the Brand Manager, Andrew should be proud of Salvatore's creations to enhance the Prada brand.

"I'll give you a hand, *bella*." The designer moved toward the door.

"Salvatore, she's a big girl. She's managed a lot without you so far." Andrew caught his arm. "Besides, I have a few things to run by you."

Relieved to be getting out from between them before she started drooling, she clutched her papers to her chest, calmed her hammering heartbeat, and said, "I'll see you both in a little while."

Not to mention Andrew needed a shower. A long, hot one... Oh to be a drop of Los Angeles County water right now. Gwen rushed out of the suite, wishing she had time to take a *cold* shower.

The private dining room was the most beautiful and exquisitely decorated room she'd ever seen. She hadn't known rooms like this even existed in hotels. Like hers and Andrew's suites, one wall was entirely made of glass. The sun had set, but a wavy line of deep blue speckled with pink and gold stretched over the horizon. The smog blurred all the tones like a Monet watercolor painting. North Fork residents enjoyed rare sunsets over the Sound. But this West Coast version took her breath away.

The beauty and elegance around her gave way however, to the overpowering aroma of roasted garlic and sweet basil. On the back wall a long sideboard held trays and trays of food. With a phone tucked into the crook of his shoulder, Salvatore was filling a plate with folded slices of Italian prosciutto and salami. Thalia was picking at an olive and cheese platter. Enrico was swirling linguine onto a fork.

At a chrome tray, Gwen lifted the cover and her stomach rumbled in delight. Raviolis in tomato-cream sauce were her favorite. On another sideboard were loaves of thickly sliced bread, and an assortment of oils for dipping. This was all Thalia's doing. And she was excellent at her job.

Gwen made up a healthy plate, in lieu of going back for seconds and thirds which would only draw attention to how much she was eating. She turned to take a seat at the elegant table, but where to sit perplexed her. She really wanted to sit next to Thalia. But her role as a PR executive meant she needed to sit with management. Not gossip with an assistant.

The seat across from Andrew was the most inviting, with the panoramic scenery of Downtown L.A. behind him. As she sat, his carbon eyes locked on hers. *Much better view.* His dark brows cinched together, sneaking a peek at her plate and the large amount of food. She would expect a man that handsome to snort in derision at how much she was eating. But he smiled and gave a slight nod, like he was pleased by her healthy appetite.

His hair was wet and combed back, not slicked and flat against his head. It still had some fullness. The shirt he wore was one of the more casual Prada dress shirts, pale yellow with a thin blue pinstripe running through it. No tie. On his plate, a half-eaten hamburger sat next to a pile of fries. He wiped his mouth and winked. *He doesn't like Italian food?*

Enrico brushed crumbs from his hands and wiped his mouth. "All right, the show is Friday but before we discuss who, what and where on that...Gwendolyn where are we with the events for tomorrow?"

With her mouth open ready to nibble on her first scrumptious steaming ravioli, Gwen panicked seeing *all* eyes at the table were on her.

"Enrico, let her take *one* bite," Andrew interjected. "I'll start with some ads we had running earlier in the week." He detailed the advertising strategy. A full-page ad in the Arts section of the L.A. Times, television and radio spots, including contests to win a chance to meet Salvatore and at that point he rolled his eyes. Andrew finished with the event he and Gwen had planned together: a special preview for L.A. media and fashion bloggers. "Salvatore, I assume everything made it here okay?"

"My team is going through all of the trunks now." He took a huge bite of bread. "I am not worried."

"I think we should include more of the ready-to-wear samples for the preview tomorrow," Gwen added.

"Good call." Andrew nodded. "L.A. is not New York."

Gwen wiped the corners of her mouth. "I can go over the other events if you're ready."

"Yes, *bella*." Salvatore sneaked a look at Andrew. "I am yours to command this week."

"It's not really like that. This collection is your vision. It's not just blouses, trousers and dresses. It's you, Salvatore. You've put who you are into these clothes. You deserve to be celebrated."

"Salvatore likes to be *adorato*," Andrew quickly quipped.

"Why shouldn't I be worshipped?" He leaned forward waving a fork.

Here we go. Gwen forced down a few more raviolis while her rams banged horns.

CHAPTER ELEVEN

Andrew watched Gwen leave the private dining room while typing into her phone.

She'd received her marching orders from Enrico and *whoosh*; off she went. Without even saying goodbye. He thought she would need hand-holding.

Nope.

The following day, she was busy carting Salvatore around. At least she answered his texts. His own day was busy as well, meeting with corporate retailers and investors.

Things had finally calmed down enough that maybe he could take her out to dinner — to properly thank her for all she'd done for the show and their brand. But before he could ask her, he received a text from Enrico saying he should meet him in the Mixing Room for a drink.

Barely seeing Gwen yesterday because of the flight, and then not seeing her most of today, had created an emptiness in him he hadn't been expecting. Not having her around made him antsy and anxious. He...he missed her.

That's when Andrew stopped feeling like a widower. He'd been licking his wounds, and now they were clean and ready to heal. Gwen did that. He had locked his emotions away. Like live wires, if exposed they were dangerous to be around.

He wanted to move his life forward and he wouldn't enter another relationship closed down and hidden. That's not what someone like Gwen deserved.

It was always Gwen. From the moment he saw her, she yanked him from the shell he'd been in, enticing him to laugh again and feel like it's okay to love again. She was entitled to see the man he *used* to be.

For so long he'd not considered a relationship between co-workers wise. But that was before he'd found someone who was worth the risk.

Now Andrew just needed to get to her before Salvatore drowned her with his oily charm.

* * * *

Gwen kept in touch with Andrew all day.

Mostly through texts. That *most handsome man behind the scenes at Prada* emerged — the elusive stranger who wanted to stay a mystery. But the way he spoke with her, she sensed the human Andrew was still there. The gentle side that always existed behind the closed door of their office.

While getting Salvatore off to an interview that morning, she'd received a message from Andrew: *And where are you right now?*

She playfully responded: Wishing I were dead.

Ha! Another Salvatore interview?

He just drags them out.

Adorato. I warned you.

I see what you mean.

Good.

Back in her suite, Gwen fell onto the elaborately made up bed where she squirmed and stretched. It was so comfortable. *So much better than the old, lumpy floor-mattress she had at home.*

She had been on the go from sunrise, passed a gorgeous California sunset, and now was ready to call it a night. Whatever the time actually was.

She was exhausted and delighted to close her eyes. Happy. Until she heard a knock at her door. *Grrr.* But a spark shot through her. That could be Andrew!

Gwen leapt off the bed in eager anticipation.

* * * *

Andrew entered the Mixing Room and his senses immediately went into overload.

He'd been deep inside himself, thinking and musing, but now all the people, all the voices, the televisions above the bar, made him feel open and exposed. Hopefully this would be quick — he'd had enough roadblocks and interruptions. As soon as this meeting with Enrico was done, Andrew planned to see Gwen.

80

Enrico waved from a bulky leather sofa in the corner. The second he arrived a tall server, almost taller than Andrew, approached to take his drink order.

"Nothing for me," he said politely. Kissing Gwen for the first time shouldn't be under the influence of alcohol. That thought stilled him cold. Had he planned to *kiss* her? Tonight?

"He'll have what I'm having," Enrico said waving a short crystal glass filled with what looked like vodka. A lime wedge had sunk to the bottom, because he was almost finished. "And bring me another too."

Andrew folded himself into the seat opposite Enrico, still shaken. "So, what's up?"

"I have no way to ease into this Andrew. I need you to go back to Milan." His boss was stern but held a twang of guilt in his accented voice. "I am not happy with how Marcello is progressing. If it gets to the point where the Creative Director starts noticing…" He tipped his glass back.

Marcello had been Enrico's hire. Usually, the Milan Brand Manager was hired by, and reported to, the Creative Director in Italy. But in a power-play, Enrico convinced her to have Marcello and his team report to the New York Marketing group. If Marcello failed, it would be on Enrico.

Andrew hadn't made it any better. He had been a contributing factor, an accomplice. He'd trained Marcello while still in the throes of heartbreak and despair. He was equally responsible.

"Sure." He didn't mind another brief trip, but couldn't this request have waited? "When?"

"After the show."

"*Straight* from L.A.?"

"We have all the clothes you need in Milan."

Andrew hid his irritation. "For how long?"

"Until the end of the year, at least."

His body froze. *End of the year? After tomorrow?* Tomorrow. That was going to be the last time he would see Gwen until *the end of the year!* The day he wanted to spend with her had been stolen from him by Salvatore, and now Enrico was taking *the rest of the year?*

His boss sipped his drink and then rolled his eyes. "Fine, you can stop home to collect your things."

"It's not just things at my apartment. Don't you think there are things in my office that I will need to take with me too?" *Like Gwen.*

Enrico put his head down. "At least Gwendolyn has worked out."

Yes, she worked out all right. It had taken less than a month for the feelings to bubble inside him, ready to spill over the edge. Could a cork be put back in this bottle…for two months?

Drinks turned into dinner, the dinner he'd wanted to have with Gwen. And by the time Andrew made it to her floor to speak to her, there was an unbearable tension in his shoulders that rivaled any he usually felt the night before a show. But the pain right now meant much more. His whole plan had been thwarted, hijacked. How could he do something, like tell her how he felt or…kiss her…now, if he was leaving for Milan right after the show?

His legs still moved him forward, but he was going to have to do this unscripted. It was a lot later than he would have preferred. And the box in his hand would be a sorry consolation for the fact that he would be leaving.

After a heavy knock, he couldn't shake that familiar bout of excitement sneaking into his bones from Gwen's bright smile.

But when the door opened Andrews's hands curled into tight fists. "Salvatore."

"Morgan. Come look."

He stepped in, wildly curious but also afraid he'd see something that would upset him. Instead, the vision of elegant beauty made that pang of longing shoot through him. "Gwen?"

Her eyes lit up. "Andrew!"

She twirled in an emerald green full length gown that cinched at her waist. Her body filled out the bodice perfectly and the upper swells of her full breasts peeked through the asymmetrical cutouts in the neckline. "Isn't this the most gorgeous thing you've ever seen?"

Yes. But he wasn't thinking of the dress. "Salvatore. You've outdone yourself. I don't want to sound like a jerk, but why isn't something as beautiful as this in the show?"

The designer rubbed a chin that hadn't seen a razor in a couple of days. "Do you know one of our models who could fill out a dress like this as well as our Gwen?"

Our Gwen?

"Salvatore, thank you." The gown gave way at the slit, showing a firm thigh as Gwen stepped toward the designer to hug him.

Andrew's blood boiled when Salvatore's scandalous hands sat on her waist. She was *not* his. The tentative hesitation in her hug however, cooled his fever. And the smile on her lips as she bounded in his direction reminded him of the woman she really was. Not all made up in a gown. As if Salvatore was trying to make her one of his models. A doll he could play dress-up with.

"Did you need something, Andrew?"

"Actually…" He could use a set of defibrillator paddles. "I have a gift for you too." He swayed further into the room, his confidence returning with every step. From a linen sack, he removed a shoebox. "She should be in Prada from head to toe, should she not, Salvatore?"

The designer grumbled, appearing to regret he hadn't thought of the obvious accessory.

"Andrew, what have you done?" Gwen asked resting her hands on round curvy hips.

"Come here, Gwen," he commanded and pointed to her suite's desk chair. "Sit."

At the chair, she swept aside the long skirt made of raw silk and sat with her knees pinned together. Andrew's jaw trembled as he sank to one knee. The shoe he removed from the box was not a new design he could have swiped from the sample floor before they left. It was one of his favorites, a classic that had been around for years. The deep black suede gladiator sandal with satin nickel studs suited Gwen's edgy personality. It was also the perfect complement to an elegant full length gown. The moderate heel would also cushion her ankles as she moved through the show tomorrow.

Andrew unfolded the soft tissue paper and held the shoe in front of Gwen.

"The Filettra sandal?" She looked at him, stunned.

"You know the name of this shoe?" Salvatore asked.

But before she could answer, Andrew turned to the designer. "She obviously did her homework on our products."

"You boys really know how to make a girl feel like Cinderella!" She slipped her foot into the insole while it was still in Andrew's hand. He leaned forward to buckle the small strap around her ankle, his chest leaning against her knee. After he repeated the same for the other foot, she stood. He'd worked for Prada long enough to know when a woman was comfortable in one of their shoes. Her toes sat perfectly against the vamp without looking crushed.

He had a feeling Gwen had stopped breathing. Andrew lifted his chin slowly. On her face was a look of controlled satisfaction. Like maybe she would wait to show how much this really meant to her until they were alone.

And why *weren't* they alone?

Andrew ran his tongue against his dry lips to speak, and for the first time the obnoxious ring of Salvatore's phone was a welcome interruption.

"*Che cosa?*" he blurted. In Italian, he ranted into the phone for several seconds. Pulling the device from his face, he turned back to Gwen, who hadn't taken her eyes off Andrew. "I have a situation to deal with."

The way Salvatore stomped to the door and slammed it shut, Andrew knew *he'd* won.

* * * *

Captivated was the only way Gwen could describe how she felt at the moment. The dress was an amazing gift, but she saw right through Salvatore's motives. She'd been turning down his near-daily invitations, so this must have been his way to see her curves. Pretty desperate.

While Salvatore had stormed in with his big personality, Andrew's presence alone — his height, his shoulders — *he* commanded the room. He filled it with his masculinity. An honorable and loyal man, regardless of how gorgeous he was, was the right man. Any man who knew he could have anyone…but wanted *her*. That was the kind of man she wanted.

OMG, the Filettra sandal! Feet were so intimate. And given the length of the skirt, even with the slit, the shoes would be hidden. It was a secret she'd keep throughout the day. A secret for her and Andrew to share.

Gwen and Andrew… That did have a nice ring to it.

"So, he takes up a lot of oxygen in the room, doesn't he?" Andrew pushed on one of his knees and stood.

"Salvatore's all showy though." Gwen fingered the skirt and swooshed the fabric back and forth.

"Do you prefer a man who is more subtle?"

It was the first time he'd dared to ask her personal preferences for a mate, and before he could retract his question or dilute it, she said firmly, "Yes, on the surface." *And smoldering underneath. Like you Andrew.*

He stepped a few inches away. "I'm still concerned all the attention will be on *you* in that dress." He held his chin, smooth and fresh.

"I was planning on wearing my hair up." She gathered a handful of waves and swept them away from her face. But when he only stared at her bracelets as they clanged together, she let the bundle fall. "Or—"

"No. No." The words caught in his throat. His fingers brushed past her cheek, lifting the hair off her shoulders again. "This is perfect."

Yes, it is perfect. And he should be kissing her by now. Those amazing lips, pink and full on hers...and on other parts of her body, making her feel alive.

His eyes bore into hers, but he said nothing. Gwen preferred to *not* have to make the first move. How would she know if Andrew really wanted her in the first place, and wasn't just taking advantage of a willing partner? But how long could she wait for him, before a crazy impulse took hold of her?

"I guess it's settled. I'm wearing my hair up tomorrow," she whispered, locking eyes with him.

He cleared his throat and stepped back, letting her hair fall. The weight of so many waves warmed her skin, even though she preferred the heat coming off his body. She stepped back as well and slipped into co-worker mode. "Andrew, be honest. Is this dress...too much? I prefer clothes that are simple and classic. Conservative even."

"I would call you classic, Gwen. But not simple. You wear our clothes beautifully." He ran his hand over the suit jacket she had draped on a desk chair. "The way they sit on you tells a story of...of the woman we know other women want to be."

The compliment left her breathless. Prada had been in business for more than one hundred years. That certainly made up for what he'd said about Starlight Elegance. "Thank you, Andrew."

"No, Gwen. I want to thank you." His shoulders softened. "I need you to know, I couldn't have done this without you."

"That's not true." She swiped at eyes she suspected were shiny with tears, she wouldn't let fall. Better to be respected as an equal, and not thought of as a weepy lightweight. "You've run plenty of these shows."

"Yes, and I know what it takes to pull this off. There was no way I could have done what you've done...for *this* show." He ran a hand through his hair, his wedding band was—gone!

The sight took Gwen's own breath away. She twisted her hair to the side, to keep her hands busy. "Did you want to do one final walk through for tomorrow?"

"No. We're set." He bent down to the pick up the shoebox. His back straightened, emphasizing his dramatic height.

She moved toward Andrew to hug him. Immediately there was a different feel to his touch from the night of their first drink. The night when everything had turned around. And upside down. His fingers pressed into her skin. His body molded against hers. Oh, the smell of him, musky and woodsy. Masculine. There it was, his heart, beating wildly. There was so much of this man, his heart must work so hard to pump his rich blood through so many veins.

The feel of his grip softening, meant it was time for her to let go. "Have a good night Andrew." She touched his hands and leaned upward for a kiss on the cheek. The edge of his mouth—warm and tender as she remembered—caught the corner of her lips. *Tickle, Tickle* went her stomach.

A strand of her long hair caught in his collar, binding them together for a brief moment. Creating a bridge that could bring them together…if someone was brave enough to cross.

Andrew snagged and looped the strand of her hair in his fingers. He held his gaze into hers, breathed and exhaled. "I believe this belongs to you."

It wasn't *exactly* what she wanted in her hand, but she took it from him and let it fall against her breast, his eyes following. It was as if he was biting the inside of his mouth, confused or holding back. "Andrew, is something wrong?"

His fingers pulled at his collar. "No. I just…I feel…"

His indecisiveness sent a pang of alarm. If he didn't really *know* what he wanted, forcing the issue could have disastrous consequences. "It's late, I guess, right?" she asked softly, drawing his eyes back up to hers.

"I guess." He pressed his eyes closed and turned around, headed for the door.

After another look passed between them, and a nod, the door closed, taking her breath with it.

CHAPTER TWELVE

The next morning, when everyone else seemed preoccupied, Gwen sneaked out onto the runway.

A hundred plus folding chairs were being set up for the guests. Assistants were removing Salvatore's collection from black garment bags and hanging them up in dressing rooms. The backstage area was twice the size of the room for the show.

The lighting team hadn't arrived yet and only yellow emergency lights poured down on the white ceramic platform. This would be her only chance. She put her hands on her hips and glided down the runway. One foot crossing in front of the other just as the models did at the interviews and the rehearsals. The way a model moved down a runway wasn't how an ordinary human walked. After a few steps, Gwen was already cramping up.

Still, she couldn't help but feel beautiful tilting her hips and projecting her shoulders, right then left. At the end of the platform, she did the quarter turns — one side, then the other — swung her hair in a dramatic swoop and sailed back up toward the AV screen in the front. She closed her eyes feeling elated.

Until she slammed into a wall. A wall of flesh and bone. The man's body was tall and lean and smelled of fresh cotton and spicy musk. "Omigosh," she said, putting her hands on Andrew's chest.

"I hope our models don't do that." He peeked at the two foot drop just inches away from where she'd been headed.

"Has that ever happened?"

"A model sailing over the edge?" He shifted her back to the center of the platform, his hands firm on her waist. "Not at any of my shows."

"I just wanted to do this once. Was I not allowed to do that?" She wanted to know where *all* the boundaries were.

"Gwen..." He put his hands on her arms. "You're an executive with Prada. This is a Prada fashion show. You have full venue access." He took the laminated card hanging around her neck in his strong hands, and her breasts warmed from how close he'd come to brushing against them.

"Okay." Not wanting him to feel what he did to her, she repositioned her body.

"But please don't do that while the show is going on," he joked.

"Can I do one more lap?" She tented her fingers in prayer.

"Why don't you practice walking out there and taking your bow?"

Gwen tripped over her sneakers. "My *what?*"

"We all come out." Andrew laughed. "I usually go after Enrico. And with all the work you've put into the show, it wouldn't seem right to come out here alone."

"So, you mean I *have* to come out here later?" She swallowed. "In front of actual…people?"

"Yep, so practice some more." Andrew smiled and ducked back into the controlled chaos behind the large screen.

It took several more seconds before Gwen could move.

By noon the viewing room was ready. The lighting team had set up the spotlights and color filters. The AV dudes had done two rehearsals with the video and music. And the security team supplied by List LA had set up tables at the entrance for guests to check in.

Gwen confidently carried her clipboard around the backstage area looking for disasters to mitigate. She just didn't consider herself to be one of them, until her boss stood before her with a horrified look on his face.

"You are not wearing *that,* are you?" Enrico asked looking at her black stretch pants and bulky sweatshirt.

"No, of course not." She self-consciously tucked a loose hair from a messy bun behind her ear. She'd seen first-hand what a crack hairstylist could do with unwashed hair. "I have a dress with me to change into."

"Better you go now." He gave her a concerned once over. "Your makeover may take some time."

"Hey!" she protested.

But he'd already been whisked off, leaving Thalia standing there. "I saw the beautiful dress Salvatore made for you."

"You mean *designed* for me."

"I heard he sewed it himself," Thalia said leaning in, like it was a secret.

"I'm sure that's not the case." But Gwen bit her lower lip. Why would such a rumor be circulating? "Thalia, was it wrong of me to accept the dress? I mean, I'm not…interested in him that way. Did I send the wrong message?"

"That's not really a fair test though. Who would turn down a dress from him?"

"Exactly." She took Thalia to a corner. "I don't want to hurt his feelings. But you don't think he's expecting anything in return?"

"Of course he is." Thalia gathered her folders like she'd been addressing a work issue. "He always expects something. There's no such thing as give and take with Salvatore. There's one give and then take, take, take, take…"

Gwen could not have articulated the man better. Perhaps at one time there had been a romance between Thalia and Salvatore. They had a lot in common. They were both from Northern Italy and educated in the United Kingdom. She rubbed the girl's shoulders. "Thank you, Thalia. You've done a great job this week. You've really kept us all on track. We wouldn't be on schedule if it weren't for you."

Thalia looked as if she'd never been complimented before. Andrew had found the time and the words to let Gwen know how *she* was doing. It only seemed right to pay that forward. She smiled one last time as Thalia skipped away. Gwen only wished she had told Andrew what she thought of the job *he'd* done.

But there was no time. An assistant on the hair and makeup team found her and dragged her through a sea of bodies to a small corner dressing room. There, her dress hung on a velvet lined hanger. It had been freshly steamed and smelled of pressing chemicals with a trace of…Salvatore's cologne. It also appeared he had made some last-minute adjustments. One of his minions had taken the dress from her the moment she had arrived, bristling about having to shorten the hemline, but the neckline was now lower and the slit was even higher!

In the back of the dressing room was a makeup table, where Gwen took a seat. The ambient colored round bulbs made her skin look flawless. "I'm taking you home," she said touching the lighted mirror.

"You read my mind." Salvatore's wicked smile reflecting back at her sent an uneasy chill up her spine.

"Excuse me?" Gwen stood and turned around to face him. "Salvatore, I could have been dressing."

He stepped in, ignoring her concern. "I hope you will give me the credit when people tell you how beautiful you look today?"

"With all the models dressed in your other clothes, I doubt anyone will find the time or inclination to remark on what *I'm* wearing." The wash of grays and whites of Salvatore's collection however was going to make the bright green dress stand out. And Gwen. Something that made her empty stomach flop. "But now that you mention it," she began but was interrupted by a tall thin man swooshing the black curtain aside and stepping in. He had a blonde wave on the top of his head and the rest was shaved. Gwen crossed her arms. "Doesn't anyone knock?"

"Check your modesty at the door, girlfriend," the man said. "I'm here to do you."

Do me? "Oh right, my hair and makeup." She ran her fingers on the table and touched the eye shadow palette plate. "I have done this before you know. Don't you have models to tend to?"

"We always hire additional people, Gwen," Andrew said holding the curtain away. The small dressing room was starting to feel like a clown car. The expression he turned toward Salvatore was sheer annoyance. "Signor Corella, there are people looking to interview you."

"Oh right," Gwen said, stepping away from the table. "Let me go find them."

"I got it, Gwen." Andrew spoke without looking at her. He clearly wanted Salvatore away from her. She tingled all over, imagining Andrew as her protector.

Salvatore briskly walked past Andrew, nearly taking the curtain with him. Looking victorious, Andrew winked at her and followed the designer through the crowd.

The stylist, whose name was Carey, fanned himself. "What I wouldn't give to have those two specimens fighting over *me*."

"They're not *fighting* over me." She sat in the chair and faced the lighted mirror again. "Andrew is just making sure his designer doesn't get distracted before the show."

"Yeah, sure." Carey pulled her hair out of the bun and began brushing out the tangles. "Girl, that man positively sizzled when he looked at you."

Gwen watched in amazement as Carey meticulously captured every bent strand and smoothed it out. *I may take Carey home too!* "That's Salvatore's shtick."

"I was talking about the tall yummy one with hair as dark as a sinful night."

Gwen met Carey's eyes in the mirror and smiled. If her plan to make Andrew want her continued to work...hopefully she'd have a *sinful* night of her own.

* * * *

The bass of the opening music vibrated inside Andrew's chest.

His production team was a well-oiled machine, but that didn't mean something couldn't go horribly wrong. Runway models like Mira, who had been giving him *come hither* looks all day, were fragile; a meltdown was possible at any moment. They were all lined up and looked like North Korean soldiers; standing up straight and expressionless. The room that had once swirled with people and voices was now nearly empty and silent.

The guests had arrived and been seated. Gwen, in her stunning dress had greeted everyone at the door with a look of welcome and comfort as if she knew each and every one of them. She had even taken the time to sit briefly with a few VIPs to make sure they were satisfied with their seats.

In other shows, he had to hire professional greeters dressed in black with headsets who robotically walked guests in and then dashed away for the next one. What a difference it made to have an actual Prada person do this. It was clear the room was set at ease and Gwen had made the guests feel privileged. Prada was a private company and did not let many people behind its walls.

She floated through the room, crowded with the media, buyers and celebrities, with effortless grace and sophistication. She was gorgeous enough to have walked the red carpet out front.

Hmm. Andrew didn't like the idea of *that* at all. Still, he raised his phone discretely and took a picture of her; zooming in on her face and then out to capture all of her. In his shoes, she glided up and down the rows, elegantly whooshing the skirt from side to side. Each step made Andrew's shirt collar feel tighter and tighter.

Caught in his own head, it took a moment to recognize the muffled sound of Salvatore's voice on the stage. His accent was always a little thicker when he addressed his fans. Prada never tried to hide its heritage and Salvatore was the best face for the design arm of the company. He liked to pretend to forget certain words in English in order to slip in as much Italian as he could into his introductions.

Andrew had discovered a few years back, reading a tear-jerking interview with *Vogue*, that Salvatore had grown up intensely poor. His father had run a small farm, and while Salvatore never came out and verbalized it, Andrew suspected the man beat him...and his mother at times. It had been hard for him to practice his calling, designing and sewing.

Andrew would have liked to see Salvatore be more charitable with his gifts and not act like...well, like such an asshole at times.

In the monitors above, he caught a glimpse of Gwen sitting with the editor-in-chief at *Vogue*. Smart. Her legs were crossed but that damn slit, which looked higher than last night, showed way too much of her thigh.

To her left was Enrico. And behind him Thalia.

So why was he backstage alone?

In a minute the entire line of models would be gone, only to return and change into their next outfits. He'd seen enough boy-boobs, and decided he'd rather be with Gwen. In the viewing area, Andrew noticed she had moved to the other side of the room. The way her head twisted from side to side, suggested she was looking for someone. Couldn't have been Salvatore, he was on stage. Catching sight of Andrew made her body language change. The curves of her face told him she was…satisfied.

He crossed the room with confidence, basking in her blue eyes. "Hey, I saw you sitting with Anna."

"Yeah, I couldn't get away from her fast enough. She scares the crap out of me."

Andrew laughed. "Well, we want her to concentrate on the show."

"Where do you usually watch all this from?"

Andrew squared his shoulders and took Gwen's hand. "Come with me. I'll show you the best seat in the house."

CHAPTER THIRTEEN

"This is amazing!" Gwen clasped her hands together in front of her.

The view from the lighting designer's booth really *was* the best seat in the house.

The space was no bigger than a fireman's rescue bucket, leaving her no choice but to be pinned up against him for most of the show. At times, his hands brushed against her arms as she swiped her hair away from her neck. As the lighting team passed by again and again, her body fell into his. On and off, his fingers pressed into her waist. The hold went from soft and gentle, as if he had no other place to put his hands, to a tighter sensation. Demanding.

Or was she just imaging all of this?

The temperature was several degrees warmer due to their elevation and the lights around them. Small trickles of sweat were beading down her back, and when Andrew leaned in to make comments during the show, his breath was hot on her shoulder, sending tingles all over her skin. She feared her nipples were raging and the small cups Salvatore had sewn into the gown would not be enough fabric to camouflage how Gwen was feeling at the moment.

Watching the show, Andrew's head bobbed in a rhythm that matched the beat by beat steps of the models. *He* should go back to modeling. Sales would soar. Gwen loved that he usually skipped a jacket in the office. Prada's men's shirts were designed for his build. Wide shoulders and a broad chest tapered down to a narrow waist. Brick red was his favorite color; the fabric made his skin look paler than it was, accentuating his cheek bones.

And this man could rock dress slacks, even if Prada's pants weren't made for his high round butt. The fabric stretched tight across his delicious derrière. He stood out from other men in the room the way a black stallion looks prancing among broken down work mules.

Andrew may still look like a top model but he had down to earth qualities. Everyone had a work persona, and at a high-profile company like Prada, image was everything. She'd seen many sides of Andrew. The man who stood up to Salvatore. The man who respected Enrico. And then…there was the man who worked with her. That was the most human side she'd seen.

Salvatore's models began marching down the stage together — signaling the show was over. Gwen sighed and erased all of the inappropriate thoughts from her mind. All she'd wanted was a few minutes to be close to Andrew and dream about what it would be like to be his. It had become a guilty pleasure to fantasize about him.

Gwen wasn't a glitzy glamor girl. Or a model. She was real. Told it like it was. Even to her detriment. She was honest, raised by a cop and a housewife in a small town. It didn't get more real than that. But she still wasn't sure if *that* was the woman Andrew wanted.

After a deep cleansing breath to get her libido in check, she smoothed her skirt ready to go back to work.

"We'd better get down there," Andrew whispered in her ear. It registered loud and clear, even over the roar of clapping from below. Again, he took her hand, but this time his grip was tighter.

Hand in hand, they crossed behind the crowd as Salvatore walked at the end of the line with Mira.

Enrico's voice came over the loudspeaker; he thanked Salvatore and made sure to kiss some media butt and even embarrass some of the celebs.

"Ready?" Andrew asked, as if he knew Enrico's routine.

"And finally, I want to present the two people who made this event happen. Our U.S. Brand Manager, Andrew Morgan and PR Executive, a woman new to Prada, Gwendolyn Foley!"

With the full lighting package shining down on her, the lights were almost blinding. The models had easily glided under the sharp beams of illumination with heavy laden bedroom eyes. Gwen just hoped her erratic blinking wouldn't be mistaken for a stroke.

She'd been walking a little slower loving the feel of Andrew leading her. At the end of the platform they waved with their free hands—but he let go to whistle at her, commanding more applause.

People were standing and clapping. She recognized all the faces she'd said hello to earlier. It was exhilarating to feel the admiration. Better than that, however, was the feeling of Andrew's hand in hers again as he whisked her away; like she was his, and he wanted her all to himself.

They returned to the area behind the stage and Gwen's one-word description of what she was witnessing was *madness*. It made her grasp his hand tighter. Nearly all of the people out front had teemed into the back. Her breath became labored. So many faces all over the place. Like a swarm. But then all she saw was Andrew's beautiful eyes.

"Gwen, are you okay?" He touched her cheek. "You look worried."

"What…" She swallowed. "What do I do now? I wasn't anticipating all this." She pointed to the swelling crowds. No one ever wanted to meet a Starlight designer.

"I tried organizing this craziness once. We have to let this part of the show flow. Don't worry, security is only letting those with the right passes in." He looked around, letting Gwen lean into his shoulder. "And Salvatore loves this. Remember I said he wants to be worshipped? Let it happen. All of these people are going to be uploading tons of pictures. It's the best free publicity we can hope for."

"Okay. Um, I'll let you do what you need to do." Gwen tried to let go of his hand.

Tried.

* * * *

Andrew couldn't bring himself to let go.

Perhaps the assignment in Milan wasn't the deal-breaker he had originally made it out to be.

He wanted Gwen. Period. He wanted to overwhelm her with his passion, take her, feel her soften in his arms. There was enough evidence to suggest she felt the same.

Deborah Garland

She stood watching him. Her chest heaving. Her eyes begging. "What do you…what do you want to do now Andrew?" she asked, her head tilted in a seductive way.

"I'd rather show you, than tell you." The swell of people in the room concerned him. Squeezing her hand, he said, "Come with me."

In her dressing room, he let go of her hand. She took a few steps inside, but turned around. She straightened her back, projecting those amazing breasts. They sat under that damn dress so perfectly, and he was ready to become better acquainted with everything underneath. He stepped an inch closer, her head lowering in passive invitation. *I'm here if you want me.*

Oh, did he ever. His arm wound around her waist, tugging her body against his. Soft against hard. The fingers of his free hand cradled her chin, gently pulling it to a more upright angle. As he bent down to kiss her, their eyes connected, her lids lowering in silent consent.

His mouth sealed over hers, gentle at first; but his eagerness ate through him. His tongue slid past her lips, to find hers, soft, wet, waiting and equally ready for him. Every cell in his body felt alive. Her hands found his waist and she pulled him toward her, grinding.

"Gwen," he said. "Oh, Gwen." He opened his mouth for air, but didn't want to waste the time away from her lips.

He backed up into the makeup chair, and without coaxing she was on his lap, her legs spread wide. But she gasped.

"What?"

"The chair's arm handles, they're cold."

He looked down. The backs of her thighs were resting on metal. Andrew smiled and slid both hands under her knees, lifting her so she wouldn't experience any discomfort. With his hands occupied at the moment, he kissed her neck and ran his lips under her jawline, while her fingers threaded through the back of his hair. He settled her lower on his lap. She was light as a feather, a surprise since she looked so full and strong. He set her down just enough to rub against the hard lump behind his zipper. The flash of her eyes showed she knew how she'd made him feel, how aroused he was.

98

"My, my. Mr. Morgan." Her voice deepened to a husky drawl.

"*My, my* is right, boys and girls," a voice from the front of the dressing room clucked. "What *have* I interrupted?"

Gwen jerked around. "Oh, hi Carey."

Andrew couldn't have said *get out* if he wanted to, he was so breathless and stunned.

"I'm just getting my bags. You two kids have fun." Carey grabbed a black suitcase and winked at Gwen. "Told ya!"

Andrew held her in the chair and caught her chin. "Told you what?"

"That you wanted me."

"Was I that obvious?"

"To him. I wasn't always sure."

He looked down. "Because I was a jerk to you at times?"

"That." She smiled and ran a finger across his cheek. The edge of her fingernail teasing him, as if she were hinting at what else she could do with those nails to his body. "I also wanted to make sure you were ready."

"I'm ready, Gwen." His one hand settled into her hair, while the other slid under her skirt.

The wet, throbbing flesh he encountered meant she was ready too.

CHAPTER FOURTEEN

Having sex in a makeup chair with only a thin black curtain to separate what was certain to be Gwen's writhing body from hordes of people—people with whom she had shaken hands and seated earlier—was probably not a wise move.

But with Andrew sliding a finger inside her and her hips grinding against his hand, it was impossible to stop.

"We should stop," he said, winded, his eyes dark and wild.

"Wha—? Why?"

"'Cuz you're moaning a little too loud." He kissed her neck.

"Was I?"

He nodded and lifted her off the chair, whispering, "Let's go someplace where I can hear you scream."

Dizzy, she twirled around the small space. Everything she brought with her was in that dressing room. She thanked God, for Andrew's good sense, to have booked one of the JW's ballrooms for the show. Even if she forgot something behind, she only needed to take an elevator ride to come collect it. Not a horrible Uber ride on a crowded L.A. freeway.

"I can't wait much longer." Andrew's warm body, holding her from behind, his lips nuzzling against her ear would make it easy to leave everything behind.

"I have to get my stuff."

He looked down and with one swoop, it was all in his massive arms. "Got it. Let's go!"

She turned to check her appearance in the lighted mirror, mostly to make sure her dress wasn't tucked into her thong, exposing red butt cheeks from a fire burning inside her body. Her appearance was a little on the disheveled side, but with all that was going on, no one would notice a *few* of her hairs out of place.

She stepped out first to have a look. As suspected, no one was watching. Andrew followed behind, and they slipped out the closest exit. That meant they had to walk completely around the building to get to the guest rooms' elevator bank.

His free hand took hers, and just like on the runway, he walked ahead, leading her. Taking her. *Taking* her.

With so many people on this side of the hotel, and all the meeting and ballrooms mashed together, Andrew grunted. It would take forever to get through this mass and at this time, the elevators would be jammed.

A faint ding behind Gwen, caught her attention. A bell hop was rolling a cart down the hall. "Freight elevator!"

Andrew spun around and as the large brass doors were closing, he used his body to stop their motion. *She* would have preferred to bang into him. Once they were opened, she slipped in and jammed her fingers against the panel to the close the doors.

It took a minute before they noticed a stack of banquet chairs in the corner. "I hope that guy wasn't coming back for these."

"He's going to have to wait," Andrew said, sliding her pile of things on the top chair. He took another chair and sat, pulling her onto his lap. "Get over here."

She released a low, throaty laugh. Girls giggle. Women do not. Andrew held her in a way she had always wanted. His large hands wrapped around her ribcage, his thumbs brushing against the sides of breasts. She lowered her head to kiss him. His lips were so full, she couldn't get enough. As each minute passed, her hidden, sensual side emerged. Andrew opened his mouth, gasping for air. Touching his face, she glided her tongue along his lips and then slowly slid a finger in and out of his mouth. His wolfish white teeth closed around her knuckle and playfully bit down.

"Touch me again," she whispered.

"Where?" he teased, kissing her neck.

"You know where."

He smiled, but the doors opened up.

"Who took this elevator!" a bell man huffed, but turned white when Andrew stood up. "Sorry about that. But we do need this elevator to accommodate our guests, sir."

"No problem." Andrew scooped her things back up and stepped out on to her floor.

They were whisper quiet as they walked to her room. In the dressing room and then in the elevator, there had been a sense of restrictions. Inside the walls of her hotel suite, anything could happen. And, she had the feeling, Andrew wasn't the kind of man to hold back. He would want to fulfil her every desire — like a genie granting not just three wishes, but any number of them. What does a woman pick first?

Her hands were trembling as she slid the key card into the reader at her suite's door. She was either shaking from nerves, or the absence of Andrew's body jammed against hers made her cold. It was a toss-up.

Inside the room, he placed her things on the dining table and turned to find her watching him. Holy crap — was he beautiful. A man that tall must be…blessed. He moved slowly toward her, his head dipped as if she was his prey.

She had no intention of running away.

His hands reached her first; his fingers gliding across the neckline of her dress, his thumb sliding into one of the cutouts. "There are so many reasons I want to rip this dress off of you."

"Go ahead," she said dotting small kisses on his face.

"I have faith in Salvatore's sewing that it won't separate at the seams too easily." He gently squeezed her heavy breasts, filling his open palms.

"Then here." She turned her back to him. As the zipper skated down, the gathered shoulder straps parted and slid away. If that hadn't been sexy enough, Andrew ran a knuckle across her exposed skin. The dim lamp light a few feet away would soften the appearance of parts of her she knew weren't perfect. She turned holding the fabric against her body, waiting for his nod to release it. When he did, she let the fabric fall.

Andrew staggered back. "Jesus, Gwen. You are so…so Goddamn *beautiful*."

She kicked the dress away from her ankles, and in nothing but her thong and his black sandals, she walked to him. He dropped to his knees and kissed her stomach, his fingers tickling her oblique muscles. He clasped the sides of her thong and the fabric slid past her hips making her feel more desirable than she could have ever imagined.

Her instincts nudged at her hands to cover herself, but not with Andrew. He stood, running the pads of his fingers across her skin. Slow and measured, watching her. Her raging nipples were warm from his heat, a convulsion of pleasure from the stroke of his fingers.

"Kiss me," she begged.

He tasted so sweet, not a trace of any food she'd seen him eat, even the coffee smell she loved on his breath was gone. His hands continued their exploration, finding her waist and her hips. "God, I love your body. I knew it would look and feel this good."

She ran her hand through his hair. "Oh yeah, and when did you first imagine it?"

"The second I saw you."

"*What?*" she screeched.

He stepped back and caught his breath. "Gwendolyn, do you really not have any idea how fucking gorgeous you are?"

The words caught her by surprise. Gwen still had moments where her confidence was short-circuited by a husband walking out on her, with no explanation. No post-mortem.

"Gwen?" Andrew's voice was concerned.

She shook her head and stepped back. "You're behind, by a few layers," she said, crossing her arms.

"I thought you'd never notice." He undid his belt. It slid out of his trousers but before he tossed it aside, she caught it.

She held the ends together, reduced the slack and snapped the sides, creating a *crack* sound. Andrew's eyes widened. "That's what you're gonna get if you're a bad boy again."

He scooped her back in his arms. "That kind of makes me want to be a little bad." His kiss was rougher this time, his lips harder against hers.

"Let me help you with this. It seems you just don't want to get undressed." She unzipped his fly and let the trousers slide down long muscular legs. A light fuzz of hair covered his skin. He was such a...*man*. Was he the mold?

Peeking at the bulge in his boxer-briefs, she became startled. No, *she* was the one who was blessed. Thank. You. God!

In a voice shockingly low and raspy, he said, "Take off my shirt, Gwen."

A delicious chill ran through her at his command. She stepped forward, and slid her finger in the folds of his tie, loosening the knot. A hand curled around her wrist, tight. Dominant.

With the tie gone, her fingers slid along the vertical hem of the shirt, releasing every button from their hole, while he lifted his arms around her to unfasten his cuffs. He tore the shirt off, but there was a V-neck undershirt.

When will I see that body already? She was completely naked yet he could still run out of the room if it caught fire!

Still, in an undershirt and boxer briefs, this man was a sight to behold. Seeing his biceps earlier in the week and not being able to touch them had left her wondering what his skin felt like. She had every right to feel his muscles now. Heat radiated from his body, even *beneath* expensive clothes. The surface of his bare skin scorched under her touch. His biceps weren't rock-hard but she didn't care to compete with dumbbells for a man's time. He was nicely contoured and his skin had a velvety texture dotted with several dark beauty marks.

Yes, they marked him well. Her fingers slid along the hem of the undershirt and with his help it slid cleanly over this head.

Gwen stood back to catch her breath. She wanted to give herself to this man. Regardless of what it meant or didn't mean. He was worth it. She craved his heat and passion. This was the best part; discovering every inch of a man. Testing the limits of provocativeness, she lifted her leg and set her foot on the desk chair, completely exposing everything she was to him. "Do you want to undo the straps?"

"No fucking way." He vaulted forward, lifted her on his shoulder and carried her to the bed. His movement was fluid and confident.

The feeling of expensive bedding against her bare skin heightened her aching need for him. Andrew hovered over her body, brushing his full and sexy lips over hers, back and forth. His tongue rimmed the edge of her lips, and dipped inside, swirling hot sweetness inside her mouth.

She pushed her own tongue forward to capture the tangle outside her mouth. Her fingers touched his face, letting them slide past his lips.

His nose glided across her jaw as his mouth slid down her neck. She marveled at the slow descent down her body. She cupped her own breasts giving him full access to taste her skin. There had never been a time when her nipples were so hard. Even her areolas had puffed out for Andrew. Every inch of her was hard.

Gwen's hands slid down his body to find out how hard *he* was at the moment.

* * * *

Andrew wanted Gwen to address the steel hard bulge inside his boxers, but first he wanted to feel and taste every inch of her.

Her body had teased him all these weeks, making him imagine what she'd been hiding behind her clothes. Were push-up bras keeping those curves in place under her blouses? Nope. When that gown fell away, her breasts bobbed in place, so firm and full and fucking perfect. His body heated, touching her nipples. Cute little reddish-brown nubbins on a swollen areola. Oh, what heaven.

The faint glow of light a few feet away made her skin look angelic. Smooth. Delicious.

His mouth closed around one hard nipple and her back shot into a deep arch. The groan she released was fucking intoxicating. He could stay there forever but he had another place he wanted her to feel his tongue. He dipped his fingers between her legs, synchronizing the rhythm of his hands with his tongue.

"Jesus, Andrew. You're making me insane."

"Wait. There's more." His face skidded down her torso, taking in the scent of her body. Vanilla and feminine musk. The rose scent was isolated to her hair, but she had so much of it, the smell often overwhelmed him. He was pleased to discover the hidden traces of what her body released when she was aroused. Rich and earthy.

"Taste me," Gwen whispered, her hips lifting to position her wet flesh as an offering for this mouth. His fingers already told him what he would find between her legs. Soft black curls, wet now, easily parted so he could get at the tender delectable damp folds.

Oh, how sweet to the taste and soft to the touch. At first lick, Gwen's hips bucked. "Easy, girl. I've got you." But he couldn't wait anymore. Her skin was so taut, to gain complete access he needed to spread her. Wide. He probed and penetrated her skin seductively with his tongue, showing her how he made love. *This is your preview, Gwen.* He got into a steady rhythm with the roll of her hips. His hair being pulled didn't slow him down, and her cries of pleasure only made him more determined. She released soft pants that sounded magical. He already couldn't wait to hear the sound again.

"Wait! Andrew. No. Stop. Stop. Andrew, *stop*," she cried out, pushing his head away.

A shudder ran through his body. He'd heard of this. Getting a woman so close and then they say no. And if you keep going, that's... "Gwen, what's the matter?"

She sat up and closed her legs. "That's not how I want to come...tonight." Her mouth closed over his, kissing his lips with a wild hunger, like she desired the taste of her own skin. "I want to savor you too, you know." She kissed his chest, teasing his nipples the way he teased her.

His hips bucked reminding her of the lump inside his boxers that could no longer be ignored. She slid back and ran her lips over the fabric. He released a cry of delight.

"I have to see it."

At her request, he roughly tugged his boxers down. His manhood filled her waiting hands.

"The skin is like silk," she said with wonder. "And smooth. You have the most beautiful veins. So thick and such length." She swallowed and glided her hands up and down.

Andrew kissed her roughly, pressing harder with every tightening grip of her hand. "It's all yours."

"Really, it's mine?"

He licked his lips planning to pleasure her to her wits end with his erection. "Yes, Gwen."

She leaned back and spread her legs for him. "*Take* me, Andrew. I'm yours."

Eagerly, he moved toward her, but his heart spiked, freezing him to stillness. He backed away, shaken. "I don't..." He ran a nervous hand through this thick black hair. "I don't *have* anything."

"Oh." Gwen caught her breath. "You didn't bring condoms with you on this trip?"

"I haven't bought condoms in almost three years."

The look on her face begged for more of an explanation, but that would have to wait. "So that means you haven't been with anyone since your wife?"

"No, of course not."

"I haven't been with anyone since my husband."

"Good." Andrew had had enough one-night-stands when he was in his twenties. The idea of that type of meaningless exchange felt hollow. Since then he'd been settled down, and *liked* being married.

"Well, I was supposed to get my period a couple of days ago. I guess with all the excitement and the time change..." When his hands closed around her swollen breasts, she kissed his mouth to calm him down and said, "Yeah, they're not usually this plump. Make love to me Andrew."

He got up on his knees and settled between her legs. He trusted her. He wanted her. Before anything else, he kissed her again. She ran her hands along his shoulders, nails digging into his skin.

Christ. He licked the tips of his fingers and stroked a coat of moisture across his erection, just in case. He settled against her damp heat and pushed forward. Nope. Not needed. He entered her cleanly, the tip sliding past the gorgeous mass of deep black curls. Further in, he hit resistance. Tight. Oh God, she felt incredible. She angled her hips and pressed her fingers on his ass, urging him in further.

"Jesus, Gwen."

The quiet, sweet woman melted away and a vixen came through. She wrapped her right leg around his waist. The cool metal studs of the Filettra sandal dug into his lower back as she commanded the rhythm she wanted him to take. He'd never felt more like a man. She cried out in response to his long slow thrusts. He couldn't remember a woman feeling so hot, so tight. Gwen's muscles gripped him as he pulled away to torture her. Oh, the way she responded to him. Like she was made for him.

Her body was firm yet soft and those curves were intoxicating. She was a woman. A real woman. But raw and primal. Her hips and back bucked wildly like a bronco. She wiggled and grinded against him to match his rhythm. Soon her body was covered in a layer of mist. Women can moan and fake orgasms, but they can't fake sweat. The thought of making her come made his own sanity start to slip away.

"Get on top of me," he commanded in a voice raw with lust. It would buy him a few moments. He wanted to watch her body bend and squirm, taking the pleasure she wanted.

She obliged instantly. He took an extra moment to kiss her heavy breasts before she slid back on to him. Her groan nearly did him in.

"Ride me, Gwen."

Her hips rolled back and forth like a sexy belly dancer. To think she'd been denied the ability to give this pleasure to anyone. Then again, so had he. And yet, they'd found each other. Not two strangers hooking up out of desperation or drunken need. But mature adults who wanted each other and acted. With her grinding into him, there was little for him to do at this point except watch this gorgeous creature gyrate above him.

Her head jerked forward, all that glorious thick dark hair fell in front of her face and then it all spilled back as she arched above him. "Andrew…Andrew… Yes, right there…I'm gonna come."

"Let it go," he grunted, squeezing, trying to hold on. The pulses were strong, making her even tighter if that was possible. Griping him, choking him. The more she jerked and squealed, the closer he came to shooting his pleasure into her. And he was sure that was *not* the right thing to do.

Her body went soft and draped on top of his chest. He took this wet noodle of a woman and flipped her over, hoping he still had an active participant. "How was that?"

"Holy crap," she blurted grasping on to his shoulders. "Did you…?"

"Not yet," he whispered, returning to his rhythm, watching how every move affected her sensitive skin. He kissed her shoulders; the sweat of her body was deliciously salty. To gain maximum penetration, he hooked her right leg in the crook of his arm, and buried himself deep, deep inside her, and rocked until he felt the shivers of his climax.

He groaned at the signal and leaned forward, rose up onto his elbows, and sealed their bodies together. At the right moment, he slid out and rested his raging erection on her stomach, using the weight of his body to finish. But he wasn't expecting it to feel so powerful. He gasped and choked, "Gwen. Jesus, Gwendolyn."

"Yes. Yes," she whispered, still writhing. It was clear she knew what was happening, but she took it, wanted it.

He finished while kissing her and stroking her hair. She kissed him back with passion. Connected passion. This was not the end.

It was the new beginning Andrew had prayed for.

CHAPTER FIFTEEN

Gwen wasn't sure her breathing would ever return to normal.

And there might be plenty of more to this, so she'd better get her lungs in shape. It certainly hadn't felt like a one-night-stand. You can't do that with a co-worker. If that's all he wanted, he would have pounced sooner. And back in New York, where he could escape behind the door of a locked apartment.

No, their attractions had grown and simmered on the stove. It just needed a shot of heat to bring it to a boil. And did it ever!

"Wow." Andrew lifted his head out of the bundle of her hair, keeping her pinned. "Let me go get a wash cloth." He kissed her nose and peeled away. The way he groaned told her he didn't want to be away from her.

The urge to peek at what he'd spilled on her was too strong to ignore. He'd not been with anyone since… And from the pictures on her blog, Cate had been too sick months before her death. Gwen's neck crammed forward. "Yikes, that's a lot."

"I wouldn't move if I were you," he said returning. He sat next to her comfortable in his nakedness. What a specimen this man was. He'd be another prime example to aliens that earth had already been occupied. Every inch of him was magnificent.

The washcloth was warm and wet on her skin. He'd run it under warm water! Gently he rubbed it against her stomach. She looked down. "You may need to get another one."

"Probably should have just doused a towel."

With his hand firmly on her stomach, she leaned over and put the nightstand lamp on to help him see what he was doing.

He turned the cloth over a few times. "That should do it." He leaned forward and kissed her.

She held his face when he did, his anxious tongue penetrating her mouth. *There's gonna be a round two!*

"Gwen?"

"Yes," she said coyly, hoping he was thinking the same thing.

"Do you… With your husband, did you…come often?"

She bit her lip. "Not really. He didn't seem too interested in my pleasure."

"Idiot." Andrew sat back, ready to discard the washcloth. His face was caught in the light of the lamp. Any shadow of gloom was gone. He was glowing, happy.

"Um. You missed a spot." She circled her fingers over the soft skin of her breast.

"Oh," he said smiling. "Don't want to leave…" His hand jerked away as if something bit him. When she looked down at her own skin, he was gaping, his mouth open. "Gwen, what are these scars?"

Uh oh. Her hands immediately covered her right breast, which was riddled with small faint puncture marks. Without the light shining down on her, her damaged skin was shadowed. But in the stark light of an LED bulb, his eyes were fixed on what she perhaps should have mentioned weeks ago, when the subject of her mother had come up. But they were still getting to know each other, professionally. It didn't seem to be an "officey" subject. With a male, no less.

Yet, they just crossed the line. Wildly humped across it.

"Gwendolyn, what's going on here?" He pointed, sitting back.

Any moisture left in her mouth turned as dry as the desert mountains off in the distance. Her gaze fell upon her own skin, joining Andrew's stare.

"I've had some biopsies," she choked out.

"*Some* biopsies?" He moved his beautiful body away.

She tried to touch him. "Andrew, wait, listen."

"I'm listening, Gwen." But his touch was gone.

"I keep having abnormal mammograms."

"Abnormal?" The panic in his voice was hard to hide. "Do you have breast cancer in your family?"

She bit the inside of her mouth, choosing not to respond to his question. "Look, all these scars are from biopsies proving that I'm fine." Gwen pointed to the faded crescent around her areola and several smaller puncture wounds.

"Why are there so many?"

"Because my radiology doctor is biopsy-happy. Every piece of tissue has come back negative. Andrew, please, I'm fine."

"One of those looks fresh."

"Yes, they're just routine procedures."

The rich color in Andrew's skin from his arousal was fading. "You didn't answer me. You told me weeks ago, your mother is passed. How did she die, Gwen?" He stood.

"That was a long time ago," she snapped and rolled off the bed.

"She died of breast cancer, didn't she?" Andrew asked holding his boxers.

"There wasn't regular screening back then. She had lumps the size of golf balls in both breasts for years. She just never did anything about it."

"But Gwen, you know what that means." The man was frozen watching her.

"Yes. I *know* what it means. But every test has come back negative." With only the gown lying close by, she'd have to dig through her luggage to put something on. She didn't want to have this conversation naked, but Andrew didn't seem interested in waiting to have a rational discussion.

"I...I went through so much, Gwen. I may not be able to do all that again."

"But *I* am *fine*, damn it." She spun around and faced the lights of Downtown L.A. The windows were tinted in bright blue; no one could see her bare body. Or the tears starting to roll down her cheeks.

"Gwen, talk to me."

The picture came into focus. She hadn't connected any dots of what Andrew's experience and what she had gone through would mean if they… The concept of her and Andrew had only sharpened a few days ago. And this whole sex-capade didn't start with a discussion, it started with a kissing assault.

The photos of Cate from the blog flashed through Gwen's mind. What the disease did to her. How it mangled her body. And Andrew had to watch it all happen. When Gwen said losing a mother was different from a spouse she meant it. Yes, she watched her mother wither away too, but her father had been

112

there to bathe her, to hold her head when she vomited. Gwen also had Greg and Skye to help out when her father needed a break.

There had been no break for Andrew.

Andrew… If this went forward, he'd be on *their* side. The family she loved who'd been hounding her, treating her differently, keeping things from her, thinking she had too much going on to take being told her father had shot someone. *We didn't want to upset you, Gwen.*

It would have made sense to sell that stupid house and move in with her dad, or even Skye. But their worried faces would be staring at her every day. No, her house was a sanctuary. It had a front door she could close and lock to get away from their constant needling. She understood they were afraid and they didn't want to lose her too.

"I'm not sick!" Gwen yelled at the people who weren't in the room.

"I know you're not." Andrew approached her; his body reflecting in the glass panels. "But it seems you're taking a very cavalier attitude toward something that could be—"

She whipped around and pulled the coverlet off the bed. "It's late. And I think this was a mistake."

"Gwen wait!" He raised his hands but dropped them to his side. After a few more seconds of silence, he rubbed his face. "Okay. Maybe you're…right."

Her breath clipped like she'd been hoping for more of a fight from him. Don't all women want that? They want the upper hand to say *no*, yet want to be begged to say *yes*. "I'm sorry." She nodded, agreeing with him.

When he didn't acknowledge her apology, Gwen stepped inside her bathroom and slammed the door shut.

* * * *

Andrew inched toward the bathroom door, and rested his palm against the smooth satiny wood.

Was this a mistake? It didn't *feel* like a mistake. How could something that felt so right, turn out this bad?

113

His hand raised to the door to knock on it. He had to tell her about Milan. The extended trip sat in the corner of his mind, while they made love. *No, by all means, continue with your fun.*

He had looked forward to more intimate passion, and then he was going to gently break it to her.

Life was short—he'd learned that the hard way. Andrew had no intention of letting these coming weeks apart derail what could have been his second chance.

But what if Gwen *did* become sick? The horrors he'd witnessed with Cate were buried inside him. PTSD comes out in nefarious ways, he'd been told. What if he committed to Gwen and *then* something happened? Could he see it through?

He reluctantly left her suite. *What a mess.*

By the time he made it back to his room, a twinge of anger started seeping into the mix. Gwen ended this. *She* shut down, refused to talk about it. *She* let *him* go.

At two am, he held his phone, Gwen's number on the screen. Would she even pick up? His head was clouded with too many thoughts, the loudest being his flight to Milan tomorrow night.

If Marcello couldn't get up to speed by the end of the year, Andrew would be trapped in Milan permanently; and Gwen, with her few faded biopsy scars, was much preferable to that.

CHAPTER SIXTEEN

Gwen waited for Andrew at the airport gate the next afternoon.

They were on this flight alone. Enrico and Thalia were staying until Sunday. And Salvatore was staying until the following week. Gwen had left him in the hands of List LA to finish his interviews, and his personal assistant could get him to his meetings. The taxi she took sailed to the airport, since Saturday morning traffic in Downtown L.A. was non-existent.

Nerves pooled in her stomach. She'd hoped Andrew would have tried to make contact, either last night or this morning. This was unchartered territory for her. She'd never had a fling with a co-worker.

A fling? This wasn't supposed to *be* a fling. It was clear that Andrew was a noble man. Honorable. If this was something else, he would have just pulled her thong aside, unzipped his pants and had her right there in the dressing room. Could her judgment have been that off?

If this was going to work out, there had to be a clear understanding of one thing: her health was *her* business. When there would be something to worry about, she would let him know.

She gasped at that thought. *Something*. Something real. A real problem. Could she do that to him? How could she have not seen this conflict? She'd been so deep in her own denial that there was nothing wrong. Worry wasn't going to get the better of her, poisoning her thoughts. There was a life to be lived. There had even been studies; worrying could increase her chances. The immune system lowers from stress.

It was clear, Andrew was going to be on Team Skye and relentlessly hound Gwen. He would be the perfect partner for her sister. And the pressure to get the genetic testing would be ratcheted up. Oh, *hell* no.

Slowly, Gwen backed away from the gate and took off to find another flight home.

* * * *

Andrew checked his phone after the attendant said, "We're boarding, sir."

Gwen never showed up for the flight. How was that possible? He had summoned the courage to go back to her suite that morning, but all he'd found was a cleaning cart outside an empty suite. Gwen had already checked out. And instead of waiting for him to share a taxi, she got herself to the airport. Strong independent women could be infuriating at times.

So how could she have missed the flight?

He cursed under his breath and got on the plane.

It was excruciating to sit in that damn middle seat. He considered getting plastered, except he had approximately six hours to go to his apartment, pack up enough clothes for two months, go to the office, pack that whole mess up and get back to the airport for a red-eye to Milan. *Meelano.*

The jet stream got him to New York in less than five hours, and in his office if he had enough time, he would stare at Gwen's desk for another five. It was so neat, not a paper out of place. He'd managed to keep his own desk almost as tidy. He scanned the surface making sure he had everything. He'd been back and forth to Italy so often, he had a complete second set of materials in his office there.

Andrew swiped one last item from his desk and stuck it into his canvas bag.

Maybe all of this was for the best.

* * * *

Walking into her house in the harsh Sunday morning light, Gwen felt like she'd *walked* home from L.A. Exhaustion passed her doing ninety, hours ago. She was on fumes at this point.

Ditching her flight with Andrew was cowardly, she admitted that to herself…eventually. And paying a crazy amount of money out of her own pocket — money she couldn't spare — to take a flight that made *two* God-awful stops was evidence she'd screwed up.

The final leg was a red eye out of Chicago. The whole time, Skye had been texting her. *Where are you? You said you'd be home around five pm.* If Gwen hadn't messed up or overreacted, the answer could have been, *I'm in Andrew's apartment. Naked. Leave me alone.* ☺

It wasn't surprising that as soon as Gwen was two steps into her living room there was a knock at the door.

When she took off for California, she was on her way to her first major fashion show in an exciting city she'd never visited. The focus had been completely on that triumph; that milestone. It had been all she could talk about. She left L.A. with a different narrative. There was certainly a better story to tell now and any professional success was going to be overshadowed by falling into bed with Andrew.

She spun on her Prada heels to answer the door, catching a glimpse of her appearance in the starburst mirror. Her skin was shockingly pale. She opened the door, her teeth jammed together for strength.

"Well finally!" Skye said holding a cup of Dunkin Donuts coffee. Her shoulder length hair swung free under a wide brimmed hat. A striking turquois peacock feather cascaded off the left side. She'd been going to church every Sunday since their mother died. "So, how was it?"

"It was good." Gwen stepped aside to let her sister in. Even in her near-delusional state, she could appreciate a nice dress. "That's a great outfit," Gwen commented on Skye's cream and red sweater dress under a stylish blazer.

"Thank you." Skye put her coffee on Gwen's kitchen table filled with newspapers and junk mail. "It's not Prada though, Miss Fancy-pants."

Gwen picked at the pile, distressed at all the magazines she hadn't read. "Thanks for taking all of this in for me."

"No problem. So-o-o? How was the show?"

"Fine," she answered coldly, while pulling apart the newspaper sections to figure out what had happened in the world while her head was in the clouds with Andrew. And his was between her legs.

"Gwen!"

"What?"

"What's wrong?"

"I'm just tired." She wiped her eyes. "I didn't sleep on the plane."

"No." Skye put her hands on her slender hips and tilted her head. It wasn't surprising her sister could tell she was lying. "I've seen you tired. Did something happen?"

Unlike the seams of Salvatore's dress, Gwen busted open; easily letting go of the tears she'd been holding back for nearly eighteen hours. "I messed up..." Dragging herself onto three different planes made that abundantly clear.

"Oh sweetie." Skye rushed to her side. The scent of their mother's perfume, which her sister had been wearing for years, immediately comforted Gwen and for a moment eased her pain. "Talk to me."

"Let me go put on a pot of coffee." Gwen wiped her nose, wishing she could open a bottle of wine instead.

Clutching a mug, Gwen described the beautiful hotel and how it felt to sleep in that fantastic suite. How Salvatore surprised her with a gorgeous dress, but Andrew one-upped him with the amazing shoes. And how intense the moment was when he slipped the sandals on her feet.

Skye was shaking her head. "Okay. And did something *happen* with Andrew?"

Gwen drew a sharp breath and began to let the post-fashion show story unfold. As she spoke, she was alarmed at how *un*-alarmed her sister looked, being told how she had been so overtaken by Andrew Morgan. How he made her feel.

Looking away, Gwen gruffly said to the woman who'd just returned from church, "I slept with him. Skye, it was so fantastic. Not just the sex but the connection we had. It was so...real." She would keep the dirty details of what he did to her body to herself...and Ben & Jerry. They would savor and cry over that one together. Later. Alone.

Before Gwen let her sister draw the wrong conclusion about Andrew, she backtracked to fill her sister in on what had happened to him. What had shaped this man to react the way he did to her scars.

Skye touched her chin and focused her rich brown eyes at Gwen—who'd been expecting *I told ya so*, and *See, we're not freaks for worrying*. Or words of rational wisdom about what to do in this precarious situation. Instead, Skye asked, "Can I see the shoes?"

"Really?" Gwen bit out, while rubbing what had to be a nose as red as Rudolph's. "That's all you got?"

Skye took a deep breath, clearing the emotion from her voice. Certainly, seeing her little sister hurt should ignite a momma-bear, bone-crushing response. But attorneys were trained to look at matters from all sides. And despite the high-drama legal shows where everything seems to end up in court, most attorneys prefer to negotiate and settle disputes.

"Okay," Skye finally said. Her tone was smooth and even. "You'll see him in the office tomorrow. You need to be strong and firm about how you feel. And ditch that ice-queen who snapped at him."

"Speaking of ice, I need a drink." Gwen stood, grabbed her suitcase and climbed the stairs to her sad bedroom. She rolled her luggage into the room, unconcerned that it had fallen over.

"So what do *you* think you should do?" Skye asked, following. "What's your plan, little sister?"

Gwen crouched down to her lumpy mattress. "Maybe I should just call in sick."

Hours after Skye left, Gwen sat at her kitchen island trying to force down some take-out food. After thinking about it, the idea of an explosion in the office was worth swallowing her pride to make the first call. *Put your big girl pants on, Gwendolyn.*

For now, it was nothing else but a *let's get the awkwardness out of the way* call about how to work together going forward. But every call went right to voicemail. Each *Hello. You've reached Andrew Morgan at Prada. I can't take your call right now, but please...* in that deep sexy voice of his was maddening. Especially since she didn't know when he created that message. Which Andrew was she listening to? The man who still had a wife? The recent widower? The man who'd met her? She began calling the number just analyze the damn message, listening to voices in the background to give her a clue.

At four am, Gwen gave up.

CHAPTER SEVENTEEN

On the long monotonous train ride into the city the next morning, Gwen sat with wet hair she'd been too lazy to blow-dry and turned numb.

Her phone was still clutched to her palm, praying for a call or even a text from Andrew. Nothing. Silence.

Except several emails from Enrico, laying out her next assignments. He had asked her to work with the advertising team for a holiday campaign and set up the promotional VIP parties and events. This was something she took issue with. At Starlight those tasks went to the greenest employees. But this was Prada. No event or campaign was unimportant. And Gwen had a feeling Prada's holiday marketing budgets were huge.

Enrico was also putting her in charge of Salvatore's new collection. Her experience certainly qualified her to develop a strategic plan. But Andrew wasn't copied on any of the emails, nor was he mentioned in any way as far as *Work with Andrew on this*, or *Get with Andrew for that*.

Good God! Had he told Enrico what happened? She'd be mortified!

Her stomach churned on the elevator to the marketing floor. She planned to walk into her office, give Andrew a stiff nod and not speak to him after all. Still, her legs wobbled in that direction. The stainless-steel lever was colder than she remembered. Andrew must have already iced it over.

"Gwendolyn!"

She blinked and turned around. "Hi, Enrico. I'm sorry I'm late. I'm still jet-lagged."

"*Cara*, you look like you flew home on the wings of the plane!"

Which one of the *three*, she wondered? Probably all of them, based on how she felt at the moment. The muted steel blue sweater dress and dark stockings she'd put on this morning fit her somber mood. And to make this the perfect start of a new week, her period had arrived and the pain bordered on unbearable.

But Enrico standing at the door made a small dose of relief slice through her. She wouldn't have to face Andrew alone this morning. It would be too jarring. Searching for something to say out of stress was when people did and said stupid shit. "Do you need something, Enrico?"

"Yes, I want to talk to you about Andrew." Unless the third party wasn't neutral.

Andrew *did* say something. *Son of a bitch,* she screamed in her head, but in a calm voice said, "Okay. Do you want to go in your office?"

"No, your office is fine." He tapped on the wood, encouraging her to open the door.

Oh. Dear. God! This was going to be a face to face intervention. But her heart rate lowered when she realized the door was locked. Andrew wouldn't be sitting in his chair with a pissed off look on his face.

Inside, his familiar scent made her stomach clench. It wasn't even cologne. It turned out to be a combination of his soap, fresh laundered shirts and his intense masculinity that left a taste of him in the air. Oh God! She missed him. She got her control in check and turned to her boss. "What did you want to talk to me about?"

"Sit down, *cara.*"

The fear that something might have happened to Andrew hit her so swiftly she *had* to sit down. If she didn't get a grip on her emotions, the terrible Chinese food from last night was going to end up all over her desk. "I'm sitting," she managed through clenched teeth.

Enrico took Andrew's chair from his desk and glided it next to her. "Unfortunately, Marcello in Milan has not been working out the way we had hoped."

She swallowed. "We?"

"Andrew and I." Enrico pressed his lips together. "I have sent him back to Milan."

Andrew was in Italy. He wasn't even on *this continent!* "For…" She stumbled. "For how long?"

"This may be good news for you, Gwendolyn."

"How can any of this be good news for me?" Her eyes shot open wide. *Did I just say that out loud?*

"*Cara?*" Enrico's warm hand covered hers.

She swiped at the lashes she hadn't bothered coating with mascara that morning, from exhaustion. "I'm sorry. I'm just not feeling well."

"If Marcello does not work out and we have to let him go, Andrew will have to resume the position." He studied Gwen's face. "I have given him until the end of the year."

The end of the year. She turned slowly to the small puppy calendar tacked to the corkboard next to her desk. Thanksgiving was the following week. She wouldn't see Andrew until next year? Or… A choking sensation tickled the back of her throat. Or not at all if this Marcello didn't get his Italian act together. She'd been biting her lip so hard she feared she would break the skin. "So *why* is this good news for me?"

"You have far exceeded our expectations. On Thursday night, Andrew and I had dinner and we spoke about you at length."

Thursday night. The night before the show. The night before he made love to her. "What did he say exactly?"

"He said the work you have been doing showed him you could handle both yours and his position here in New York, if he were to remain in Milan permanently."

"On Thursday you asked him to go to Milan?"

"Yes, *cara.*" Enrico nodded. "It was a last-minute request, but Andrew was happy to accommodate me."

That was when Gwen could have sworn she was going to be sick. *Happy.* He was *happy* to take off.

"You and I will talk more about the other matter if it becomes necessary. We have not made any final decisions."

"Enrico, these were just dropped off." Thalia came into the office and placed a stack of photos from the show on Gwen's desk.

"Ah, yes. Thank you, Thalia."

Gwen couldn't make eye contact with the girl just yet. They'd been talking about how Salvatore may or may not have expected something for the dress. Then Gwen left with Andrew.

Now *he* was nowhere to be found. This was why people shouldn't shit where they eat! "What's this for, Enrico?"

"For today, we would like you to review these proofs and work with the art department to create the media kits for Salvatore's collection."

Every 'we' cut deep crevices, but still Gwen said, "Okay. I'll get that done today."

"Then go home if you are still not feeling well, *cara*." He stood and walked toward the door.

"I'll be fine." Gwen closed the door behind him and spun around the office.

Andrew was in Milan until the end of the year. *And* he knew all of this when he made love to her. Even though he wouldn't be walking in any moment, his absence left a gaping void that was turning out to be greater than his presence. The powerful lingering scent he'd left behind had enough energy to rise up and create a translucent form of the man. A part of Andrew was still there. Watching her.

She picked up the stack of photos, carelessly letting pictures of model after model slide past her fingers. Buried in the pile was a photo of her from the show. The green dress stood out from all the neutral colors in the other pictures. Gwen yanked that photo out, balancing the others. But it wasn't just of her, it was of her *and Andrew*. She studied his face for the truth he'd been keeping from her. She hoped to see a man who was hiding a secret and who had been planning a massive getaway. Instead all she saw was adoration.

Yet...he took off to Milan. So why didn't he tell her? Before, or...after.

There wasn't much of an after, though. He'd been cleaning her up and that's when the argument started about her medical issues. And *she'd* finished it by storming away. No resolution.

In a burst of frustration, Gwen threw the photos in the air not wanting to think about that day ever again. The glossy prints rained down around her; flashes of white from the photo paper sides fluttering like doves released at a wedding. But this felt more like a funeral.

Her hands were shaking, rolling Andrew's chair back to his side of the office. She slammed the executive swivel so hard into the desk that a small glass container of paper clips fell over. She debated leaving the mess but took the high ground and cleaned them up.

She reached over and was jarred by the empty space in front of his phone. The gaping hole was surrounded by folders, pens and sketches.

The picture of Andrew and Cate was gone.

Gwen braced her body against the desk, staring at where the photo had been. Just the week before, Andrew had moved the frame to make room for art layouts they had been looking at. It had struck Gwen how he had picked it up with no emotion as if it were his stapler.

Yet now that stupid frame, the one *Gwen* purchased, was in Milan. With Andrew.

* * * *

In his Milan office, Andrew's arms were folded, his chin leaning against his wrists as he listened to rain pounding against the windows.

He stared at the photo of him and Cate, and all he could see was his own reflection in the glass. He didn't like what he saw. And Cate's eyes seemed to narrow at him, disapproving what he'd done.

It ate at him that *Enrico* would be telling Gwen he was in Milan. It ached how the news was going to be received. His phone was dark, cold and dead, only coming back to life since he'd plugged it into his laptop.

Somewhere in the twelve thousand miles he traveled and the multiple stops he made, his charger had gone missing. He clicked on his laptop to do some work, and the Auto Play icon popped open. He took a breath. Managing his photos from the show would be delegated to his Milan assistant. Knowing she would sort and file them into the Dropbox accessible to the entire department to use on the company's website and other materials, Andrew hit *[Open folder to view files.]*

With a few more clicks pictures dotted the screen slowly, due to the megabyte size making the process crawl. He passed the monitor several times walking around his office, getting resituated while the last set of photos materialized.

Gwen's face appeared in one small box after another, creating a flipbook. His jaw quivered as they came into focus. They weren't just pictures of a colleague at an event, smiling or pointing. There were ones he'd snapped as he watched her from the shadows. Her face, her hair, her shoulders swallowed up the frame. It was all he saw of her. It was all he *had* of her, now.

How she'd smiled at him only reminded him how much she had wanted him. The feeling of being wanted wasn't foreign. But for Andrew, most times he felt *hunted*. He wasn't a game to Gwen. With her, the feeling was different. Natural.

What he would have trouble shaking the most was the feel of her beneath him, powerful and supple. Her combination of curves and strength brought out another side to his passion. Feral and wild. She took every ounce of what he had to give and gave back just as much. He could be himself with her…and that made her impossible to resist.

Gwen could handle the *real* Andrew.

Yet, he couldn't ignore feeling blindsided by the news of her health. It still would have been startling to hear had she'd been upfront. But she'd made it seem like it was no big deal. Either she was being careless with her health or she hadn't intended on opening up to him.

Even if they were in a…a relationship. He'd been so ready to take that step forward. With Gwen.

But now his hopes for a new start had evaporated. Like his patience.

The rest of the photos had loaded, but he grabbed his mouse, highlighted the ones of Gwen—and sent them all into the Recycle Bin.

He stared at the bin for several minutes, something nagging at him over that decision for the rest of the afternoon.

By the time he made it back to the flat, the rain hadn't let up and he was soaked. In the center of the hallway, the black cat sat…also wet from the rain.

Andrew looked around, curious about why it was just sitting there. The mischief in the fuzzy little face made Andrew smile for the first time since leaving Gwen. He tapped the owner's door but the one across the hall opened up instead. The attractive older woman who always watched him with intensity called out in her broken English, "Signora Morelli passed away last week."

Andrew glanced down at the soggy feline. "I'm sorry."

"My daughter...she is allergy to cats."

"Allergic," Andrew corrected. And now he owned a cat.

"I have been feeding him out here and I think he likes to sleep outside anyways." She disappeared into her apartment, the large black lacquered door slamming behind her. When it opened again she was balancing two dishes and a small bag of dry food. He rushed to help her, catching a glimpse of what was under her robe. Her dark eyes met his. "*Scusa.*"

The moment hit him like he'd been slammed into a wall. There, a beautiful willing woman. And him...single, technically. He could drop the bag of food and pull her into his apartment.

But that's not what he wanted. That woman was not *who* he wanted. He cleared his throat and moved his eyes away. Fast.

"I'll do my best to take care of him. But I live in America. I'm only here until the end of the year."

"I will see if another neighbor can take him after that. But he is looking, how you say...lonely right now?"

He was indeed. Andrew knew the look. It's what he saw in his own mirror. "*Grazi.*"

Without a formal invitation, the cat scampered into his flat. Andrew followed him in and grabbed a small towel to dry him off. The cat purred happily at his touch.

He set up the two bowls under the window his friend preferred to climb through. The tin bowl was filled with water and placed on the floor. The cat lapped at it as if he'd been in a desert. The other bowl was made of ceramic and badly chipped. Still, Andrew poured the contents of an unknown brand of food into it. It would top his shopping list, to get the little guy something better to eat. And new bowls. But upon placing the food down, the writing on the side caught Andrew's attention. "Your name is Casper?"

He purred loudly, his body stretching up to get to the food.

"That's a strange name for a black cat." Andrew pet his back while Casper crunched on little fish shaped nuggets.

"I'm going to get cleaned up." He paused, realizing he'd said so little in that flat in all the time he'd been staying there. When Cate passed, he disappeared inside himself, alone in his head with only his thoughts. He could already feel himself slipping back into that abyss because of Gwen. But the large yellow eyes staring at him were begging for conversation. And it felt good to have someone to talk to.

After a shower that wasn't as hot as he would have liked, one that wiped away the last remnants of Gwen's perfume, Andrew sat on the velvet sofa. He turned on the television, but soon dipped his head back to close his eyes.

He dreamed of Cate for the first time in more than a year. It had always felt like he was underwater, her image so blurry. Probably his brain was unable to conjure the right memory of her. The beautiful healthy woman, or the mangled mess.

Even her voice was muted, but Andrew recalled her speaking about Gwen. *She is your second chance. Don't give up on her.* The kiss Cate left on his cheek was a warm, moist peck pressing against his skin. She was still his wife, but his heart belonged elsewhere at this point.

Drew?

Yes?

In two minutes and ten seconds that update you approved will wipe out your Recycle Bin. All of her pictures will be deleted. Her image dissolved and a fresh burst of lemon scent filled his senses. Andrew's eyes shot open to find the cat on his chest, meowing. Casper turned around, giving Andrew a view of his behind while he clawed at his legs.

"Ouch! What did you do that for?"

The cat sprung off the couch, sailed across his desk, flickering his laptop to life. A timer appeared against the dark background.

"That doesn't answer my… Oh shit, that update!" Andrew leapt up and sloppily signed into the software. "Wait, how do I stop the update?"

Casper jumped back on to the sofa and yawned lazily.

"Great. I'm asking a cat." He released a series of hard and frustrated breaths. "Wait." He went to the Recycle Bin itself. When a page full of files poured down, his legs gave out. But he clicked the [Date Modified] bar and mercifully, all of the pictures of Gwen appeared on top. He quickly highlighted them all and scrolled to the [Restore] option.

A soft purr hummed from the arm of the sofa where the cat had sprawled out, satisfied from his cheap dinner. A small pink tongue hanging out, a furry chest rising and falling. Andrew hung his head, feeling relief as well. A few more key strokes created a new folder on his desktop.

With shaking hands, Andrew typed: *My Gwen*.

CHAPTER EIGHTEEN

The smell of a fresh baked turkey always made Gwen think of her mother. It was still hard to spend Thanksgiving Day without her.

With too many miles between the North Fork and Manhattan and the Expressway jammed with cars, Darling Cove and its residents had their own parade. It was pretty crummy compared to the real one. Gwen pressed away the mixed feelings of whether or not she should have accepted Salvatore's invitation to watch the Macy's parade from his apartment.

But waking up with the Darling Cove sunshine across her bed satisfied Gwen that she had made the right decision. Besides if she weren't around, who would feed the rest of the Mallorys?

The morning held on to the chilly temperatures from the bay waters, previewing the cold winter months ahead. But the afternoon sun was warm on Gwen's shoulders by the time she texted her sister that she was heading home to check on the bird.

Her dad was monitoring the traffic from Sound Avenue and even though Greg was technically off duty he was never really *off*. He stood on the next block, his arms folded, his face stern, watching out for trouble. Even without his uniform, his six-foot stocky build turned heads in this town. His eyes were as green as hers were blue, and his golden brown hair was long enough now to curl up at his collar.

Gwen smiled at his dedication but behind the mirrored shades she knew her brother was lonely. His wedding had been scheduled for Thanksgiving weekend ten years ago, so this holiday was always hard on him. He'd been so in love with Faith Copeland. It was still a mystery why she ran off.

An hour later Greg and Skye streamed into Gwen's living room. "How was the rest of the parade?" she asked, grinding at the potatoes with a beat-up mixer.

Greg gave her a sarcastic look that said, *I'm forty years old and it's a kid's parade.*

"Who was that man playing Santa?" Skye, who clearly had been drinking too much coffee, swirled into the kitchen. "Even with that fake beard, I could tell he was hot, hot, hot."

"Makes sense, I think it was one of the volunteer firemen," Gwen said, manually mashing the potatoes.

Skye had been single since the beginning of the year when her two-year relationship with singer Miles Benjamin ended. Skye loved the man despite his faults and the complications of dating someone in show business. If anyone could have tamed and handled music's bad boy it was Skye. She was disarmingly beautiful, mixed with that hometown good girl charm from growing up in Darling Cove. But that wasn't enough for Miles.

Martin came in and embraced Gwen, his cheeks refreshingly cold against her warm skin. The stove and oven had made her kitchen feel like a sweat shop. And on his collar lingered a trace of sweet smoke from nearby fireplaces. "Do you have any beer?"

"In the fridge."

"What can I do?" Skye asked.

"Can you go to the diner and get the pie?"

"You got it. Greg, go to Sadie's and get us the pie."

He grunted and put his coat on. "Are you sure you don't want to come and leer at anymore hot firemen today?" Greg snapped as if *he* never looked in the mirror or noticed women gawking at him.

"Oh please. I don't *leer* at men. Besides, I'm single. I'm allowed to look."

Martin stared at his bickering children. "What the heck are you two doing with your lives anyway?" He pointed to Gwen. "At least your sister's been married. Which is more than I can say for the two of you."

"Dad, I'm still getting over this thing with Miles. Besides my law practice is doing very well now."

"Oh, save it. You do real estate closings. I drive by your office at night and it's dark."

Martin's eyes drifted to Greg, who'd been rocking on his heels. "Don't either of you want kids someday? I never thought my youngest child would be my best chance to have a grandchild."

"Me?" Gwen gasped.

"I was *supposed* to be married. In case you have all forgotten," Greg said bitterly.

"You were left at the altar years ago, Greg." Martin waved his hands, dismissively. "Get over it."

Gwen wisely chose not to mention that she'd seen Faith on the train, nor question if she's moved back to Darling Cove for good.

Greg asked his father, with a questioning look, "Since when do you want grandkids anyway?"

"Based on the women I see leaving your house, fat chance of *you* giving me any." Martin was looking at Greg in a way Gwen hadn't seen before and her brother was turning white.

"Ho, ho," Skye released under her breath. The spotlight had been taken off her for a moment.

Greg pressed his lips together, but said nothing to Skye. Instead, he kept his eyes on his father. "Are you spying on me now?"

"It's called patrol, Greg." Martin cracked open his beer. "Are there no available women under fifty in this town anymore?"

"Under fifty?" Gwen interjected. "Greg, what's he talking about?"

"Oh, our brother's been *dating* ladies on the older side," Skye whispered.

"Really?" Gwen looked up at her brother.

But before he could respond, Skye began laughing. "He probably figures if they're using a walker, they can't run off the way Faith did."

"Why am I just hearing about this nugget of gossip now?" Gwen hated how so much had been kept from her while she'd been dealing with mammograms and biopsies.

"Because that's my private business, Gwen."

"This coming from the people who hover over me like a busted parade balloon." She smashed at the potatoes in the pot so hard, a lump came flying back out at her.

"Gwen, come on—it's only because we love you." Skye rubbed her back.

"Yeah, well like Dad said, go find someone else to love for a while." She cleaned herself up. "And will someone go pick up that damn pie!"

"Sheesh. Greg come on, I'll buy you a scone."

After her brother and sister left, her father stood watching her.

"Dad, I'm sorry. I've just been…stressed at work."

He took a long breath. "I know you hate that we keep things from you."

"I don't want to be treated differently, Dad. Mom didn't want that either."

The pained look on her father's face, had Gwen ready to back track, but he lifted his chin and said, "Okay. Here's something you don't know…since you want to know everything."

"Dad, what is it?"

He put a hand on her arm. "Your sister knows, and of course Greg."

"They know what, Dad?" Fear drove Gwen's heart into quick staccato beats.

"The state prosecutor is re-opening my shooting case."

"Okay," she answered and then cleared her throat. "But the first two prosecutors found nothing. I'm sure this one will look at all the evidence and make the same determination."

"We'll see, pumpkin." Martin took his beer and settled on the shit-brown loveseat to watch football. "We'll just have to see."

Gwen leaned against the counter, her face turned away from her dad. And she thought her problems were serious.

Besides Andrew, her biggest dilemma was all the food that was going to sit in her freezer for weeks.

* * * *

After going through reports with Marcello all morning, Andrew ate lunch and left early.

It was Thanksgiving for him, even if he was celebrating it alone. Casper had been coming and going at his own leisure. With no one to eat dinner with, Andrew chose to walk the streets of Milan's shopping district. Anything to make the hours pass by quicker.

In Italy, it was just another Thursday. But *Black Friday* was an international event, and even the smallest of merchants were gearing up.

Every day was starting to feel black without Gwen.

Wishing Italy was warm all year round, he jammed his chilled hands in his pockets. Milan enjoyed seasonal changes like New York. He played a daily game of watching New York's temperature to compare. Of course, every look at the Tri-State weather tugged at his gut knowing what Gwen was experiencing and that he wasn't there to go through it with her. It made Italy feel like forty thousand miles away, not four thousand.

His mother was chipper calling from Bermuda. When he'd told his parents he'd be gone for the holiday, Sarah pouted for a week. But she got over the sting by planning to drag his father out of town for a long weekend.

"Is Dad at least enjoying the pool?" Andrew asked.

Sarah sardonically said, "No. He's playing golf. I'm here by myself!"

Andrew sat on a bench facing a park. School had let out, and kids were playing. Their delicate voices tolled in Italian. He crossed his legs and pivoted his body away, fearing someone would call the *polizia* and complain about a strange man watching small children. "Can I talk to you for a moment, Ma?"

"Of course, my handsome boy. Do you need something? Do you need me to ship anything to you over there?" She said *over there* like he was on a military base in Kabul, Afghanistan.

"No. I assure you Milan has stores and I have everything I need." Except Gwen. "So..." *I can't believe I'm going to say this.* "I met someone, Ma." The intake of air in his mother's lungs was shockingly audible. "Ma, are you all right?"

"Hang on. I'm checking my phone to make sure I have the best signal possible. Because I don't want to miss a word of this." But she huffed, and said, "Hmm, well it looks like three bars is the best this five-star resort can offer. Go!"

"Okay, *met* someone was probably not a correct characterization." He took a breath. "There's a woman I work with. She—"

"In Milan? Let me tell you something right now mister. If you think I'm going to be continent hopping on a plane to visit you and my grandkids in Italy, you are mistaken."

His fingers gripped the phone tighter. "No Ma. In the office in New York."

"Oh!" She squealed in delight but then released an, "*Oh-h-h.* How is that working, long-distance and all?"

"Distance is not the problem at the moment, Ma. We…got together while I was in L.A. for the fashion show. She's the woman who sits in my New York office. You were looking at her pictures."

"Oh her. The girl from 'No.'" She laughed and he laughed with her. "Okay, and?"

"I didn't notice until after… She's got scars. Biopsy scars. Her mother died of breast cancer. Gwen doesn't have it. But I started to panic and asked all these questions. She…asked me to leave and I haven't spoken to her since."

His mother didn't say anything for a moment. They were fiercely alike, which made sense because he was made of the cells in her body. He inherited his father's sense of business, but when it came to matters of the heart, he was all his mother. This was also why Cate was able to drive a wedge between them. And it often bewildered him why Cate was the only woman he'd ever loved, yet his mother despised her. Like his Id had tried to be his own man when it came to relationships but forgot to tell him. Finally, she said, "Well then, you have to fight for her."

"How do I do that from Italy?"

"You're in the country of love. Put her on a plane and show her how you feel."

He remained silent for a moment. In the past two weeks since he'd seen Gwen, he'd brought up her number on his phone so many times and just stared at it. His fingers hovered above the call icon. But he had never pressed it. And there were several emails he'd written that were sitting in his draft folder.

What stopped him every time was that he didn't think he could do the right thing by Gwen if she were to get sick. Could he stick around *again* to watch the horror of someone wasting away? In the end, he was completely dumbfounded, and didn't trust himself to make the right decision. He thought the scars from losing Cate were healed, and he was tougher now. Deep inside he wished he knew for certain if he could handle it.

"What if I'm not really the best man for her?"

His mother cleared her throat.

Here it comes.

"Andrew, if you've even had the notion to talk to me about this woman after all the *other* women in your life I never met..."

He wasn't proud of the whoring days that overshadowed much of his twenties. As Lanvin's top male model he had his pick of women. Plenty of beauties fell at his feet and into his bed. "Okay Ma. You made your point."

"You're so like me. You know that don't you, my boy?"

"Yes. Ma, I gotta go. I have..."

"Work? You've been hiding behind that for more than a year now." Sarah finally got the timeframe correct.

"I have some serious thinking to do."

"Call back if you need me. I love you, my handsome boy." Sarah cleared her throat, after he grumbled. "Oh Andrew, you'll always be my handsome boy. But you *are* a man now. Whatever you decide, I trust you and...I will never abandon you again." Her voice drifted off at the end; hiding the pain of how she'd once alienated herself from him.

Opening up to her was an enormous weight off his shoulders. It sounded like a blessing to pursue Gwen, given the risks. But that was life. Life had no meaning without risks. The best things in life were *not* free.

The Milan ATM bus system, however, should have been free the following Monday morning. The way the driver was taking the turns on Via Giuseppe Ripamonti made Andrew wonder if she was Cyber-Monday shopping on her iPhone.

His stomach was still queasy settling into his office. But the meeting invitation via email he opened from Enrico made his shoulders ache with stress. It wasn't the agenda, it was the other attendee:

Gwendolyn Foley.

Andrew swallowed. Hard. Most of Western Europe and an ocean just dissolved into a voice on the phone. He suspected Enrico chose to monitor the call to gauge Gwen's performance and for all his boss knew, there was still tension. Perhaps Enrico feared Andrew would be biased. The only bias he felt was he wanted to do his own Goddamn job. In New York. *With* Gwen.

If only Enrico knew the truth.

"Okay, okay," Andrew said, calming himself down, reading through the meeting notes.

Gwen would provide an update on the menswear lines and the new jewelry designs. Andrew maintained responsibility for the women's apparel, the Prada accessories and the entire Miu Miu brand.

He nodded, and said, "I can do this. It's not like she'll see how nervous I am."

He attempted to eat lunch, but the update sent by Enrico, changing the meeting to a teleconference via Skype, made him toss the rest of his panini in the trash.

Andrew was scarcely prepared to hear Gwen's voice, even though he had all day to stress over the matter, thanks to a time difference that was not in his favor.

It wasn't the first time he had to face an ex-lover. No, that's not what Gwen was. Despite only spending one night with her, it felt deeper than that. She had meant more to him than that.

With shaking hands, he logged into Prada's Skype account. It was excruciating to watch the buffering icon.

"Andrew!" Enrico's face filled the screen. "How are you? We miss you."

Immediately his throat tingled. *We?* "Hi there. Yes. I'm missing New York too."

"I have Gwendolyn here," Enrico said, but didn't turn the monitor around.

Andrew swallowed a few more breaths in preparation for seeing her face. "Okay," he said softly.

"Hello...Um...Gwendolyn." It hurt to just say her name out loud.

He'd been calling her Gwen because she had asked him too. He wasn't sure if he still had that right.

The room spun behind Enrico, making Andrew grip the seat beneath him. Gwen's eyes had been focused on her lap when she came into view. Her hair was pulled back into a tight bun and her cheeks seemed to have lost some volume. It pained him how thin she looked. That was not the same woman he left two weeks ago.

Her lids lifted to the camera briefly and it was like an entire colony of butterflies had hatched at the same time in his stomach. "Hello, Andrew," she said with caution. She began her status updates, holding and staring at a yellow legal pad teetering on her lap. "I've collected progress reports from Gus, Stephan and Antonia for the menswear lines. They will have at least a dozen prototypes ready to ship to Milan for review by the end of the month. The new jewelry line however has had some issues. Their schedule has been set back, I'm afraid." Her head lifted briefly. "Enrico and I have been trying to mitigate the effect it would have on their deadline but a shortage in the non-corrosive, environmentally friendly metals we've specified have been more of a problem to source than the team's initial estimates."

Enrico jumped in, but the monitor stayed on Gwen. "Without assigning blame, we think one of the production assistants did not provide the manufacturer with our exact volumes and specifications. But Gwendolyn here is on it. I have her working with the strategic sourcing group in Paris to find another vendor."

"Okay, but…" Andrew paused. "I was part of the initial negotiation. So, I'd like to be on any calls you, or she, might be on."

There was silence, followed by mumbling. Gwen looked up as Enrico sat next to her, so he could see and speak to them both at the same time.

"I would like this matter addressed immediately." Enrico shifted in his seat. "Perhaps it would be best to do the call together in person."

"In person?" Gwen asked.

Andrew crumpled the paper at his fingertips. *Put that woman on a plane.*

"Gwendolyn, I know this is short notice, but could you fly out to Milan tonight?"

"*Tonight?*" Both he and Gwen asked Enrico at the same time.

"*Sì.* And Andrew, when she is there, perhaps she could meet with Marcello. Have her sit with him…give him a hand."

Gwen turned to Enrico, leaving only her profile visible. Andrew's fingers touched the monitor outlining her face, and grunted when the camera shifted back to his boss as he resumed his seat behind his desk.

"Andrew, are you okay with this?" Enrico asked.

He swallowed. *Very,* except…he was still anxious to see her and be alone with her. "Sure. So, tomorrow?"

Enrico took a call on his cell before answering. "*Prego,*" he said into the phone and turned back to Andrew. "I'll let you two work out the details. I am needed on the designer floor."

The monitor swung back around. The look on Gwen's face could only be described as panic-stricken.

* * * *

Gwen stared into Andrew's dark gray eyes. And she was pretty sure her mouth was gaping open.

In the last two minutes, she'd just been told to go to Italy. *Tonight.* To fix a jewelry mess she could easily take care of with a phone call. But what about this business with meeting Marcello?

"So…" Andrew said, brushing his hand through his hair. The ring was still gone. "Hi."

"Hi," she replied back, preferring to keep her voice even to gauge *his* reaction.

"Um. How are you?"

God, she hated that question. *Great. Never better.* "Okay. You? How is Milan?"

"Cold. Make sure you bring your winter coat."

138

And we're gonna talk about the weather now. Her nerves had her stomach in knots. She drew in a ragged breath, unable to deal with the tension rising up in her. "Listen, Andrew—"

"Gwen, I went back to your room Saturday morning."

The air trapped in her lungs escaped like an overfilled balloon. And…he called her Gwen. "You did?"

"Of course. I wanted to tell you myself I was coming back here."

"Oh." Not to try to smooth things out. But to just deliver the news that either way, they weren't going to be together in any meaningful way. Right. Message received.

"And why weren't you on our flight?"

Our. That little detail stabbed at her. She looked down, guilt creeping in. "I ended up taking a different flight home."

The way he pursed his lips, meant he understood why. He looked down as well, clearly agitated. "Okay."

"Andrew, I'm sorry—"

"No! *I'm* sorry. You didn't do anything wrong. I was coming at you with a bunch of invasive questions about something obviously personal and sensitive. I know I overreacted." His large hands, hands that had been all over body, covered his beautiful face. She touched the monitor trying to lower them. "Because of what happened…to me, with Cate. I just freaked out. I'm sorry."

"So am I." The explanations were out of the way. But the ugly and gritty residue sat like tea leaves at the bottom of a saucer, telling her that she and Andrew may be at some kind of an impasse. Perhaps it was all for the best. "Hey, it was only one night. We're adults."

"I didn't want just one night." His voice was just above a whisper. They were on company time and Prada's internet. For all she knew this was being recorded.

The ball was just tossed back in her court. Last time she dropped it by shutting him out and hiding. Too many thoughts were fighting for position in her head, from *Run to that airport, now,* to *Run away.* Somewhere in between was the right response, but the words were caught in her throat.

"I guess…I guess you just didn't feel the same way." Andrew sat back, sounding sorrier than she had been prepared for.

"I don't know how to do this," she groaned.

"Do what?"

Her hands pointed back and forth between them. "This. A relationship, like this."

"Gwen, you were married."

"Yes, to the second man I ever slept with. Who I met the first week I was out of college."

Andrew's eyes were in a fast blinking pattern, calculating what that meant. His lips widened into a smile and his body shook with a laughing fit.

"What's so funny?"

"You have a lot to make up for."

"Was I that bad?"

He coughed. "Are you kidding—" He cut his words short as his eyes drifted over her shoulder. "Um, can you call me back from *our* office?"

She twisted around. A group of women had gathered by Thalia's desk, holding papers, but watching Andrew through the glass with flushed faces and puckered lips they were licking. This is what being with Andrew would be like… The man who can have anyone.

She turned back and sat up straight. "We can finish this when I see you tomorrow."

"We'd better." His bold confidence stilled her and a smile curled his lips.

He *wanted her*. Still.

"There's an 11 pm out of JFK by the way. It's usually full, so you'd better call now to make sure you get a seat." His eyebrows dipped, their seductive promise crashed a wave sensation under her skirt.

"Okay then. I have to go. Apparently, I've got a plane to catch."

CHAPTER NINETEEN

"Andrew Morgan," he answered his desk phone the following day hoping it would be Gwen.

"*Suono*, can you speak for a few minutes?"

Andrew glanced at the time. It had been excruciating waiting for her to arrive. Her plane landed nearly two hours ago. Every call he made to her cell went straight to voice mail. Even the driver who was sent to pick her up wasn't responding. Andrew had this overblown visualization that she'd been kidnapped. Or some Gucci agent had spotted her and lured Gwen away.

"Sure. What's up?"

"I have been doing some thinking."

Uh oh. That was how he ended up in Milan in the first place, training Marcello. "What about?"

"I haven't said anything to Gwendolyn. She is doing a great job here, but I need you in New York, Andrew."

"I need to be there too. Being here for these extended periods of time…" He didn't want to sound petulant.

"*Lo so, lo so.*"

"I know you know, Enrico. What's your idea?"

"What do you think of Gwendolyn replacing Marcello if he does not work out?"

Andrew thought about that for a moment. "I think she can do the job. But having Marcello report to us was already a gift from the Creative Director. Now you want to move that position to New York all together?"

"No, no. You misunderstand. We will transfer Gwendolyn there."

Andrew froze. Fuck! The words *Gwen, you may have to move here to Italy* would have a hard time coming out of Andrew's mouth, fearing she may run him over to get a Work Visa.

No, that was not an option. At all. He would sacrifice himself and agree to stay in Milan first; do both jobs if he had to. As the U.S. Brand Manager, he had autonomy to travel back to New York. But if Gwen was here in Milan and he was in New York…

That would be a disaster.

"Andrew?"

"Yeah. I don't think that will go over so well. Putting a New York person in that position. I can't see the Creative Directory agreeing to that."

"You let me worry about that."

Andrew held his head.

"Why so glum?" a soft voice echoed from the doorway.

His head shot up and his throat suddenly went tight. "Gwen!"

"Ah, she is there," Enrico said into the phone. "I will leave you to it then, *suono. Caio. In bocca al lupo.*"

"I'm gonna need it," Andrew said under his breath as he hung up. It took him another moment to look back at Gwen.

Before he said anything, she swayed into the room. A camel car coat hung on her shoulders. Underneath, she was wearing the winter white wool sleeveless dress he'd seen on her desk last month. It sat on her body as fine as he thought it would. "Everything all right?"

It is now. "Yeah, that was our boss."

"Oh." She pulled off brown leather gloves. "Did you need to finish speaking to him?"

"No, he's said enough."

"Ha! I bet you don't miss him."

"No, I miss you."

Her body froze. "Andrew, I..." She slowly lifted her eyes to his.

"I mean, I miss working with you." The way she looked at him made him wonder if he'd have to start back at square-one with her.

Her shoulders softened. "Oh. Okay. Yeah, it's not the same without you in the office."

"Enjoying all the space?"

"That, and no faces pressed against the glass like when we were meeting with Enrico."

"Stop it. That didn't happen." He turned to look out his open door to the rest of the department. There was a woman staring at Gwen with a frown. "Anyway...let me show you around." He stood to slide his suit jacket over his shoulders; he dressed more formally in Milan.

Gwen moved further into the office with her luggage, walking backwards, and their bodies collided. "Oops sorry."

I'm not. "It's okay," he whispered instead.

"Your um…tie is crooked." She stepped closer, her scent surrounded him like a warm hug. Her fingers tugged on the knot; the memory of how she'd slid it off in L.A. flashed by, sending a firestorm to his groin. He could lift her up right now, lay her on the desk and penetrate her easily.

The way she tugged on his tie, the way she held on to it… It was like she didn't want to let go. "There," she said softly looking up at him. In her eyes, were the answers he'd wanted. There was the longing, and need, he'd seen before.

He'd not anticipated being this close to her so soon into the visit. If only he knew how she felt. *Ask her, you dummy.* A little voice that sounded oddly like his mother's, rang in his ear. "Gwen?"

"Yes?" Her body inched away so her eyes could meet his; her height compared to his was something he'd been enjoying. It had brought out the protective side to him.

Before he could consider whether her replacing Marcello was something he was supposed to keep to himself, his mouth opened and the words tumbled out. "One of the reasons you're here is because Enrico may want *you* to take over for Marcello if we have to fire him." He sneaked a look through his lashes. "And Gwen, I'm sorry, but it's looking like that's going to happen."

Gwen's chest heaved taking in the news. "And that means you're back in New York." When he nodded she quickly gave voice to his worst fear. "And I'm here."

"Those would be the logistics."

She turned away. "Either way we're…in two different offices," came out in a delicate whisper laced with sadness.

He released a sharp breath and spun her back around, his fingers gripping into her shoulders. "Gwen…"

Her body softened against his. "Andrew?"

They were in the land of *Amore* but this was still the workplace. As much as he wanted to kiss her — and suspected she wanted that too, he couldn't. He stepped back.

It was too soon.

* * * *

Only when Andrew touched Gwen had the knot from the last few weeks inside her stomach loosened.

It stung when he let go, but this was an office. The idea it was all fun and no work on this side of the world was absurd. The people she'd passed looked just as determined as those in New York. No siestas for this bunch.

Andrew held his door open. "Let's walk around for a bit. It's almost the end of the day, but I think Marcello should still be here."

"Should I leave my things in your office?"

"Sure. I'll lock the door." Andrew peeked over her shoulder, his gaze settling on the woman outside who had not moved and now looked even more upset. "Of course, you could have just packed a toothbrush and hopped on the plane. If you think there are plenty of clothes lying around the office in New York, wait till you see the production floor here."

"Show me. I can't wait to see the world you've been a part of for so many months, Andrew."

"This isn't my world. My world is home in New York." Andrew bit his tongue as if he wanted to say more, but continued to escort her through the corridors.

It was surreal to walk through the corridors of Prada's Milan headquarters. Italian purred all around her. This was where it all began! So much history, even though this was a new complex. The campus was in the Largo Isarco section south of the city and it was *stunning*. It looked more like a museum, but not in a formal way.

The large concrete entrance ended with a tower of glass, and while it only rose up two or three stories, it sprawled out for acres behind her. There were several wings, each with classic red tiled rooftops, one of which spanned an entire city block. And the arch shaped windows reminded Gwen of a church.

"You look like you belong here." Andrew tugged on the curled end of her long dark hair. "Stop it!"

She smiled behind her gold rim shades. "Does Marcello know I'm here?"

"*Sì, lo fa.* I mean, yes he does. But as far as Enrico's little scheme? Let's just say you're still getting familiar with the company, and you want to share some ideas."

She refrained from rolling her eyes and instead gave an encouraging nod, thinking: *The man works for Prada, he can't be that dumb.* "I'm sure there were subtle hints of what's wrong that you missed." She followed Andrew into Marcello's office.

The man was on the phone speaking Italian. By the look on Andrew's face it was clearly a personal call. After he hung up the phone, he turned to Gwen. "*Scusa.*"

Marcello was tall, but lankier than Andrew. His body had not bulked up yet, the way a man's body fills out when he's in his thirties. Dark brown curls flopped on a thin and bony forehead and his cheekbones cast a shadow on the lower half of his face.

"Marcello, this is Gwendolyn from the New York office." Andrew rested his hand against the small of her back.

She leaned across the desk, which was filled with papers and folders. Worse than Andrew's used to be. "It's nice to meet you."

"*Così meraviglioso di conoscerla.*" He cleared his throat. "I mean, it is wonderful to meet you…Gwendolyn."

His eyes lingered on hers for a moment, but were dragged away by the sound of Andrew's voice. They conversed in Italian for a few moments, giving Gwen the opportunity to look around. She took an inventory of the rest of his office. Messy, like his desk. It had a haphazard look to it, like it had once been neat but then Marcello just gave up.

After looking at the pictures on his bookshelf, Gwen was certain she had a good diagnosis of the problem. Photo after photo of Marcello on ski-slopes, on a yacht with beautiful girls, in front of a roulette wheel in a casino, a motorbike…the frames were several rows deep and she couldn't see them all, but it was clear. Marcello was a party animal.

* * * *

After work, Andrew hoped for some kind of flinching objection when he suggested they check Gwen into the hotel.

Nope.

And she'd been up in that damn room for nearly an hour getting settled and ready for dinner. He sipped his third cocktail at the lobby bar, wondering what the hell he was doing there and not up in the room getting her ready...for him. The way he wanted her.

He looked up, and there she was. His eyes hurt seeing her stride through the lobby with confidence. She smiled with the look of a cat who swallowed an entire pet store of canaries, showing off her first clothing score from the production floor earlier. But the red and black wrap dress she changed into was too low cut, and too damn tight. It showed every luscious curve of her body.

"Ready?" she asked with a smile that was going to kill him.

He tossed a few Euros on the bar and led her out of the hotel. His hand was on her back; he had not planned to stop touching her until they got to work tomorrow. On the walk to the restaurant, she was silent. But inside at the table, she would not shut up.

About Marcello.

After she placed her drink order and looked at him oddly when he asked for water, she lifted a yellow legal pad out of the work bag she'd hidden under her coat.

"Okay. Here's what we need to do. We need to put Marcello on a performance plan."

He sighed, figuring there was no way to divert the conversation to *them* without getting this part out of the way. The woman was on a mission. Unless Andrew planned to take the Kamikaze route, he decided to nod and listen to her. "And what is a performance plan?"

"We're gonna give him small assignments." She sipped her wine, her fingers lifting the glass softly. Perhaps she'd be better at his job, managing a staff. Clearly this was her forté. "I had this awful assistant at Starlight. But the woman had been there forever, so I had to make it work."

"So, what did you do?" Andrew's face was smashed into his palm and he was trying not to seem bored as hell with this topic.

"Micro-micro-micro managing. It's awful, and it made me feel like I was the one being punished. I had to give her small daily tasks. And at the end of each day, I had to sit and review what she did right and what she did wrong. I used some reverse psychology here and there, but I really tried to beef up what she did right. And then I played the active listening game to get her to figure out what she had done wrong, and why."

Why? Why were they still in the restaurant?

Finally, Gwen finished her meal; she'd talked more than she'd eaten. Walking back to her hotel, he should have paced his steps slower to let her enjoy a view of the city.

But Andrew wanted, no *needed,* to be with Gwen. In her hotel room. In her bed. He'd been given a second chance, and he wasn't going to let anything mess this up. That included not letting her turn away or give into doubts.

Under the marquis, he knocked into her back when trying to get to the hotel's lobby door. "Why did you stop?"

She spun to face him. "Where do you think you're going?" she asked, her hands on his chest.

"Inside."

She crossed her arms. "Really? For what?"

He *hoped* this was some odd role-playing game. He leaned in closer. "Okay, I'll play along and buy you a drink first."

Her body jerked back. "You realize that we just can't pick up where we left off in L.A."

"Why not?"

"Why not?" She blinked in astonishment.

"Because there never should have been this stupid gap of time." His expression was pinched, filled with tension. "L.A. was supposed to be the beginning for us Gwen. Not the end."

"Either way, we would have had to re-set this whole thing to base it on reality. That night was a fairy tale." After she pulled the collar of her coat closer, she drew a fist to her mouth. "I was a princess and you were—"

"Look at me." He lifted her hand away and leaned it against his lips. "Gwen, I don't want a princess. *Or* a model. I want *you*. The real you and everything you are."

"How do you really know you want someone like me?"

He moved closer and set his lips against the curtain of smooth brown hair and whispered into her ear. "Don't you remember what you did to me in L.A.?" When she released a slight nod he said, "Just trust me, please."

He didn't care if he sounded pathetic. If he expected Gwen to open up and take a risk, to be vulnerable, he needed to set the example of what that looked like.

But he realized there may be other emotions lurking under the surface. Perhaps they would come out in time. Andrew didn't have time. Didn't want any more time…to think…to wonder. He wanted to move forward with his life. With Gwen. He exhaled and stepped back.

"Fine, let's do this. Let's get this ugly part out of the way so we can get on with our life together. I don't want anything festering."

"Okay." She took a deep breath. "Did you even consider that I wanted to wait to tell you about what had been going on with me *after* I got to know you better? And *after* I figured out it was not just a one-night-stand?"

He crossed his arms, certain there was more, and it was best to let her get it all out.

"Meanwhile," she continued. "You climbed into my bed harboring your own secret. My health didn't really have anything to do with it, did it? You were leaving me either way. When were you going to tell me you weren't coming back to New York?"

"So, you were allowed to withhold information until after we had sex; but my doing it meant I was purposely keeping something from you?"

"That was a big deal to me, Andrew. How could you, running off to Milan after fucking me, not come off as anything but you considering me a one-night-stand?"

"Gwen, if I wanted just a one-night-stand, there's a shit-load of women I would pick before you." *That came out wrong.*

"Because I'm not good enough for you, is that it?" Her jaw quivered. "I can't believe I thought you were—"

"Wait!" He pulled her against his chest. "That's not how I wanted that to come out. What I meant was I wouldn't *use* you. I wanted something more with you. And if I just wanted to get laid I would pick someone I didn't care about."

She sniffed and squirmed away.

"Please, don't walk away from me, Gwen." Andrew's voice cracked as if a wall burst. "You did that the last time, and I wasn't strong enough to stop you."

"What's changed?" She touched his shaking arms.

"I was miserable without you. With you, every day I laughed and felt happy and excited. Do you know I hadn't smiled, or at least it didn't feel like I had…in so long before I met you?" When she drew a breath, he moved a lock of hair out of her eyes. "And without you, I couldn't… Sometimes you don't realize what a hole you have in your life until someone has actually filled it."

"Andrew, that means so much. But…" She flicked away the loose tear skidding down her cheek. "I can't promise you I'll *never* get sick."

"No matter what happens I'm here for you, Gwen." He held her tight. "This is only going to work if we can open up to each other."

"I'm trying, Andrew," she said, putting her head down.

"We're in this together. This was meant to be. It has to be. If you recall, you had a choice in L.A. Salvatore clearly wanted you. But you left the show with *me*. I was the one who ended up in your bed."

A burning sensation spread across his face when her shameful eyes looked away.

"Wait a minute." With a hand over his mouth, he asked, "Did you hook up with him while I was away?"

"He invited me to his apartment to watch the parade." She threaded her hands together.

"Yeah, okay I guess I don't need to hear any more." He leaned against the canopy pole. Mentioning Salvatore made him feel so flushed with fury that he could set the entire marquis on fire.

"Andrew! I'm not seeing him. I'm not anything with him." He took a deep breath. "Why?"

"Because I want *you*, you *jerk!* And I couldn't bear another man's hands on me after what we had in L.A. Even if I didn't think I'd ever see you, or be with you again." She swallowed.

He took hold of her face, and when there wasn't the slightest hint of resistance from her body, he lowered his head to take a much-needed kiss of her lips. But she met him more than half way and kissed his mouth. Hard. He tugged her by the waist, drawing her hips against him. Even through layers of cashmere and merino wool, she would know he was aroused.

Her kiss was both hot and sweet. He finally became re-acquainted with her tongue. Soft, yet powerful. Demanding, yet hesitant. The feeling that he was totally at ease with her but also raw with anticipation of what her body was capable of doing to him was an enthralling paradox.

They stopped kissing, but he kept his head bent down, his eyes fixed on the blue pools of light he had missed. With his forehead resting against hers, he decided he'd rather not be in that hotel tonight after all. "Gwen, what do I have to do to get you to come back to my flat tonight?"

"Ask."

CHAPTER TWENTY

At Andrew's door, where on the other side he wasn't sure if he could control himself, he collected his raging thoughts that were starting to spill over like a pot of boiled water.

The months he'd spent alone in Milan before meeting Gwen flew by like an anxious flock of birds looking for warm weather. But the time apart had scraped along like metal on concrete—smoking and clanging, leaving nothing but a piercing shrill.

Gwen grasped at him, clawed under his coat, her nails digging into his Prada dress shirt. He didn't care if she tore right through the damn thing. The way her fingers repeatedly slipped inside his trousers made it hard to keep a clear head. He was crazed with hunger for her as well.

He opened the door and the look on Gwen's face taking in the simple but authentic Italian flat was warming. If things didn't work out with Marcello, it would be hers. It was one of the many flats Prada had permanent leases with for those on extended assignments like Andrew. If she had to live in Milan, this was where he would want her. The building was safe, and he knew many of the neighbors. All hard-working decent people.

And his new roommate would watch over her.

"Who is this?" she squealed, pointing to the cat sitting on the floor in the middle of the living room.

"That's Casper."

"That's exactly what I would name a black cat." She lifted the tiny bundle of fur into her arms. Cradled like a baby, Casper patted her cheeks with white tipped paws.

"Yeah, I thought the same thing." He laughed, softly twisting a white foot around his fingers. "I think he likes you."

"I love cats. Dan was allergic." Gwen pressed her face against the small patch of white above Casper's nose. "How old is he?"

"I don't know. He belonged to a neighbor. But she died recently. Now he's mine." Andrew smiled. "*Ours*."

Her eyes rose at his comment. That simple word held a wealth of meaning. He put his arms around her and kissed her with fierce passion. A gentle whine from between them interrupted the moment. "Are you done with him?" he asked, sliding his hand under Casper's back.

"For now."

The cat's long body stretched as he was released to the floor. Casper pranced across the parquet squares and curled into a ball on a new bed filled with plush toys. "He's as happy that you're here as I am."

Gwen's mouth was hard against his. To match her enthusiasm, he lifted her up. The way her legs immediately wrapped around his waist sent him into a fit of lust.

Andrew carried Gwen to the bed he had slept in alone for weeks wishing she was there.

* * * *

Andrew's long strong arms were around Gwen's ribcage like he was a caveman.

She even detected a grunt.

He put her down and twisted her around. Being kissed on the neck from behind made her legs rubbery. This man was so intoxicating. She couldn't hold back anymore. She turned around and slid her fingers into his thick hair. His arms came up, engulfing her as he kissed her with a sense of urgency, bringing a rush of heat to her face.

His tongue pushed past her lips, softly enveloping her in a deeper, more passionate kiss. Her body softened with the sense of relief and warmth, even though she was still a little ball of need.

Sometimes half-dressed sex is hot, but she wanted to be naked and exposed. Andrew must have had the same thought. He ripped off his tie, undid a few buttons on his shirt and wrenched it over his head.

She reached back to slide the dress zipper down, but her arms weren't long enough. "Need. Help."

"Got it," he said robotically, duck walking with his trousers around his ankles to reach her. He unzipped the dress and kicked the slacks away at the same time. Someone else would have paid six hundred dollars for those pants, but he chucked them in a corner.

The same went for her dress. It was still a prototype, but others like it were topping twelve hundred dollars. Yet she couldn't get it off her body fast enough. The soft jersey fabric slid down her legs and his hot furnace of a body leaned against her, clutching her from behind again. Oh, the heat, and the power. The sense of him. He was so large, yet he moved so elegantly. Those modeling years went to good use. But his form didn't belong to anyone else. It was hers. *He* was hers.

His arousal was raging, pressing into her back. Begging for attention. Release. He kissed the back of her neck, biting and nipping at the skin while his hands roamed across her breasts. The bra straps slid down over her shoulders, but she twisted around, letting him see the fabric drop away.

Andrew fell to his knees and kissed her body as if he worshipped her. Every press of his lips was followed by a small pant, a moan from him. Like she was water and he'd just wandered out of the desert. There was such relief in the sound. His shoulders went on for miles, her hands glided along his smooth skin. What a specimen.

The sides of her satin cheeky panties were secured in his manly hands sliding down her hips. He buried his face in every inch he exposed. Kissing, nuzzling, smelling, and tasting. He dragged the panties all the way past her ankles and without being asked she lifted one leg onto the edge of the bed. His fingers trailed back up, curving into the heat between her thighs.

Her head fell back in pleasure, while he rubbed the sensitive bit of flesh that drove to her to dream about this man.

"Oh. Oh," she cried out, even though it was hard to breathe. It wasn't clear if he had lifted her up on to the bed, or if she fell into his arms. She was in a trance, a spell cast by his fingers. Circling, dipping, withdrawing her wetness and heat and using her own juices to lubricate her throbbing clit.

"Lay back," he whispered.

"No." She sat up. "I want to watch you do this to me."

153

While kneeling on the floor his tongue hit her skin. Scorching. She grabbed onto his hair, thankful he'd let it grow in for the coming winter. There was plenty to tangle around her fingers. His tongue worked up and down, in and out and along the sides, slow and then fast. It was clear he had no intention of stopping until she was done.

That thought sent rocket waves through her. A man who wants to give her pleasure to the point of madness.

"Andrew, yes. Right there. Like that. Don't stop. Keep—" Her mind fell into a thousand pieces. Blood rushing through her ears. Pulsing and shaking. And he didn't let up even after her orgasm. He'd been with enough women to know how sensitive the skin is right at the end, and he kept going, even harder. More.

He wanted her to come again.

The very idea made her back slam into the mattress. She was a short, half-lit fuse five minutes ago. Ready to blow, but now she needed time—and he seemed to recognize that. He kissed the insides of her thighs, his fingers massaging her clit again.

He pulled her closer to the edge of the bed and spread her legs wide. She wished she had stuck with ballet so she was more flexible. His hand cupped her ass, tilting it toward him. What she could only discern to be a full open mouth kiss was placed upon her entire swollen cleft. His tongue flicked at the opening, swirling around sensitive skin that she needed him to touch.

Oh Jesus!

All the while, his fingers still massaged her with the same intoxicating pace he started with. Deep thrusts in, and then smooth swirls.

"Oh Andrew," she cried out, biting her own fingers.

"God, Gwen, you're incredible. You feel so good. So hot, so tight." His tongue curled around the rim of her belly button, while his fingers did all the work. "I don't know how long I can wait. I need to feel you come again. I need it."

A man who didn't want to wait. Couldn't wait. Needed it. It was too much. And for the first time *ever*, she came again. This was deeper and stronger than the first climax.

Holy shit! This was what she'd been denied all these years. Her voice cracked and all she could get out was "Yes. Yes, yes!"

This time he did stop. But there was only one second between all the attentions given below her waist, until his body blanketed hers.

"You're sweaty," she said.

"That's you, my dear."

"I have to do that to you. You have to let me."

"Wait," he tugged at her shoulders and treated her to an open mouth kiss; the salty sweetness was so delicious.

Her hand skidded down his long hard body. She'd futz with his nipples another time, she wanted to touch him and feel him. There wasn't a chance to become very well acquainted with his manhood in L.A., it'd been too eager to be inside her.

He deserved love and kisses too.

As her lips made their way down his body, Andrew's hand roughly tugged down the fabric of his boxers to his upper thighs, revealing a massive erection. The startling proof of his desire.

The boxers clung to his hips. Her nose trailed down his body the same way her hand had. Smelling him, kissing him. Woodsy and musk and fresh soap and sweat.

She bit at the tiny patch of hair that sat above his magnificent length, while her fingers massaged him.

"Oh God, Gwen," he groaned.

"You better start thinking of other deities to call out to." Her tongue circled the tip, which had already released a dab of translucent salty goodness. She lapped it right up and then in one quick movement, she took him entirely in her mouth to the base.

His back jerked. "You're gonna kill me."

She released him in a slow torturous trail, trading her tongue for her lips. But stopped to say, "I can't kill you. I need you."

She repeated soft licks and swirls of her tongue, until her hair was being pulled so tight, it hurt. Hurt so good, though. He was so strong. Such a man. A real man. Her palms took hold of him, her mouth made him so wet and slick.

He jerked again. "Gwen, unless this is how you want this to end, I suggest you stop." Bending down, he kissed her mouth roughly. "I want to be inside you when I come this time." He twisted toward his nightstand and removed a shiny foil packet from the top drawer.

While he bit it open, a move which made her gasp, she asked, "And when did you buy those?"

"Yesterday." He removed the condom. "After our call."

The idea of him leaving work to buy condoms gave her an erotic thrill. "You expected this to happen?"

He lurched forward—his large body made the bed scrape along the hardwood floor, and pushed her back. "Do you always shave your legs and trim this hair so short?" His fingers tugged at little wet curls.

"No." She laughed. "But I'll do anything you desire down there." She'd go completely bald if he asked her to.

"Hair or no hair, I plan to spend a lot of time there." He kneeled against her and with the condom fastened, he settled at the base of her wet waiting notch.

At first, only the massive bulbous tip slipped past her knotted nerves. She was still quivering from his mouth and hands. He leaned forward resting on an elbow to keep his face close to hers. His breath was hot and she loved dragging it deep into her own lungs.

"Ready?" he asked with a devilish humor. The short break brought things back into perspective. He smiled, touching her face.

"You'd think this was our first time."

He drew her near. "I want L.A. to be *our* last first time."

"I want you Andrew. All of you. *Please.*" A tingling sensation that bordered on pain, rushed through her body as he filled her, quick and with command.

"God," he groaned into her hair. "You're going to think I'm terrible at this."

"Why?" she panted, her chest falling as his rose up to meet hers.

"I feel so close the moment I'm inside you." His hips rolled in a perfect sweet rhythm.

"That's 'cuz it's been a while."

He kissed her lips. "No. I take care of myself daily. This…" He gasped for air. "This is you."

"*Daily*, huh?"

"It's how I'm built. It's always been that way."

"I'd like to see that sometime."

"That would be a waste."

"I'll bring you back to life."

"You already have, honey." He buried his face in her shoulders, his teeth gliding along the bone, nipping at her skin. "Oh God, Gwen. I'm coming."

He was so massive that his pulses felt like a vibrator hitting a button the back of her. When pressed, she slipped into her own orgasm. Her third! She ran her nails down his back and yelled his name. Again.

She took his orgasm and raised him one, her hips curling and circling to maximize his pleasure. Increasing her own. Their tongues locked as their bodies spun out of control together in harmony.

When Andrew stopped shuddering, his head lifted and his eyes squinted. *Daily*. That was a sight she'd have to implant into her head and take home to feast on.

Slowly he slid out; she jerked again.

"Let me go toss this. Don't move." He kissed her cheek before he rolled off the bed.

"I'm not quite sure I can move." Still, she stretched and propped on her elbows, not wanting to miss seeing that Adonis of a man walking around naked. The sight was as good as she remembered; tall and lean. Against the lights coming in from the window, a halo shimmered against his pristine figure.

He peeked his head out of the bathroom. Even with a faint light she could see him blush. "I'll get us something to put on. It's a little chilly."

Could have fooled me.

Out of curiosity, she leaned forward to peek into the nightstand that condom came from. Her fingers slid into the brass handle to open the drawer and gasped. Gold packages as far as the eye can see.

"Holy shit, I'm in trouble."

CHAPTER TWENTY-ONE

Andrew woke Gwen the next morning with his body on hers like a blanket.

"What time is it," she moaned, holding his ass.

"It's early," he whispered, taking long glides in and out of her. Slow and deep.

"Is this how I can expect to wake up all week?"

"If you let me. This is who I am, Gwen." He bent his back to take a hardened nipple between his wet lips. "I think this is who you are too. You just didn't know it."

"I wouldn't have wanted to be like this with anyone else."

"Good." That swelling, falling over the edge feeling came on again. But he lasted a little longer this time. With each encounter, his self-control was returning to him. "Ah-h-h," he released, and properly kissed her good morning.

"Is there coffee?" She stretched, her pale body luminous against a faint lamp light outside.

"Yes, but we have to get you back to the hotel." His fingers ran across her stomach.

"Oh right. Can't keeping showing up in the same dress, can I?"

"Don't think of me as a pervert." He snapped off the condom, *wet* – God she was soaked. "But I would like nothing more than to walk you through that building, your hair all fucked up, your mascara smeared, your dress wrinkled –"

"Don't forget the limp from you riding me so hard."

"Oh, I didn't think of that."

"That will garner a lot of respect for me if I *do* become the Brand Manager here. Thanks."

That reality bit into him. He didn't want to hold her back from her career. But he'd rather see her rise the ladder in New York – so he'd be there to look up under her skirt.

Just that thought made him hard. Again.

An hour later, Andrew stood over Casper's bed. "He's never done that to my clothes."

"That's so cute." The cat was sprawled out on top of her dress.

Andrew bent down to retrieve it but snapped his hand back when Casper hissed. "Hmm."

Looking around she asked, "What do you think he did with my shoes?"

"Um," Andrew said reaching under the sofa and pulling out one of the red leather sling-backs.

"What is it?" She gasped at what looked like a dozen little claw and bite marks in the heel.

Andrew ran his hands through his hair. "Let me get your dress."

But the cat spun around in a circle twisting his little body, the fabric curled around him. He released a happy sigh.

"Do you think that means he likes me?" Gwen asked petting his head.

Andrew bent down. "I have a feeling he's not letting this go." His eyes flashed to her. The cat can have the dress, Andrew was keeping Gwen. But she needed something to wear.

Damn, why had he been so anxious last night? He wouldn't even let her up to her room to get her suitcase. "I have an idea. Grab the shoes and put on your coat."

"I'm gonna walk around the office all day in a bra and panties? I'll just stop at the hotel."

"It's getting late."

"And whose fault is that, Mr. *I-love-shower-sex?*"

Instead of answering, Andrew looked away, embarrassed. He was getting out of control with her. Was there a boundary that would push her too far, too soon?

She stepped toward him and touched his face. "What's the matter?"

He cleared his throat and addressed another issue that had been haunting the back of his mind.

"Even if Marcello is gone and one of us has to live here, Gwen, I'm not giving up on the idea of us." He looked around the flat. "We can make this work. It'll just be…expensive."

Gwen looked away and exhaled, considering his words. "I'm already drowning, Andrew. I mean this job is helping. I don't know if I can add thousands of dollars in airplane tickets to my monthly expenses."

"I meant it will be expensive for me. I'll take care of it. If anyone is going to go broke, it'll be me. If anyone is going to lose sleep to be on the phone, it'll be me. If anyone will be dragged back and forth across the Atlantic—"

"Andrew, I get it." Her hands were shaking. "And is all this punishment you're willing to inflict upon yourself because you're the man?"

"Yes," he said boldly. "Do you have a problem with me wanting to be strong for us?"

She brushed his cheek. "When you put it like that, no."

"Plus, I have more seniority. I have more autonomy to travel. Especially here." He sat on the sofa. "This is all my fault anyway."

She crouched in front of him and took his face in her hands. "How is this your fault?"

"I couldn't make Marcello better at his job."

The corner of her mouth pulled into a small crease. "I'm here to help you now. Let me at him!"

"You need something to wear first." Andrew's eyes roamed her naked body. "I know just the place."

* * * *

Gwen's heart fluttered stepping into the original Prada store that had opened in 1913. Located on Galleria Vittorio Emanuele II, it was a narrow shop that once only sold leather goods, steam trunks and handbags. Andrew was making calls, accounting for their time, while she browsed the store. Even at the early hour, there were bodies buzzing around her. Tourists mostly, she could tell.

The flagship store in Downtown, New York City was an architectural marvel, its massive square footage seemed even more colossal by the long walls on the second floor that were all murals. This shop, however was small and intimate. Andrew had said he couldn't wait to show it to her, and since she was in need of a dress, it made sense to see it sooner rather than later.

Getting there had been unnerving, never mind chilly walking around in a bra and panties under the short car coat. Her exposed legs caught many looks, as if people knew their secret, but smiles abounded as if this happened all the time. Americans really were way too uptight.

She was loving Milan.

While she couldn't place the exact smell of the store, there was a juicy pool of green envy emitting from every sales girl Andrew said hello to. "You've been in here before?" she whispered.

"Of course. I'm in here all the time."

Hmm. All the sales girls were young, had great skin and must be contestants in a hair growing contest. Each of them had long smooth tresses running down their backs. The sleek but easy chignon resting at the base of Gwen's neck received a self-conscious tug. It was the easiest style she could come with since their time was so limited thanks to the ravenous man she had woken up next to.

Gwen pursed her lips to be strong. If she played the role of a woman who belonged with Andrew Morgan, maybe she could convince these Alpine Ibexes who were eyeing her like she was a wounded wildebeest. With her head held high, she followed him to one of the rear counters with graceful steps. But her footing faltered when he pulled out a measuring tape.

"Oh no you don't." She put her hands up. "I'll find something that fits." Nervously she searched through a rack of dresses fearing a scale might be behind the counter too.

Andrew's warm hand covered hers. "Get into the dressing room," he whispered in her ear.

"Let me pick something out," she whispered back.

"That's not how it works in *this* store," came out of his motionless mouth like he was a ventriloquist.

"What?" She looked at the sales girls whose shades of green envy had turned ghostly white. "How...how does it work?"

"They undress you." Andrew moved her away from the rack, his knuckles against the small of her back. "They measure you. And bring you options."

"Options?"

"Yes, and champagne." He turned and snapped his fingers. "Girls!"

"Okay, but they aren't measuring me," she said loud enough for at least one of the Ibexes to hear.

"I wouldn't dream of it," he said closing the full-length dressing room door with him on the inside. "Now take off your coat."

She pouted, shrugging out of the sleeves.

"Please breath." Andrew slid the measuring tape around her waist. "I assume you can't hold your breath for eight hours."

"Air is overrated." She twisted her arms together. "Besides you made me eat that croissant!"

"*Made* you? You practically ripped the last bite out of my hand."

"That's what happens if you put yourself between me and buttery flaky goodness."

"I'll remember that." Andrew put the tape around his neck. "I'll be right back."

"Um, I don't know what my retail allowance is up to." She futzed with her bun. "But remember I have a mortgage to pay for."

He rolled his eyes and left.

Alone in a dressing room that looked like it hadn't seen a fresh coat of paint in a few years, Gwen swiveled her hips from side to side. *This has to be some kind of bogus mirror,* she thought, noting how lean and slim she looked. *This must be how we trick people into spending so much money.*

When the door opened, she assumed it was Andrew and said, "Hey do we jury-rig these mirrors to—" She threw her hands across her chest.

"*Ecco qui.*" A girl with a down-turned gaze handed over a flute of champagne.

"*Grazi.*" Gwen accepted the glass. She narrowed her eyes as the girl closed the door. "As if I'm drinking this." She poured the bubbling golden liquid into the garbage. The sales girls had probably taken turns spitting into it.

"Wow, you must have been thirsty." Andrew stepped into the room, his hands full of black fabric. After she pulled her

162

shoulders to her ears and said *Yum*, he placed the dresses on an aluminum bar. "Your measurements were a little uneven, so I got you multiple sizes."

"This is the best you could do?" She held up something she might wear to a funeral in the Middle East. "Where's the shroud that's supposed to go over my head?"

"I'm not sending you back to the office showing any more skin and curves than I have to." He unzipped the first option. "And are you opposed to a *burqa?*"

Gwen stepped into the dress. "I should tell you, I have a lot sleeveless dresses in my suitcase. Someone's gonna see my shoulders."

"No they won't." The stuck zipper gave way when Andrew reached in and shifted her breasts into place. "My hands will be there."

Hopefully he didn't mean his hands would be *there*. She smoothed the torso running her fingers along seams under the bust line. The boat neck, three-quarter sleeves and hemline that skimmed past her knees made her look ten years older. *Something I could lend one of Greg's dates.* "God this is ugly."

"We'll take the first one," Andrew shouted.

After leaving the shop they walked two blocks north to a bus stop.

Andrew held her hand and pointed to various landmarks, his voice somber. Gwen sipped a steaming latte; even the milk tasted extra fresh. He pointed out that the public transportation was fairly reliable and put his head down to hide his frustration. Like he was having trouble thinking of her being in that city all by herself. It gave her pause as well. In Darling Cove each member of her family was no more than a five-minute drive away.

The best part of that day was that Andrew had not let go of her hand. He walked the Prada corridors with strong shoulders, proud that she was his. If he was a new man now, it showed more than ever. She was introduced to everyone they passed. They greeted her in Italian, to which she replied with warm nods and lots of *Grazis*. Andrew chuckled walking away from the Creative Director.

"What?" She poked his ribs.

"She asked how the weather was in New York. She's going there next week. You said, '*thank you*.'"

She decided to work harder to increase her knowledge of the beautiful language. The rest of the morning Andrew whispered the words she'd been struggling to recall into her ear. For every word she got right, she was treated to a kiss. Talk about positive reinforcement!

All delight, enjoyment and out-of-this-world sex aside, this was still a business trip.

Andrew parked her in his office and booted up his laptop. "I got an email back from the Paris team. They can do a call tomorrow morning."

"Right." From her work bag, she pulled out her spiral notebook.

"Um, ever hear about this thing called the computer?" He mocked.

She smiled and tugged his laptop closer, pretending to tap on the keys the way he did, in a series of one finger movements. "When you learn to type properly—" She halted mid-sentence, her breath sucked in by a startled gasp. Slapping at the keys had opened a folder chock full of photos. And they were all of *her*.

The name on the folder was even more startling. *My Gwen*.

She looked at him.

"I took those in L.A."

Her fingers brought the cursor to one of the photos to look at the date stamp. She swallowed. "You had just gotten back here and with all that had happened...you still considered me yours?"

"Does that scare you?"

Without Andrew, the days in New York after L.A. had been suffocating and dark. Now being with him, that dead feeling inside had been flipped on its side, cartwheeled and split apart into a thousand unrecognizable pieces.

Thank God! Andrew had brought her back to life too.

"It takes a lot more than that to scare me."

"Good."

At lunch time, she checked out of her hotel and after work she settled into the flat, taking over most of the closet.

Andrew sat on the velvet sofa looking at dinner menus from local *trattorias*. She considered sitting next to him to have a look as well, but a wild burst of passion overtook her. She stood in front of him and began to strip away her clothes.

"Is your dress really that uncomfortable?" Andrew's jaw dropped looking at her.

Fully nude, she lay down on the sofa and spread her legs, wanting to feel the velvet upholstery against her body while… "You can keep looking at those menus if you want. I'll be right here."

Andrew tossed them in the air and reached to loosen his tie.

"No!" she cried out and covered his hand. "Keep it on. Keep it *all* on and take me."

Andrew's massive body sprang off the sofa and into the bedroom. He came out with a condom wrapper in his mouth and lowered his zipper with anxious hands.

With his Prada slacks lowered just under his beautiful ass, he cupped a hand beneath her bottom and started a slow rhythm that eventually exploded into blinding ecstasy. Twice.

* * * *

During the conference call with Paris on Thursday, Andrew kept having to shift in his seat.

It was the only downside to being with Gwen like this. He'd been walking around half erect most of the time because he couldn't stop thinking about her. If there was a way to brand *Gwen*, he would.

By noon the scent of her perfume had dissolved from his clothes and he needed to be on top of her again. Soon.

She stood and addressed the team, pacing, as if that made it easier for her to think. He'd seen her do this back in New York. She was commanding the conversation and driving him crazy while she did it. The tight pencil skirt showed off her figure a little too nicely. Damn, her curves made him melt. Every rounded edge was flesh he wanted to sink his teeth into. She offered him an easy smile and a wink. Her demeanor was soft, and the languid way she moved her hands as she spoke was eating away at all rational thinking.

The paradox finally hit Andrew. That was *him* when they had been apart. Being in the same office with her, seeing how she interacted with others, other men, Italian men who clearly wanted her was unnerving. Each one Gwen got to know, Andrew could tell they wanted her too. And if she were going to be in Milan alone, they'd be hounding her non-stop.

He pulled at his shirt collar for air, watching her. Every breath she took and every rise and fall in the tone of her voice spelled her out perfectly to him. He finally had it figured out, who she was and what she was about.

He was hooked.

And by the cattle prod sticking out of his pants, it was clear *Andrew* was the one branded.

* * * *

The fingernail splitting sex from holding on to the bed sheets so tight had been dinner *and* dessert that night for Gwen.

Being with Andrew, knowing they would be apart soon made him feel like a meal she needed to shove in her mouth before the plate was taken away. He was a deep soothing gulp of wine needed to melt the ache of their pending separation.

Before she came to Milan, she could only imagine his life here, this flat, this bed. Now she had memories, real and raw to bring home and obsess over. The sight before her now — Andrew lying in that bed, face down, still naked with the top sheet resting just above his ass, stilled her. Made her lose her breath. It hurt *not* to touch him.

She pulled the sheet away and ran her fingernails along the entire length of his body. Up his rock-hard calf, over his perfectly round butt, and across his back.

"Hey!" He squirmed and rolled over. "That tickles."
Much better view.

She lifted her leg, straddled his hips and danced her fingers up his torso. Small beads of sweat from their lovemaking moments earlier dotted his shoulders. She loved how the hair around his navel darkened when it was wet. "Better?"

"No. You're going in the wrong direction."

Pressing her bare chest into his, she stroked his cheek. "Are you sure?" She smoothed the skin under his eyes.

"I like that."

She'd been ready to respond, but the sound of his cell phone cut her off. Understanding that sometimes Prada came first, she un-wedged his phone from between the pillows and looked at the screen. "It's your mother."

He swiped the call to voicemail stopping the annoying clatter. "I'll call her back tomorrow."

Gwen had mixed feelings about him blowing off his mother, just because she was there. But they were naked, sweat still dripping from their bodies. Her nipples were still hard and she could tell Andrew was getting ready for another go at her. "Does she know about me?"

"Yes." Andrew smiled.

"And does she know I'm in the middle of a divorce?"

"I'm not sure I mentioned that. But only because it's not important."

Gwen brought her long hair to one side, the curled tips tickled her sensitive nipple. "I'm sure a woman who's been married so long might think of me as a failure."

Andrew sat up and kissed her with an urgent passion she'd not felt before. "Your husband left *you*. You didn't fail Gwen."

He leaned back as his foot dangled over the side of the bed. It allowed Gwen to rest firmly against his chest. "Did she like Cate?" It was a question she'd been dying to ask.

"No." He was definitive and deliberate.

The answer floored her; that he could be so direct about something that had to be an issue in his marriage. It also rose the stakes for Gwen; she had to make sure his mother would be on her side. Except she already felt weakened by her wishy-washy marital status. She'd been ready to ask for more details but the sudden tension in Andrew's shoulders meant he'd slipped into his own head.

Finally, he filled the silence and said, "If I had one complaint about Cate, it was that she didn't even try to make my parents like her."

"Do you think they would like me? I mean, you went from a beautiful successful model to a..."

"To a what?" He looked confounded. "How exactly do you see yourself Gwen?"

"Just a small-town girl from the North Fork." She watched in amusement as Andrew pressed his lips together, which meant he may have dismissed women here and there for being geographically undesirable. However, since he was technically working out of Milan at the moment, Gwen did at least have the New York home court advantage. "Never mind. We're just getting started here. Who even knows—"

"I know. I know what I want. And I know what my mother and my father want in a...a wife for me."

"When you find her, let me know."

"I'm gonna ignore that." He pitched his body forward hooking her legs around his waist, raw sexual fury overtaking him. With a soft thud, she landed on her back. From the nightstand, he grabbed at the mountain of condoms. God it was amazing to watch him roll one on. He was so long. It was a miracle they fit! After several sweet licks from a tongue that was anxious to please, he drove deep inside her, rhythmically rolling his hips.

The sex was getting better and better. He'd been learning her body and she was figuring out all the little spots that made him shiver. Running her hands from his navel to the pelvis, drove him wild. She didn't even have to move further down. But oh, when she did, it was as if Andrew had been lit on fire. Especially the touches she'd been sneaking all week; on the bus, under the desk; or when *she* decided she needed sex and initiated it, stroking him to life.

There was so much of his body to study and enjoy.

He lowered his voice to a silky softness. "Get on your knees."

She twisted her body, but before she even bent her knees to get into that position, his arm wound around her waist, propping her up, lifting her. He couldn't wait. A comforting hand ran across her back. He slid back into her; this position allowed maximum penetration and depth. God, how he filled her. Touched every inch of her. Ignited every nerve. His moves were precise and measured. Slow and torturous. This man knew what he was doing. Knew how to take her, to please her. He finished in a spectacular style while massaging her to another highly vocal completion.

The rest of the night, they lay awake, touching, caressing, and kissing. It was still early according to her body clock. She let Andrew fall into an easy sleep, so she could watch him delicately snore. The covers tangled in his long muscular legs. Yes, he would be strong for her, for them. It was primitive, but very powerful.

His chest rose and fell in dramatic high and low swells. She rested her fingers above his heart. The smooth easy beats pleased her. Although she knew he was asleep, his hand covered hers.

Andrew rolled over, her body molding against his, their legs locking beneath the covers.

So this is what forever feels like…

* * * *

In front of his office on Friday morning, Andrew was battling Gwen over who could tear themselves away first.

It was the in-person equivalent of: *No, you hang up.* Except it was: *No, you walk in first.*

Finally, he placed a soft kiss on her lips, nudged her body inside his office, and closed the door.

He had to continue his work with Marcello.

Gwen's suggestions had been working. All of them. By the end of that week, their daily review had gotten shorter and Andrew was praising Marcello more than he was criticizing him. For the tasks he was just not getting, Andrew delegated the work to an assistant in the group. Others, he automated. The man appeared energized and pleased with himself. Marcello's shoulders no longer slumped from exhaustion and his clothes looked like he'd found an iron somewhere in his house.

But a big hurdle was coming up. The yearly report of all the brands' activities and a projection for the following year was due at the end of the year and it was already early December. This report had taken Andrew months to put together his first year. Marcello didn't have months.

Andrew would have to spend the next two weeks drinking espresso well into the night using his own report as a template. After he showed it to Marcello, Andrew was relieved to hear he planned to work throughout the weekend to get started on the report.

As for Andrew, he had a better plan for *his* Saturday.

CHAPTER TWENTY-TWO

Andrew woke Gwen up early Saturday morning, resisting the urge to climb on top of her.

Reluctantly, she got up grumbling, and clawing at him as he got out of bed. *I created a monster!*

Sipping coffees, they took a bus to the center of town. By this time, he could tell she was happy and excited. He loved that he was starting to be able to read her thoughts and what every curve of her face meant.

The highlights in her hair gleamed in the sunshine even when the wind blew it all around her face. She wore very little makeup and seemed to prefer to only darken her lashes, dab nude lip gloss on her mouth and go. She was a natural beauty with fresh even skin tone that gave her face a warm shimmer. What frightened Andrew the most was the striking beauty who emerged when she spent more than five minutes on her appearance.

After a few minutes of huddling against the gentle wind, a large motor-coach rolled into view. They had been waiting with a small crowd on a nearby piazza. Italians didn't gawk on the curb craning their necks for a bus like New Yorkers. They approached life with ease and comfort. On their own terms. And when their ride arrives, they give their shoulders a shrug as if to say, *Well okay, I guess I will get on.*

He was taking Gwen to the five cliff side villages along the northeast coast known more commonly as the *Cinque Terre.* "I'm usually here alone," he had explained when they bought the tour tickets. "I always knew I would rather experience this with someone special."

Her eyes were stormy reacting to the way he said, *special.*

It was a smaller crowd than usual; the guide had explained. The tour was more popular in the spring and summer months. There was however plenty of beauty they only needed eyes for and not sunscreen.

The bus ride to the beautiful region was magnificent in its own right. At times the road was quite narrow, and all that stopped the bus from tumbling down the hillside was a white iron railing no more than three feet high. Even at this time of the year the landscape was lush, with primary pops of reds and oranges. Winter roses, the guide had said, didn't own a calendar and would continue to climb up the sides of houses with southern exposures.

Parts of the road were spent climbing mountains. And to get over a mountain, a road winds up and down, often cutting through short narrow tunnels. When that happened, the entire interior of the bus was plunged into darkness. Gwen squeezed Andrew's hand during those moments and the tight grip he returned was part of the continued affirmation of his devotion and affection.

The road flattened out. Even though it was still one lane, the scenery on the left had not changed significantly. Gwen leaned into his ear and he immediately bent to listen.

"I have to ask…if I'm leaving tomorrow, why are we spending my last day a hundred miles away from your bed?"

"Because I want a life with you that goes beyond sex." His answer was short and succinct, no room for follow up or a discussion. His brows dipped down, creating that dramatic expression he liked to lay on people to get what he wanted. "And I'm willing to sacrifice my pleasure, even in the limited moments we have to share things with you. That's the type of relationship I want Gwen."

Gwen didn't respond, because there were no words beyond what Andrew had just said.

At times, it was hard to look at him; his beauty still stopped her heart. Especially when his face caught the light a certain way or when he looked at her with intense passion in his eyes. But small flaws made him real; a scar on his chin and his left eye had a tendency to drift when he was tired. After so much time studying his face, she was able to see beyond the crushing good looks and appreciate the man underneath.

The rough stone of the mountains gave way to the ocean. In the province of La Spezia, the first stop was along the Ligurian Coast in a town called Porto Venere. While the bus made daredevil twists and turns to negotiate the cliffs between the road and the center of town, the guide provided some basic facts about the town. Andrew translated: the town was actually comprised of three villages and several barrier islands.

And it wasn't surprising by the smell...the main economy was fishing. Still the view from the bus drop off, which wasn't far from what looked like a modern day marina was breathtaking.

She settled against his chest while the guide spoke more about the town. To Gwen, the most important piece of information was when the boat to the next village would be leaving.

Her face turned downward listening to the guide say he'd be taking the group on a walking tour to see several historic churches. "I didn't come all this way to be indoors," she whispered.

"I don't think the church tour is mandatory. Let me find out where this boat is leaving from and we'll figure it out from there."

A sidewalk café still had tables outside even though the weather was brisk. Gwen loved sipping a rich, full bodied red wine in chilly temperatures.

They took a seat and Andrew ordered two glasses of their house red in Italian. Listening to him speak the language was such a huge turn on.

Small trees lined the quaint street. They could have easily been sitting on Center Street in Darling Cove. Drenched in winter sunlight, Gwen eagerly snatched the glass of wine and took a hearty sip. "Holy crap, *that* is amazing."

"Drink up. We have all day." He leaned back and crossed his legs, watching the street and cars going by. His square jaw and taut mouth made him look like he was posing in a photo shoot.

Andrew looking out at the small town with ease and pleasure, filled Gwen with hope. Perhaps this tall, gorgeous, ex-model, Prada-wearing man could one day fit into the laid back North Fork culture. Her neighbors however would have a heart-attack. She could hear the whispers now. *Did you see the handsome man from New York City yet?* They really did say 'New York City', like in that old salsa commercial. She chuckled into her wine.

"Something funny?" asked the handsome man.

"No, but can I ask you a personal question?" She leaned forward. When a startled look crossed his face, she backpedaled. "Never mind."

He clutched her hand. "Of course you can. I was just surprised you prefaced it that way. After what you've done to my body all week, there's very little personal information I have left Gwen." But he looked down and cleared his throat. "Do you want to ask me about Cate?"

She bit her lip. He still didn't know she'd stalked Cate's blog and had all the info she needed. No. Gwen had been dying to know something else. "Um. No, not right now."

"Okay." He took a relaxed sip and resumed his pose. "You can always ask me anything. So, what then?"

She pulled the glass up to her lips but before she took a sip, she tilted her head and asked, "I have to know... How did the whole modeling thing come about?"

Andrew's eyes flickered and he pursed his lips, suggesting she could ask anything *but* that.

Her chest tightened. "I'm sorry. I don't need to know."

"No." He put his glass down. "But Gwen...is that all you see when you look at me?"

"Of course not," she said dumping her hands in her lap. "I just suspect it's an interesting story. You can give me the abridged version if it led you to working behind the scenes in fashion."

He looked at her for a moment and a small smile formed. She wanted to know why he made that career choice, and had hoped to prove she was interested in peeling the layers to see beneath the surface. "I was working in my father's law firm when I was in my junior year at NYU. Yes, my father had expected me to go to law school and yes, he expected me to become a lawyer just like him. The good news was that he wasn't a dick about it. Anyway, I'd been in the law library looking for something when one of the partners who was in charge of the entertainment side of the firm introduced me to one of his clients. He gave me his card and told me to call him."

"I'll bet it was someone from Ford, wasn't it?"

"Yes. What he was proposing sounded interesting enough. I had the height and I was thinner. My hair was a little longer then too. It was a look that was in demand at the time. I got a portfolio together and I started working almost immediately. Mostly runway stuff, some catalogues. The agent was trying to push me towards commercials but that included trips to L.A. for auditions. I liked the runway work. But then it got tedious. And the scrutiny… If you think women are objectified, wrap your pretty head around this: the ratio of women to male models is six hundred to one. To say *male* modeling is competitive is an understatement."

"So how did you end up at Prada?"

"I was in a show for Lanvin and I met Enrico. We bumped into each other at other shows after that, and one day he asked me to lunch, to talk about working for him." He sipped his wine and looked at his phone for the time. "Enrico asked me brand related questions. My major in college was marketing, so he must have done some research on me. I didn't realize he was looking for a brand specialist. But he wanted my take on Lanvin. I'd been modeling for them almost exclusively and knew the Creative Director well."

The mention of Lanvin made Gwen's heart spike. Cate had modeled for them. That's how they met. Two models…who were married. What a fairy tale *that* must have looked like. She swallowed and self-consciously touched her face. Her follow up question was lost in the back of her mind. After a throat clearing, she found it. "Was it hard adjusting?"

He blew a large puff of air from his cheeks. "You have no idea."

She'd only known Andrew in his brand manager role, and he owned the position with command and power. It showed, in every facet of his marketing campaigns and strategies, just how good he was at his job. As she opened her mouth to respond, he appeared lost in his own thoughts. "Is something wrong?"

"You're better at all of this than I am. You realize that, don't you?"

That set her back. "I don't know if I would say 'better'. Maybe just different. We basically had the same education, and have worked in fashion our whole careers." A thought occurred to her. She and Andrew could be a fashion power couple too. *Prada's most beautiful couple behind the scenes.*

"Enrico wouldn't give you Marcello's job, if you weren't..."

Again, the idea that she could be the Milan Brand Manager had taken a back seat to this whirlwind romantic week with Andrew. What a boon for her. That was the whole point of walking away from Starlight Elegance. Propelling herself forward. To have the career she'd always wanted.

Andrew checked his phone. "Mmm, drink up. The boat is leaving in a few minutes."

While he scrambled to pay the check, Gwen wondered which boat in life she really wanted to catch: business or personal. And would they have different destinations?

* * * *

During the windy, high-speed boat ride to Monterosso al Mare; the largest of the five villages, Gwen's unruly mane jabbed at Andrew's face.

But he loved her hair...so long, rich and thick. He adored how it felt in his hands, how it felt spilled over parts of his body when they made love. Gwen fit perfectly everywhere. Like she'd been built for him. The way she easily snuggled against him, leaned into him, touched him without hesitation or concern if someone was watching was getting to him — driving him crazy. It had only been a few days but he suspected, he was hopelessly addicted.

Once they were in the town, the guide talked about how after World War II part of the village had been rebuilt. And during the construction they expanded the town. The landscape had been so altered, a pedestrian tunnel had to be built to put the village back together again.

At the cliff-framed beach, he turned to Gwen. "I have a question for you."

"Okay." She looked away from the five-hundred-foot rocky drop that was making him nervous. "Shoot."

He took a seat on a bench looking out over the water. "Tell me about your mother."

"That's pretty broad."

"Okay. What do you remember the most about her? What's your best overall memory of her?"

At first she delicately touched her lips with her fingers. He studied their shape, the smoothness of her skin. He didn't like that they were empty. It made her a…target—whether there in Italy, or in New York. Restlessly, he stirred in his seat waiting for a response. "Gwen, if it's too difficult to talk—"

"No. No. Not at all. I was just thinking that when I think of my *mom*, I think of how much she loved my father. I know that's boring and corny. But she adored him. She wasn't from the North Fork. They met in Chicago. She was a city girl. Her parents had money, but I'm not sure what happened. I think they didn't want her to move away. I don't recall having a relationship with my grandparents on that side." She stopped to take a breath.

It appeared she was becoming emotional. He unfolded himself off the bench to stand next to her. "It's okay." The story bore some similarity to what had happened to him. How his parents had turned their back on him, when he married someone they didn't like.

Gwen touched his hand. "But my mom loved our town. I guess because it was so different from where she grew up. She was the typical strong, dedicated, cop's wife. My dad worked all kinds of shifts. I never knew if he was coming or going, but my mom managed our schedules and his flawlessly. Even when I was older, and at the age where your parents being all fussy is kind of gross, what moved me was to see how her body just came alive when he'd drive by in his patrol car and blow his sirens just for her. She'd take whatever was in her hands and wave to him."

"That's amazing Gwen." He smoothed the skin on the hand that had been clutching onto a scarf.

"Are your parents happy?" she asked, returning the touch on his arm. "You're such a decent honorable man. Your father had to have had an influence on you."

That made him smile. "It wasn't as sugary as all that. Attorneys are serious and work long hours. My dad doesn't have much of a sense of humor. But my mother wasn't looking for a comedian. He gave her the life she wanted and as far as I know, he was always faithful."

"Everyone has their own definition of happiness, but it sounds like you grew up with two great role models."

"Now there's a modeling job I wouldn't mind having, right now." His words were amusing but his serious tone took Gwen back a few steps. She'd been ready to respond but he touched her face. "Why don't we get some lunch."

CHAPTER TWENTY-THREE

Andrew held onto Gwen's waist as they walked to a quaint trattoria.

Its dark paneled walls, its mosaic tiled floor and the red patent leather booths made him feel as if they'd been propelled back into the fifties. The server talked them into trying the truffles in a white wine reduction.

Gwen smiled diligently through a few bites, but said, "I'm sorry, I can't get it out of my mind that they use pigs to dig these up." She forked through a couple and raised one off the plate. "This could have been in a dirty swine's mouth."

Andrew pushed his plate away. "Tastes like it."

Sitting on the curb a few doors down, he and Gwen enjoyed the taste of authentic Italian pizza.

The coastal train to Manarola had wide windows, and like a dog who preferred to hang its head outside and lap up the wind, Gwen wanted to feel the ocean breezes on her face.

Her nose wiggled looking at the town, and he read her mind. *Looks the same as the others.* There they decided to shop and act like tourists, buying magnets, tee-shirts, a painted print of the marina which looked like a swimming pool for *Castello Doria*, some cooking oils and glittery cheap jewelry.

Andrew snapped some photos, most of which were of Gwen, and took her hand to find a cafe to get some more wine.

At the marina's outdoor seating tables, he chose a house Prosecco. The serving girl who made him feel like he'd stumbled upon a hidden Hooters, with her short skirt and dramatically low V-neck tee-shirt, gave him the typical looks he'd been accustomed to.

The server walked away from the table and Gwen leaned forward. "I think she purposely spilled the water on herself to have her own wet tee-shirt contest."

He'd learned not to pay attention to women like that. Especially in the presence of another woman. But he felt it wise to note, "Do women like that realize any decent man isn't going to want a woman who dresses like that?"

"Or look at your date with contempt," she countered.

"Is that what you think you are? My date?"

Gwen responded with fire. "That's just it. She doesn't know that. I could be your wife!"

Andrew wished he had a mirror. He was clueless to guess what expression sat on his face at the moment. The "wife" remark had fallen on his head like a hammer.

Gwen began biting her lip as if she regretted her comment.

He reached across the table, and was concerned when she tucked her hand in her lap. "Gwen?"

Her other hand clutched the wine glass as she swallowed another long sip. Now he'd have to get that server's attention sooner rather than later for a refill. "I have another question," she said softly.

He took a breath. "Sure." A dark expression took over her features and it alarmed him.

"Have you considered we may *not* be able to work this out?"

The weight of the words and the serious look on her face startled him into actually taking a fraction of a second to do so. "Okay," he said somberly in a deep scratchy voice that had been deprived of oxygen.

Gwen looked at him, her face contorting, taking in the changes of his own features. "What happens then?"

He swallowed a lump of bile. "Happens?"

She took what looked like a shaky breath. "The likely scenario is that I'm here." She made a small semi-circle with her head to pantomime 'here'. "And that…occasionally you will still have to come here." She broke down.

"Gwen, stop. Just stop this right now."

"No!" She sounded like she was gagging on tears. "How do I look at you then?" She flicked away moisture from her cheek. "I'm not making any promises—"

"I *am*."

"Don't expect a brave soldier sitting here on the other side of the world. You and Enrico think Marcello is doing a shitty job…" She finished her wine and collected her scarf. "Don't expect too much from me." She sprang from the table and rushed out the door behind her.

Andrew lunged across the table to grab her. His legs tightened ready to go after her but he paused. He paused to collect himself. Vernazza was a small island. He'd find her.

The inappropriately dressed server reappeared. *"Are you all right?"* she asked in Italian.

Andrew clenched his jaw and took out his credit card. *"Bene."*

"Women get..." She fumbled in English detecting his American accent. "Emotional at certain times of the month."

To that he smiled. He wished that was the case. *"Grazi. Conto per favore."*

The server smiled back and placed a hand-written check on the table. He noticed the date. If Gwen was regular, based on where she said she was with her cycle at the L.A. fashion show, she *wasn't* approaching her time of the month now.

Either way, as a modern man, he learned not to dismiss a woman's heated passion for the natural course her body takes every month.

He paid the bill and stepped outside. The sun's angle was sharp against the water and it stung his eyes. Adjusting, he didn't see the blurry figure in a tan coat materialize. "Gwen!" He wiped his eyes. "Honey, are you okay?"

She rushed into his arms, her head sliding under his jaw. "I'm sorry. I didn't mean to pressure you."

"That was hardly pressure." He touched her face. "You can always tell me what you're feeling or thinking. That's the relationship I want."

He kissed her lightly but her tongue tickled his lower lip and he pressed firmly against her face, letting her passion overwhelm him. Needing a breath of air, he rested his chin against her forehead. Before he could think, he said, "I've changed my mind, Gwen."

Her body hardened and she jerked away. "What?"

He smiled and folded her hand back into his. "You'll see."

The final town of Riomaggiore was reachable via a cliff-side walk from Manarola. The guide walked ahead, providing details about the cliffs and rocky shoreline below, what it had done to small boats in a once-in-a-lifetime storm, a hundred years ago. Gwen was getting restless, and with every hour that passed, her plane ride back to New York the following day became closer to a reality.

Once they made it into the town, Andrew searched up and down the streets, looking at each building, every sign. *There!*

After several cars passed, he took Gwen across the street.

"The rest of the group walked that way," she said pointing.

"I'd rather be here with you right now." Andrew stood under the sign for a small hotel.

* * * *

Gwen leaned against Andrew's back while he paid for the whole night, since small seaside hotels in Italy don't have short stays. Still, she knew it would be worth it.

Unbuttoning his coat, she breathed and spoke while kissing him. "We don't have much time, and we have to be super careful."

"I agree about the time, but…" He reached into his trousers and took out his wallet. A shiny gold square slid out into his long fingers. "I figured…just in case."

"I love how you think." She slid her coat off.

"I love—" He choked. "Um…"

She placed her hands over his lips. "There's time for that."

His arm wound around her waist and he carried her to the small bed. It creaked under their weight. She stripped herself bare, wanting to feel exposed. But she dragged the covers aside and slipped beneath the cool sheets to prevent the act from feeling rushed. Like…maybe they could spend the night. Like…maybe they could never leave.

As fashionable as Andrew looked, like always, watching him remove his clothes slammed her with a desire she'd never known. The jacket eased down his long arms, and when his sweater was no longer in the way, her hands ran across tight stomach muscles. She was perhaps taking too long touching the upper portion of his body, he lowered his pants and stepped out of the puddle they created at his feet. Every inch of skin he exposed rushed her with more heat. His manhood bulged through clingy boxers, she didn't have to touch him to know he was ready.

"Can I put the condom on you?"

"God, I would love that." Andrew took possession of her eager mouth, and kissed her.

"You open it though," she whispered. "I get so turned on watching you slice into these things with your teeth, like you can't wait."

"I usually can't," he mumbled with the packet in his mouth. He turned it over. "It goes on like this."

She snatched it from his hands. "I know how a condom works, Andrew."

"Kiss me while you put it on." His commands were so enthralling. Telling her what he wanted was having an effect on her she didn't think she could ever shake. So confident in how he wanted her. He groaned as she slid the thin piece of latex over his magnificent length.

There'd be no time for foreplay. Gwen's body sizzled hot when he entered her. Her cells lit up, on fire, when they became one. They were connected as never before, sharing their passion for the act and the act alone. "Oh God, Andrew."

"I know, Gwen," he said, caught between a sigh and a moan.

When he kissed her, she could smell the ocean on his skin and taste the wine on his lips. He lifted her leg to get the maximum depth. And his long legs and strong thighs gave him the power to pull all the way out and slide back in, sometimes teasing her, running his long, thick erection all across her aching flesh before dipping back inside her, deep, hitting the end of her.

This was certainly the end. The end of any rational thinking about anything. Gwen's body went wild, a burst of energy overwhelming her. "I want to be on top."

"Are you sure? I'm close."

"So am I. I want to take you, Andrew. I want to ride you."

He rolled over, but his body was so bulky they were disconnected momentarily. She leaned back, feeling, finding him…to slide him back into her wet flesh, throbbing with need.

"Wait," he said, reaching down.

"It's fine. You're inside me." Sitting back, she spread her thighs wide; her body already beginning to tingle.

He grabbed her hips and rocked her back and forth. "Jesus Gwen, that is so fucking good. Ride me. Yeah."

Her hands flew over her head, her fingers tangled in her hair. His palms roamed her body, holding her breasts, squeezing hard nipples in between anxious fingers. "Yes. Andrew. There. That's it. Yes. Yes."

His back arched in a steep curve, sending him even deeper inside her. "Gwen, I'm coming," he cried out, his legs bucking.

She was so high up, she almost fell off from his violent body jerks. His orgasm reduced him to moans and groans. When her own pulsing stopped, she fell onto him. His long arms came up and pressed her body into his. Tight.

He found her mouth and kissed her hard. "Oh my God. That was fucking, incredible."

"I never want to leave here."

"I know. But we do have to get back to Milan."

Why? She took a deep sniff of his chest. He smells different when they made love. A new scent was released. Male. Satisfaction. She leaned forward, putting her hands on the mattress in order to climb down.

He sprung forward chest first. "Uh oh."

"What," she said, thinking they'd been there too long and maybe the bus back to Milan was gone. *Too bad.*

He leaned forward and from the center of the bed he picked up the condom. "It must have fallen off when you moved."

A touch between her legs confirmed it. Warm and wet, very wet. "Oh," was all she could respond. She sneaked a peek under her lashes, thinking he'd be looking the other way. His eyes were firmly on hers. This was her fault. Sure, the girl who only had three sexual partners was a condom expert. She'd been so caught in the moment, and so loved the idea of putting it on him, she didn't want to wait for a damn lesson.

"Is this a…" He shook his head.

"Is this a bad time for me, you mean?"

"Yeah."

She waved her hand. "No. It should be fine. I'm thirty-five, not fifteen. It's not that easy to get…" She chose not the say the word, fearing a Beetlejuice experience.

"Oh, okay. Good. I guess." He closed his hands around the condom and walked to the small bathroom.

Once he was out of the room, Gwen ripped her phone out of her bag. She kept track of her cycle in her calendar. She found the little X from last month and counted to get to her *unsafe* days.

Oh no.

The ride back to the Milan was filled with silence.

Gwen's eyes were heavy but she didn't close them. Couldn't close them. Her head leaned against Andrew's shoulder while their fingers locked at the knuckles. He never let go of her hand. The silver lining was, he was coming home in a couple of weeks. He said he'd work day and night if he had to, to make sure Marcello's annual report would show Enrico he could do the job.

And if that didn't work…

They would think of something. They would make their relationship work out. Somehow. They slept that night in a tangle of sheets, legs, arms and a cat.

In the airport the next morning, Gwen reached the line for security, but Andrew pulled her aside and kissed her, gently touching her face. His fingers were soft on her skin.

"Gwen…" His face went blank, searching for a way to finish.

She swallowed. "Me too." She had no idea what he couldn't tell her, but she was sure her face looked the same as his did. Sad. In this moment, *she* would be the strong one. "I'll text you when I'm on the plane."

He nodded, his lips rolled in, tamping down his emotion. "I really want this to work, Gwen."

She smiled and kissed him softly. But in her mind she was thinking, it just may *have* to.

CHAPTER TWENTY-FOUR

It'd been almost two weeks since Gwen had seen Andrew…and her period should have arrived three days ago.

It had been the worst possible time to have un-protected sex. But she'd decided not to put that additional worry on him. What had been done was already done at that point. Andrew had enough stress with Marcello.

But how could *one* slip up…

"Give me another one." She stuck her hand around the bathroom door and waved impatiently to her sister. "The other brand. I can't believe this."

She bought several pregnancy kits. Skye handed her a wrapped stick that reminded her of a popsicle. The others rested on the edge of her sink, all positive. Gwen released a gentle stream of urine on the stick, set it beside the others on the counter, and waited.

Sitting on the edge of the tub, she clasped her hands together. When she and Dan were first married, she had become pregnant right away…but after a month lost the baby. With the passing years since, Gwen had acknowledged the miscarriage had been a hidden blessing, since Dan had turned out to be a creep. It would have been worse if he'd left her with a child. But what had stuck with her all these years was that *feeling*. She'd been sick with nausea but never *got* sick. It had just been a horrible churning in her stomach every day, all day.

She'd woken up that morning…with the same feeling.

Her nervous fingers picked up the latest stick. *Just like the others.* Two little pink lines winking at her. She slapped them all off the sink, shooting them into the shower, the cheap plastic echoing off the tiles.

"Am I opening another box?" Skye asked from behind the closed door.

"No." She scooped the sticks up and opened the door.

"I hope you're going to throw those away." Skye scrunched her face at the five wet sticks in Gwen's hand. "They do have urine on them."

"If all of these are accurate, I'm having a baby." She let the sticks fall into the trash one by one. "And I'm going to have more than urine all over me soon."

"All those pink lines and you're still not convinced?" Skye asked.

The last hour rocked Gwen's emotions all over the Richter scale. She'd just spent an amazing week with Andrew. And there was the promise of a great relationship on the horizon. Now, she felt *not* like the deer lucky enough to just be caught in the headlights, but the one who'd been hit and smashed through a windshield. And this was her own fault. She looked in the trash bin. "Oh, I'm convinced all right."

"Are you done being melodramatic? Come here!" Skye hugged her. "A baby. A teeny-tiny baby."

"Andrew is six-foot-four. I don't know how *teeny* this baby is going to be." As if there wasn't enough to worry about.

Skye released her. "When are you going to tell him?"

Gwen sunk onto her mattress. "He's four thousand miles away. Should I text him the good news?" She'd heard the term *Expectant Father.* What about an unexpectant one?

"I agree, you probably want to tell him in person." Skye sat and smoothed her back. "When is he coming home?"

"Christmas Eve."

"That's some present, Gwen."

"Surprise!" she mocked.

"I'll go make you some of that vanilla tea you never drink." Skye stood and whistled her way to the kitchen.

Gwen rolled over and took out her phone. Christmas Eve was in a few days. Andrew had arranged to fly home for the holiday. He needed the week to work on his report. His and Marcello's projections were due on the thirty-first. He'd initially been cautiously optimistic about how Marcello was doing. But the tone had since turned grim.

Gwen mashed her wet face in her pillow. Wrapped up in Andrew's arms that week and attached to his body again and again, it had been easy to dismiss the distance. But reality had been a cruel bitch since she'd been back in New York.

Deborah Garland

Phone calls were an inconvenience with the time difference. With six hours between them it always seemed just on the edge of doable. Andrew was well into his day before she woke up. Facing lonely evenings at home while he slept had been a drag. In the middle of December, the days were the shortest now. On the North Fork the sun still rose fairly early, but she'd been coming home to a dark sky. The upside was, once she was in her house, she only needed to stay awake for a couple of hours.

Nine hour flights would make weekend getaways impossible. And with U.S. holidays and Italian holidays usually not lining up, there weren't even any long weekends to take advantage of. If she had to move to Milan, it would be completely unreasonable to try to maintain a relationship or expect that they could ever grow into a real couple that way.

Now she'd added a dense, sticky layer of complication! How in the world would they raise a baby together living on two different continents?

Skye returned with two steaming mugs of tea.

"Thanks." The smell of nutmeg filled Gwen's senses. But after two sips, she put the drink down. "Skye?"

"What sweetie?" Her sister took a seat on the floor, her legs crossed facing the mattress.

"I guess I can admit to you that I'm in love with him." *First comes love. Yeah, right.*

"I hope so!" Skye sat forward and tapped her stomach. "Did you tell him?"

"No. We had just…worked things out." She looked at the ceiling. "Now I'll never know."

"Know what?"

"How he really feels about me."

"What do you mean?"

"This is going to force his hand."

"Gwen, this isn't the fifties. Men don't *automatically* feel they have to marry a woman anymore. Especially a career girl like you." Skye made sense. But that's not the man Gwen suspected Andrew was. "And just how much do you love this job, anyway?"

Here comes that *being a mother is the most important job in the world* crap. From a woman Gwen suspected secretly didn't

188

even *like* kids. "It's paying my mortgage. And…" She strained to look at her alarm clock. "It's getting late and I have to get up early to get to this job I love so much."

"Okay, okay." Skye got up.

Gwen stood as well, and walked Skye to her front door. Her sister pulled her into a hug and held her for a moment, and then she stepped back to rub her stomach again. "Six-foot-four huh?"

"Mmm. And yes, it *is* proportional."

"Bitch."

But the following day on the phone, listening to Andrew's voice penetrated Gwen deeper, since now she had a mini-version of the man growing inside her. Already her insides pulled and twitched, like a magnet drawn to its other half.

"Gwen, that's the third time you've yawned. Are you having trouble sleeping?"

Yes, because you're not here. "No. It's just that by the time I get home—"

"What time *do* you get home?" he asked.

"Around seven," she answered, even though the colder weather usually made it later. And if there's a drop of precipitation…

"And what time train do you have to take in the morning?"

"Six-thirteen." It hurt just to say it.

"That's insane. Are you in our office?"

"Yes." She loved that he still called it *their* office.

"Go to my desk and sit in my chair."

She'd been resisting that. Hers was a basic task chair, black, mesh, impersonal. But his was considered an Executive Swivel. High back, curved sides and leather. The arms had worn in places, she assumed from his strong hands gripping the sides, his nails digging into it. It hadn't meant as much the first week she was there. She didn't intimately know the ass that had been sitting in it.

Like she did now.

She wiggled her own butt against the seat trying to absorb any long lost heat. Then she remembered Enrico had technically sat in it last. And gagged.

"Hello?" Andrew called out to her. "Open my top desk drawer."

"Okay." She slid it open. Messy. Shocker. "What am I looking for?"

"My spare keys."

Tucked in the back was a batch of keys on a single stainless ring that made her jaw drop.

"What are all these for?"

"They're for everything. My building, my mailbox, my apartment, my bike lock, my car and my parents' apartment on Fifth."

Gwen had heard that a major movement in a relationship was when a man gave a woman a key. *A key.* Andrew was handing over his life. "I don't know what to say."

"I want you to stay in my apartment until I get home. I wish you would have told me about this crazy commute sooner."

"This is very trusting of you, Andrew."

"You sound surprised."

"I'll try not to trash the place." Gwen closed her fingers around the heavy key ring. With great power comes great responsibility.

"Call me tonight when you get there."

She sighed. It had been grating how protective Greg and her dad were, but this was different. This didn't have an annoying, needling quality. This felt primal and dominant. Made her feel…cherished. "But you'll be asleep."

"Doesn't matter. Do it. Okay, Ms. Foley?"

"Mallory."

"What?"

"I signed my divorce papers. In a few months, I'll be Gwendolyn Mallory again."

After a brief silence, Andrew gave his usual response, "Good."

Gwen stirred, wondering if these keys meant she'd have to change her name…*again.*

And the keys unlocked more than Andrew's apartment.

She already knew it was not where he had lived with Cate. In the blog, she mentioned a duplex on the Upper East Side. His new apartment was downtown. It was a typical pre-war layout with a small galley kitchen, white ceramic tiles and an open countertop overlooking the living room. On it, she placed the dinner she had picked up on the way home, as well as a few toiletries from Duane Reade. Thank heaven they also sold underwear. As far as clothes, she snagged a few reject dresses from the designer floor on her way out of the building.

On the far wall was a row of windows overlooking Seventh Avenue South. Her gaze wandered down the narrow hallway that opened to his bedroom. She'd save that for last.

On the refrigerator, take-out menus were held under magnets, all neatly lined up. Sure, his desk looked like it had been grabbed by Godzilla, shaken and put back, but this place was immaculate.

Thank goodness though.

The only odd thing about all of this was, she'd not slept in this apartment with him yet.

But his scent was everywhere. His bedroom held even more traces of him. Without wondering if she was allowed to or not, she opened a drawer in one of his bureaus. She fingered through the pile of clothes and it was as if Andrew himself had climbed out from the bureau. The smell she had come to associate with him still clung to the fabric. It was delicious and spicy. A wave of pleasure coursed through her as she recalled the body that produced this musky aroma.

The colors drew her attention. "Jets and Yankees huh?"

While these weren't her favorite teams, her dad would love this man. "I hope he doesn't mind me putting some Mets and Giants colors in here."

She smiled and closed the drawer. He had to know she was going to snoop. He'd not just started dating women. But where to look next. Hmm.

Andrew's closet was amazing. All Prada shirts, pressed and lined up, organized by color. Very little white. Burgundy mostly. That looked best on him. Her fingers skidded past the fabric. All of this has been on his body and they were just sitting there now waiting. "I know how you feel," she said to a pair of pants. "You'll be on him soon. And me too hopefully."

Wanting to get a better look, she pulled on a silver chain to turn on the light, but it was blinding. "Geez." She waved her hands to find the chain again, her eyes peeking through her lashes. A splash of color on a shelf way up high caught her attention. A hat box. Pink and lavender floral. Not very manly. It must have belonged to Cate. What could be in there?

Gwen shook her head. Maybe Andrew just kept the box. Gwen turned the light off and left the bedroom to try to force down some dinner.

Filled with exhaustion an hour later, she brushed her teeth listening to the two sides of her personality arguing.

You want to look in that box, don't you?

No I don't.

Come on!

It's wrong, isn't it?

Maybe…maybe not.

Unable to figure out the cable and television remote combinations, she grabbed her tablet, but couldn't even play any online games because the Wi-Fi password Andrew gave her didn't work. All there was to do was stare at the ceiling from his bed. Even though it was lonely as hell, it was comfortable.

And she was cozy in the Jets tee-shirt that nearly came down to her knees. She stretched, forcing a yawn and slapped her hands down, too restless to sleep.

"Oh, what the hell." She whisked the covers away and went back to the closet. Her fingers found the string and the bulb blazed back to life. Looking up to figure out how to maneuver the box down, made the light sting her eyes. *Okay, this is the first sign, this was wrong.*

"I guess it doesn't matter how I get it down," she said dragging his desk chair from the living room. But it was still so high up. She bet he just slid that box in no problem, he was so tall. The chair wobbled as she jumped, trying to touch it. "Great. They'll find me dead right here, and he'll know what I did."

She huffed and reached up one more time, dislodging the box. It hit her head on the way down, popped open and dozens of pictures rained down on her.

"Son of a—" She slid to the floor to gather up the contents. "A year from now he'll find one of these under his bed." She switched the main light on.

Sprawled across the floor was Andrew's whole life. In a few minutes, she watched the man she loved grow up. There were even some headshots from his modeling days. How young he was! But it was how *thin* he looked that made her short of breath. He was reedy as well when she had met him. Now his face was full and the muscles on his shoulders no longer looked like they'd been strangled tight. In her hands was the old Andrew. Thin and unhappy.

Way at the bottom of the pile were the pictures she'd really risked her life to see. The ones of him and Cate. This pile didn't match the chronological order of his life. The heartbroken Andrew tucked *these* photos away.

A brown envelope sat in the middle of the batch. She peeked inside. "Yikes." Her hands shook, going through images of Andrew undressed and in a compromising position with another woman.

It bothered Gwen that he had kept such reminders of their intimate life together. But with the rise of dumpster diving, she could understand Andrew wanting to keep these in a safe place. Cate may be gone. But he was still very much…here.

Going back to the more *respectable* photos, Gwen could see how Andrew had matured during that relationship. Cate was as beautiful as Gwen remembered from the blog. The evidence of the ideal couple she had conjured was in her hands. Lanvin's top models. Fashion's original power couple. A tall stunning blonde, next to an even taller gorgeous dark haired man. They looked happy. Natural. Like they *belong* together. If there were rows of photos of men and women and the challenge was to pair up the perfect couple…Cate and Andrew would be the first two to be picked off to be together.

Sifting through all these photos where Cate looked absolutely fabulous begged the question, why had Andrew chosen one of her looking so sick to keep on his desk. Why remember her like that?

It was just one flawless picture after the other. *Ho hum.* Where did Gwen fit in this equation? She'd known her whole life she was pretty. There had been enough attention tossed her way to support that she too had something special. But this was another level. *This* was beyond her.

She shook her head, placed everything back in the box. Tomorrow she'd get a forklift and put it back. Back where it belonged. The memory of Cate was in a box. Tucked away and stored up so high, even Andrew needed a ladder to look back.

I'm here. In his bed…and I'm having his baby.

What was all of this going to mean to Andrew? Did he even *want* kids?

There *were* people out there who didn't. Gwen was pretty sure Skye was one of those people. And men too. There were men who *didn't* do the right thing by pregnant girlfriends.

What if everything she thought she knew about Andrew was wrong?

Burning on that last thought, Gwen tossed and turned until dawn, too many horrible *what-if* questions taunting her, fracturing her, her mind racing and running away with her sanity.

CHAPTER TWENTY-FIVE

Andrew was going to have to run…if he was going to make this damn plane.

Grinding holiday traffic delayed his transport van to the Milan airport. He'd *run* all the way back to New York if he could. Being without Gwen these past two weeks after what they had in Milan, made the hours crawl by. She'd got under his skin. And over it, and under it. The best way possible. He had connected with her on a level he didn't think was possible.

In the last few days, however he detected something was wrong. The distance must have been hard on her as well. It troubled him that the miles may have torn her down. She'd brought out the best of him, excavating the man he once was. He wanted to do the same for her. He was looking forward to the coming hours of getting under *her* skin…and over it…and inside it.

While Andrew had no idea what would happen with the Milan Brand Manager position, one thing was certain, he and Gwen *were* going to be *together,* in one way or another. He was hopelessly in love with her. And there's only one thing to do when that happens.

A marked up draft of Marcello's year-end report had been left on the young Italian's desk. It was full of red ink: *Change this. Research this better. Spell this correctly.* It would come down to a razor-sharp wire, whether or not Andrew had gotten through to him enough to make proper projections for the coming year.

What would Marcello have done if Andrew wasn't there to help him? That thought stopped Andrew from running to JFK's baggage claim. "What *if* I wasn't here? What if there was no brand manager in New York?" he asked a stranger who pointed to the men's room.

If Andrew quit, Enrico would *have* to keep Gwen in New York. Being unemployed wasn't the best Christmas present he could offer Gwen, but he hoped his grandmother's engagement ring would make up for it.

What mattered almost as much was, he had his mother's support this time. Fully. And in Sarah Morgan's usual style, she'd planned the whole thing for him. He was to bring Gwen to their apartment and on the Christmas tree there would be a little mini stocking with her name on it. Inside, would be the ring.

"You'll have to change the setting," his mother had suggested. "Today's woman needs something more sophisticated."

If he didn't get there in time, she'd have that all picked out too. But that made him smile; being caught in between two strong women.

There was buzz of a blizzard coming to New York in the airport. As usual, the models varied. Some said it would hit tonight, some said tomorrow. Others none at all. Still, if all went to plan, he'd get to Prada just in time for the Holiday party to be winding down. He could speak to Enrico and then take Gwen to meet his parents.

He'd chosen not to tell her anything about his plan. He wanted it to be a surprise.

Oh, he couldn't wait to see the look on her face.

* * * *

Gwen frowned at the snow while the Prada holiday festivities went on behind her.

And her face hurt thanks to all the European style kisses, especially from Italian men with thick, overgrown five o'clock shadows. The eggnog in her hand was too sweet. It left a fuzzy feeling in her mouth and all she wanted to do was to rub her teeth with her fingers. She'd poured it right from the container since the bowl was full of alcohol. The smell stretched out across the room. The party was showing no signs of winding down. It was seven pm and people had started drinking after lunch.

Big fluffy chunks of snow swirled outside the window of the second-floor lobby. A white Christmas had always excited Gwen. Before. Now it just meant she'd have to endure a dreadful commute all the way back to the North Fork. The two feet predicted for tomorrow on Christmas Day was going to bring the suburban line to its knees, unlike New York City, which doesn't shut down. Mostly. It took a terrorist attack, a blackout and a hurricane so bad-ass it was called a Superstorm, to bring this city to a halt.

Andrew's plane had landed, according to Alitalia's website. He'd been unusually tight lipped the past couple of days. It was so hard to get any real intimacy over the phone. She knew he'd been preoccupied with Marcello's report.

That may have changed if she had told him about the baby.

She came up empty in the planning department for that one. She considered putting the pee-sticks in a box. But that seemed cold. Every other idea of how and when to tell him ended up like a crumpled piece of paper in a wastebasket.

His plan was to come to the office, meet with Enrico…and that was it. He hadn't even asked her what she was doing for Christmas, so she assumed he would be spending it with his parents. As far as Gwen could tell, he had no intention of being with her for the holiday.

And why should he? Who *was* she? Not much, except the mother of his child! But he didn't know that. She left Milan with a promise of…'something.' They'd *be* something, some day. There was no rush. And she'd been okay with that. Heck, she hadn't even known if she'd still be living in New York.

A thought violently shot through her like pain. What if Marcello *was* going to be fired and Andrew knew that. That meant, as Enrico had told him, she would be offered the position in Milan. He'd been in this business, and worked for this company long enough, to know that she would be insane to turn it down. So perhaps he was inching away from her. Rethinking things. And in his mind, he probably thought he was doing what was best for *her*. Plus, the last two weeks of separation may have convinced him the distance was just too hard.

Or perhaps…Gwen wasn't worth it. Not worth the trouble. Or the money to travel as he had so proudly offered to bear the brunt of.

Fear, doubt and anxiety circled her like the drifts of snow outside, creating a vortex of panic that was so strong that before she could stop it, Gwen was in tears.

She had dissolved into a frightened mess. How could she face Andrew like this? A dab under her eyes confirmed her mascara had smeared. No. She couldn't handle seeing him. It was best to leave. *Now.*

She turned from the window, but the elevator flashing monitor stopped her in her tracks. The arrival bell was louder than she would have expected since the lobby was filled with voices and laughter; the sound was extra metallic. Daunting and foreboding. A sensation crawled down her spine, leaving her extremities cold. The doors opened, and Andrew stepped out of the car.

Gwen's heart splash-landed into the milky eggnog sitting at the bottom of her sour stomach. She'd been on the other side of the lobby with at least a dozen people in between. Yet she saw him as if everyone else had dissolved away.

He hadn't noticed her though. His head was dipped slightly like *he* was trying to go unnoticed. As if a gorgeous man of six-foot-four could ever pull that off. Even at Prada. Perhaps he didn't even want to see her…at all.

Frantic, she slid behind a rack of coats, peeking through a dark grey trench and a fuzzy fur coat that looked like it was made from a litter of Cavalier King Charles Spaniels. A line had formed for Andrew, mostly female. The way they were smoothing their hair and checking their teeth was sickening.

Andrew's chin rose when Enrico waved to him from the other side of the room. The tall body moved, a picture of grace and elegance. Even after a nine-Goddamn-hour plane ride.

He and Enrico talked briefly. Andrew mostly listened, his head bobbing at whatever Enrico was telling him. Andrew's eyebrows cinched together and a hand lifted to his mouth as they walked in the direction of Enrico's office.

In a flash, she raced to her own office. She'd gathered her things in a pile earlier, including her coat, and only had to *smash and grab* everything to leave quickly. She couldn't however risk waiting for the elevator. She slipped out of her office, crouching down, cursing all the damn glass offices that resembled fish bowls until she got to the west staircase.

She was steps away from the stairwell door, but a voice called out to her, making her spin around.

* * * *

Andrew sat in Enrico's office, antsy, and full of concern. Where was Gwen?

He'd played it out in his mind. He would step off the elevator and she would be there. He would rush to her, pull her into his arms and kiss her senseless...in front of everyone.

But she had been nowhere to be found. It wouldn't have been surprising if she'd been in their office, working away. Her commitment was so impressive, and a huge turn on for him.

He'd tried to move in that direction, but he'd been swarmed by other women. Then Enrico found him. Hopefully this wouldn't take too long.

He had a woman to propose to!

"*Bene.*" Enrico closed his office door. "So, now we are alone, tell me, how is our friend Marcello doing?"

"He's coming along. His report will be on time. And so will mine."

"*Suono, you* I am not worried about." Enrico waved his hand. "Your report will be stellar. I am certain. You are irreplaceable to me, Andrew. Please do not ever let anything that happens make you feel otherwise."

The sentiment swelled him with guilt, considering he was now scheming to quit, in his own power-play if it came down to it. "Enrico, Marcello *is* doing better." He leaned forward. "He's not where I think he should be. Perhaps if you give him more time. Give *me* more time with him. Maybe another month?"

"But Andrew, this has been dragging out long enough, yes? I cannot reasonably extend Marcello any more time. Let's wait to see what his report shows. That will tell me if he has a full grasp of his job or not. And whether or not we need to replace him."

Andrew swallowed. "With Gwen? Is that still the plan?"

"She has proven herself extremely capable. With the Milan position not operating at its fullest potential, do you think we have time to vet another candidate? That would mean more trips for you, *suono*. And do you want to train someone from scratch all over again?"

"What if…" Andrew cleared his throat. "The position went back under the Creative Director. Maybe we bit off more than we could chew."

Enrico leaned back, his chair squeaking. He tented his fingers and looked away. Even though Andrew threw in the "we", it was really all of Enrico's doing.

He'd just insinuated that his boss made a massive blunder. Maybe he wouldn't have to quit. Maybe he'd be fired! His lower jaw clenched and he planned to back-pedal.

Enrico narrowed his eyes across the hall to his and Gwen's office. Had he seen her? Andrew slowly turned his head in that direction and exhaled. Nothing. He tapped at his phone hoping for a vibration that she'd texted or called. Nothing. And it was getting late.

"All right, *suono*. I will take everything into consideration and *we* will make a decision by the end of next week."

Andrew shot to his feet. "Good. I think in the end it will all work out. For everyone."

"You like her, don't you?" Enrico stood as well.

"Um, Gwen? Yeah. Sure."

"I knew you would like her." Enrico waved a finger and smiled. "I may be an old man, but I can tell what's best for you."

His heart fluttered. Could Enrico have known what'd been going on? Andrew had been ready to just dip his head and leave. But Enrico added, "She has done well for us here at Prada. She has a bright future. I thank you for working with her and showing her what it means to have our standard of excellence."

He released a sharp breath. Business…Enrico was talking about business. And now it was about time Andrew got to his *pleasure*. "Merry Christmas, Enrico."

"Same to you. Give your mother my best." Enrico winked.

Andrew narrowed his eyes, but smiled back.

While standing in front of Thalia's desk, he called Gwen. *Pleasure*. That's what Andrew needed tonight. Deep, sweaty, grinding, fingernails-scraping-down-his-back pleasure, with the woman who was hopefully going to agree to be his future.

* * * *

"Salvatore?" Gwen turned at the sound of his voice.

"*Bella*, you are leaving so soon?"

She exhaled. "Yes, I have a long ride back to the Island. And my *name* is Gwen."

After a grunt, he said, "American women are too hung up on such formalities."

"It's called respect," she said, backing up closer to the stairs.

"You know I am going to my house on Lake Como for New Year's Eve. Perhaps you would like to join me, yes?"

The hand on her arm may have blazed with Salvatore's heat, but a man other than Andrew touching her made Gwen feel sick. Her stomach heaved. Perhaps the tiny cells that grew and multiplied inside her, fueled by Andrew's blood, were protesting the presence of another man. As they should!

Since she hadn't answered, Salvatore must have assumed she was considering it. "At midnight, the lights in the sky burn brighter and with more brilliant *colores* than your Fourth of July. Come with me…Gwendolyn."

Lake Como. *Really?* How many women would kill for a tumble with Salvatore on one of the world's most beautiful lakes? But a snort of laughter rose to the surface at the absurdity of just the *idea* that she would go with him. She drew her hands to her face in embarrassment.

"The idea makes you giddy, Gwendolyn?"

She smiled and put her hands on her hips. "I'm sorry. I can't go to Lake Como with you." She turned around, initially thinking she didn't need to respond further. But to make sure he never propositioned her again, she added, "I'm in love with Andrew Morgan."

But did he feel the same about her?

The stairwell door opened easily, and her boot heels clicked against the concrete, sending an eerie echo all the way down to the main floor. When she got to the street level and fled out the service entrance, her phone blew up. *Andrew*. She swallowed. Her heart pounding. What was she doing?

With shaking hands, Gwen answered, but rather than waiting, and risk him asking her to come back into the building to meet him, she sloshed down the street to catch a taxi on West Side Highway.

* * * *

"Gwen! Where are you?" Andrew cried into the phone, ecstatic to hear her voice.

"Oh. I'm on my way home."

"What?" He spun around and headed to their office. "What do you mean you're going home?"

"The party was winding down. I didn't see you. When I didn't hear from you I thought maybe your plane was delayed."

A shudder went through him, but a sense of calm filtered in. "Oh, so you're going back to my apartment?" He hoped that's what she meant by *home*.

"No. Back to the Island."

"Gwen, it's Christmas Eve. I just got back into town."

"Uh, yeah. I…I, uh, figured you would be with your family."

Andrew was speechless, and couldn't think of how to respond. He placed his free hand over his mouth.

"You didn't say anything about us getting together, so I figured I would just see you on Wednesday."

Andrew fell into his office door and slid to the ground. He hadn't said anything. She was right. How stupid of him to assume that *she* would assume they would be together. It didn't matter that he'd had this whole damn surprise waiting. That's the fucking nature of a surprise. Still, he should have made it clear he expected to *be* with her. The ring was enough of a surprise.

It occurred to him, however, if Gwen wasn't even expecting to see him for the holiday, how would a ring go over?

"Hello? Andrew, are you still there. Do you need to get going?"

Andrew shook his head. "No. I mean yes. I need to get going." *To the Island to be with you.*

"Okay, I'll see you in a couple of days." Her breath came in short bursts and then the phone went dark.

"Not exactly, Gwen," he said getting to his feet, but he faced the window and cringed. The blizzard.

Fuck!

* * * *

Darling Cove was whisper quiet.

The many inches of snow that had already fallen sound-proofed the whole town. It was nearly midnight. The trains had stopped at so many additional stations, as crews brought in snow-moving engines to clear the way.

Center Street was lit in gold and green lights and the houses on the side streets also glistened brightly with twinkling lights. Gwen's feet crunched under the fresh snow. She passed on the many taxis that were waiting at the train station in favor of walking. She didn't have far to go, since she didn't plan to go home.

Midnight mass at St. Mary's always drew a big crowd. Many years she'd been long asleep and never made it to this mass. Six-year-olds were able to stay awake, as evidenced by all the seats swallowed up by people she never sees throughout the year.

You know we do this every Sunday, the priest needled the hordes who filled up the vestibule and lined up against the wall under the *Stations of the Cross* figurines. His snarky comment always got a laugh. After sitting for almost five hours, Gwen was happy to stand, but a hand in the front was waving to her.

Dad!

She excused herself and weaved through the crowds to be with her family. Greg had stood at the entrance of the pew to let her in. He offered a warm smile as she leaned into him for a hug. She squeezed between the two men she loved. The men who meant more to her than any on this planet.

Her throat went tight, thinking of Andrew. "Where's Skye?" she whispered to Greg touching his hand.

He pointed to the line of singers in front of the altar. Skye's face lit up when Gwen found her. More noticeable were the faces looking at her sister. Especially the man standing against the wall, smiling. Edward Mendelsohn, the chief of Darling Cove's volunteer fire department. The man who played Santa on Thanksgiving.

Skye could do a lot worse. Edward was handsome as hell, dark auburn hair, full and brushing against his collar. Leaning against him was a little boy, but there was no woman with them. Hopefully Skye's hidden aversion to kids wouldn't get in the way there.

The choir finished their opening hymn. Gwen's reveries drifted in and out of time. Greg's hand brushing against hers, made her think of him and Faith, and what would have been, and then Edward watching Skye, thinking of what could be someday.

Of course, threaded in between, was her and Andrew. And the mess she'd made of everything. The songs were about hope. Gwen *hoped* that with the ghost of love past, present and future, Gwen too could find her way to the morning light.

After the mass, Greg shifted on his heels outside the church and finally said he had somewhere to be. Odd, since it was one am.

But his hug was tight and yummy.

"Merry Christmas, handsome." She touched his face, round with cheeks that curved so nicely when he smiled.

"I'll stop by in the morning during my shift." He kissed her forehead. "Good night, Dad." Greg hugged his father and shuffled to the parking lot.

"'Night Gregory." Martin watched him go, shaking his head.

"Dad, I'm just gonna walk." She braced for an argument, even though her house was only a few blocks away.

Martin kicked the snow off his boots. "Can I walk you?"

A pang in her heart drew her hand to her chest. "Of course. I would love that." She looped her arm in his and they crossed the street.

"Anything you want to tell me, pumpkin?"

Gwen stopped, the cold constricting her chest. "Why…why do you think I want to tell you something?"

"I can always tell when there's something…going on with you."

Skye!

"Okay." Gwen didn't need to be afraid. This was her father. The man who would always love her no matter what. Her lips parted, but the words were caught.

Martin stepped closer and touched her shoulder. "So, when *is* this baby due?"

She looked down and grunted. "How do you feel about only having two children?"

He laughed. "Your sister didn't say anything to me. I made you, remember? I know every inch of you." His fingers slid down her arm and then back to her cheek. "And you're glowing, pumpkin."

"You said at Thanksgiving, I'd be your best shot. But are you disappointed in me?"

"Of course not. And the father?" When she knocked her head from side to side he added, "He doesn't know, does he?"

"And you know that from detective work?"

"No. I can't imagine if a man knew you were carrying his child that he wouldn't want to be here with you now."

She curled her hands around her scarf. "I'm afraid to tell him."

"Afraid he won't live up to his obligations?"

"I'll never know how he really feels about me."

"Is he a nice man?" Martin rested his hands on her shoulders.

"He is, Dad." But she sighed, absorbing the reality of the situation. "I just don't know if I'm the right person for him."

"That's for him to decide, isn't it?"

More and more tears were building up. She'd been lulled during those intimate moments with Andrew into feeling like they were the perfect couple. She didn't know how to navigate the confusing waters where she felt like people would look and judge. *Oh no,* they *don't belong together.*

The sneering thought that would stream through people's minds when they learned Andrew was *staying* with her, committing to her because she was pregnant. *Oh, he's just doing the right thing.* No one could believe a man that beautiful, that sophisticated and polished would want a simple, good girl from all the way out here.

"I guess."

"I trust you'll do what's right, and no matter what, pumpkin, I'm here for you. You can always count on me."

"I always have, and you've never let me down."

"And don't you trust that you would choose to be with a man who has the same values?"

Gwen thought about that. It was true women tend to pick men who had the same qualities as their fathers. Martin was a decent, loyal man. A man who showered his family with love. In Milan, Gwen saw those qualities in Andrew and even commented on them. How could she let her insecurities make her think she'd been wrong about him? *Damn hormones!* "You're right." Her voice cracked.

"It's cold. Let's get you and my grandchild home."

Martin and Gwen walked the last block in silence. At her door, he gave her one more hug. "Why don't we go shopping this weekend for some real bedroom furniture? You're gonna need that guest room soon."

"Dad, you don't have the money for that."

"Don't you worry about what I have and don't have." He smiled. "And the way you're talking, it's not like I'll have to pay for another wedding."

"Ha, ha." Gwen took out her keys. "Do you think he would want to live here?"

"With you?" He took the keys and unlocked the door for her. "He'd be a fool not to. And I trust you wouldn't get involved with a fool."

"*Again*, you mean." Warmth blew out from the house. At least she'd be cozy.

"Get some rest." He handed back her keys. "I'll send some town guys over to plow out your driveway. Merry Christmas, pumpkin."

"Thanks Dad, Merry Christmas." She stepped inside and crumpled on the other side of the door.

CHAPTER TWENTY-SIX

By midnight, Andrew read on his phone that the governor of New York had declared a state of emergency due to the blizzard and all the roads out to Long Island were closed.

Coming home without Gwen had caused a long, drawn out conversation. He was pretty much told, *You messed up, Son.* If his father, who was head-strong, no-nonsense, and showed as little emotion as possible said he did wrong by a woman, Andrew wasn't about to argue.

But this was just a gross misunderstanding. Once he explained what his intentions were, he was certain the woman who had revealed herself so intimately to him in Milan would emerge.

He slept at his parents' apartment in his old bed, too tired to go all the way downtown to his own. That's not the homecoming he wanted. He had planned to bring Gwen there and make crazy love to her, hopefully with his grandmother's ring on her finger. Going there alone—felt empty and hollow.

On Christmas morning, the roads were back open. Andrew decided to go to the end of the earth for Gwen—he just didn't realize she *lived* there. His eyes bulged at his phone when he put her address into Google Maps.

"Are you even going to call her to let her know you're coming?" his mother asked, pouring hot coffee into a to-go cup.

"No, I want to surprise her," he said pulling his phone off the wireless charging pad on the counter.

Sarah stopped mid-pour. "Hasn't that got you in enough trouble already?"

He raised a warning look at her.

Rolling her eyes, she said, "A least take the ring with you."

Shaking his head, he bit out a quick, "No." He didn't care to propose in a house she shared with another man. But he'd keep that objection to himself. "I'm just driving out there to bring her back here."

"This Darling Cove got a lot of snow. Take my car, so I can at least not worry about you two." Sarah handed him the keys to her Cadillac.

The roads should have been jammed, but the blizzard must have changed millions of plans for the holiday. Still the *Time to Destination* on his phone made him cringe. And it hadn't taken into account he was only going forty miles an hour in the one lane that had been plowed.

"Jesus, Gwen. Even the Expressway didn't want to go out as far as Darling Cove," he said getting off at the last exit. And he *still* had forty minutes to go.

Once he was on Sound Avenue, Andrew's breath escaped him taking in the beauty. Even covered in white, the landscape was incredible. The storm released inches of heavy wet snow and all the trees looked like its branches were holding little snowballs ready to engage in a winter battle.

The white puffs of smoke from the houses he passed made him fondly imagine families were opening presents, laughing and snacking on cookies. And a little hungry. The blankets of powder in front of all the homes were untouched, clean and smooth.

The lady in the map app told him he needed to make a right in about a mile. Looking at the screen, swaths of blue on both sides meant he was surrounded by water. The little red upside down teardrop appeared and Andrew shuddered. There was his destination.

Gwen lived right on the water.

Turning onto her street, brought a rush of anxiety he wasn't expecting. He stopped the car to catch his breath. A cop car was in front of the address on the GPS. Andrew's hackles rose on his neck, worried. But a man bundled in a cop's leather bomber jacket and hidden under a hat came to the car. He released a quick siren blast and put the lights on. But only for a brief moment and drove off. Andrew's cheeks ticked up, remembering Gwen's heart-filled story in Milan about how her father used to do that.

Her father! Andrew slapped himself in the forehead.

He threw his car into drive and raced past Gwen's house to follow the cop. As the police cruiser drove through the town, Andrew admired all the lampposts which were decorated in lights and wreaths. Darling Cove was not what he had expected. Every corner was a picture of elegant charm…like Gwen.

The car he'd been following turned and parked in front of a station house. Crap! There were several police cruisers. The cop who he'd been following got out of his car and took off his hat. That couldn't have been her father, though. Too young. *Greg.* Andrew recognized him from the pictures. He became a cop…like his father.

Andrew blew out a puff of air, got out of his mother's Cadillac and stepped into the precinct.

Inside, it smelled of fresh paint and metal. A man in a uniform stood behind a wood paneled desk, his hands resting on a shiny granite countertop. The man threw a look at another officer and turned back to Andrew.

"If you're looking for the Hamptons, you took a wrong turn about an hour ago," he said with a sly smirk.

Andrew accepted that he looked like the typical Hamptons visitor. Not all of eastern Long Island was created equally. The North Fork was very different from the Hamptons. But he'd rather fit in and be accepted here. "Actually." He wrung his hands to keep them from shaking. "I was wondering if I could speak to one of your officers."

"Who are you looking for?" a voice echoed from a side doorway.

Andrew glanced to his left; the cop he was following approached him. "Greg?"

"*Officer* Mallory," the desk captain said in a stern voice.

"Excuse me, yes. Officer Mallory. I'm actually looking for the *other* Officer Mallory."

"*Martin* Mallory is in the —"

"I got this, Carlin." Greg was formidable in his dark long sleeve shirt and matching tie held down by an American flag clip. But it was the two guns on his waist, a set of steel handcuffs dangling from his pants and a long brown stick tucked into another holder that stood out the most. Greg's chin lifted defiantly to meet Andrew's eyes, which were a few inches above his. "Who are you and what do you want with my father?"

If he'd not been surrounded by several guns, one of which Greg's hand rested on, Andrew's answer might have been a stout, *That's my business*. Instead he said, "My name is Andrew Morgan. I'm a... It's about your sister, Gwen."

Greg's probing words may have been tough, but his mouth curved and his lips trembled. "Gwen? Has something happened to my sister?"

"No, she's fine." Andrew brought his hands forward to dismiss Greg's panic. "In fact, she's more than fine. She's wonderful." He wanted so much for Martin to hear what he had to say first. That was the proper thing to do. But Andrew had to improvise, if for no other reason than to get out of that station house in one piece and not end up on the news. *Man dressed in Prada gets pounded by North Fork police officers.* He cleared his throat and continued. "I'm here to ask your father's permission to marry her."

"You have my permission!" Martin answered from the opposite corner.

Andrew breathed in relief. Ignoring the others, he walked toward Martin who was beaming. "Sir, Andrew Morgan, sir. Thank you. I promise to make her happy and do the right thing by her always."

"Hey Mallory, looks like you're getting a new brother-in-law," the officer named Carlin said. "You may not want to pick on this one so much. He's taller than you." The officers jolted with laughter at Greg, their polished silver badges gleaming with reflected light.

Andrew walked toward Greg in an effort to be the bigger man and stuck his hand out toward the officer.

Greg's eyes trailed over Andrew's shoulder. His father was probably giving him a stern look by how his expression changed. A reluctant sigh escaped Greg's tight lips. His gaze trailed to Andrew's hand. The firm grip made Andrew wince slightly. He nodded and turned back to Martin.

"I'd like to go to her house now and get her." Andrew tugged on his coat. "I have a ring for her in the city."

Martin touched Andrew's shoulder. "Why don't you let me give you an escort to her house. I think that would make up for a ring. Gregory, get your coat."

* * * *

Gwen yawned while making another pot of decaf coffee.

Her sister lounged lazily on the shit-brown loveseat. A fake log of fire burned on the television while Skye went through her Facebook feed, announcing all the holiday posts. Casey climbed up as well and curled in the crook of her knees. But the dog snapped to attention and began whining, prompting Skye to look out the living room window. "Hey Gwen, do you know someone who drives a cherry-red Cadillac SUV?"

"No," Gwen answered from the kitchen. "Probably someone who got lost going to the Hamptons."

"Wait a minute, there're two patrol cars behind it."

"Lights and sirens?" Gwen came into the living room and petted Casey's head to calm her down.

"Yeah. I guess it was someone getting pulled over." Skye started to push the curtain back but took another peek. "It's Dad *and* Greg out there."

Gwen walked toward the window, curious about the odd coincidence.

"A young guy is getting out of the Caddy." Skye sat up on her knees. "Huh, I thought only geezers drove those things. Holy crap, is he tall!"

Gwen joined her sister at the living room window. "Who is?"

"The guy. Wow. I can see from all the way back here, that man is *gorgeous*." Skye smoothed her hair and hopped off the loveseat. She opened the front door and said, "Hey, there *are* crazier ways to meet people. *And* he may need a lawyer."

"Skye I wouldn't—" Gwen's eyes sharpened. That walk. Those legs. That jet back hair. "Oh my God!"

"What?"

"That's Andrew." Gwen yanked her coat on before Greg added another police shooting to the Mallory family list of scandals.

"Wait, let me go. Greg may cuff him first and ask questions second." Skye ran out wearing only a thin sweater.

"And you think *you* can stop it?" Gwen followed, slushing through the path the town guys had made for her at four that morning.

Skye was staring at Andrew in amazement. He was leaning against his car with his hands in his pockets. *That's* his car? His face was even. Greg and her dad's cop cars hovered in front of the driveway, their blue and white lights flashing. They had their doors open, already getting out.

Gwen spun around in confusion. What the heck was happening? A wave of dizziness passed through her and she began to slip in the snow. Andrew was at her side first, even though Skye had been the closest.

"I've got you," Andrew said, his voice low. "Gwen, it's me. What's wrong?"

His hands on her arms sent a wave through her. Fear. She was so afraid to lose this man; but her instincts were telling her to push him away. "There's nothing wrong. I thought we were just spending the holidays with our families."

"Gwen," he said moving closer. "I expected to see you last night *and* today. I just never said anything because I thought it was understood. Jesus, after the week we had and what we did…in Milan."

"I can't believe you drove all the way out here."

"I can't believe you thought I wouldn't."

Gwen looked at her father. "And you just randomly pulled him over?" She turned to her brother. "Both of you?"

The men exchanged odd glances. Greg pressed his hat down. "No. We were having coffee at Sadie's and he came in."

"Yeah," Andrew said. "I stopped to make sure I was going the right way and recognized them."

"How would you recognize them?" Skye asked in her cross-examination voice.

Andrew smiled. "She has pictures of all of you on her desk."

Gwen looked down. "Oh right." She swallowed to say something else, but her father stepped toward her.

"It's cold, why don't you go in the house."

That shell of a dwelling was a house, but not a home. What would Andrew think? "Um, actually..."

Andrew stood up straight, his arm around her but he didn't say anything.

Greg and his mirrored cop shades focused on Andrew holding her, but then cast a sidelong glance at the Caddy.

Andrew rolled his eyes. "It's my mother's. She wanted me to use it. My Beamer only has front wheel drive."

"Oh, that won't do out here." Martin folded his arms smiling. "We get piles of snow."

Gwen watched them interact. Andrew's mother handed over a sixty-thousand-dollar car so he could drive all the way out to Darling Cove? The same woman who didn't like the girl he married? He'd said his mother knew about Gwen. This gesture must mean she approves. It made her cheeks tick up.

But the feeling of nausea spread through her. How would his mother feel about a knocked-up girl from the sticks trying to trap her son? Gwen stepped back, scared and confused.

"Gwen, this gentleman made a long drive. Perhaps he wants some coffee?" Martin turned to her brother and sister. "Greg and Skye, go in the house and get your gifts."

Andrew touched her face. "Gwen, what's wrong? Has something changed since you were in Milan?"

"I—" She sniffed, his touch was so warm. But everything was wrong and everything had changed.

"Are you crying? Is there something going on with your family?" He pointed to the house.

Yes. But it was the family inside of her and in front of her. It was forming and falling apart at the same time. She squirmed away. "I think we need to talk."

He released a low chuckle. "I agree. Can I come inside and get out of this wet snow?"

There was no other way to do this. "Sure." She walked up her driveway keeping a few steps between her and Andrew.

Inside, Skye was handing out gifts from under her tree. "Greg, this is yours. Dad, take these."

They collected all the wrapped packages and filed to the door.

"We'll leave you two alone," her father said, touching Andrew's arm.

Skye kissed her cheek. "If the old man got Prada and I didn't, I'll be back... Upset."

Gwen snorted. They all got Prada. Even Greg, a midnight blue tie he could wear for work instead of the stiff polyester department-issued one.

Andrew shook everyone's hand on the way out. Gwen caught one final look at Skye, who was saying, *Oh my God*, with her mouth. Greg rolled his eyes before leaving.

Andrew closed the door, but watched the crowd marching away through the sidelight. "Are they here a lot?" he asked, turning around.

"I'm afraid so."

* * * *

"Good. Now why are you standing all the way over there?" Andrew asked Gwen, but was worried to hear the answer.

She rubbed her eyebrows. "No reason. Do you want some coffee?"

"Sure." His eyes followed her as she left the living room. It gave him a minute to take in the surroundings. He turned around, realizing the room was empty except for a small sofa. All along, he'd imagined some eerie feeling would wash over him stepping inside a home she shared with another man. But every corner so far smelled of Gwen.

In front of a bay window stood a Christmas tree that made him ache. He would have loved to have been there to help her set it up. He stepped closer, the smell of pine filling his senses. A real tree. He'd never had one. It was tall and slender with colorful lights, some blinking, some not. His fingers touched the soft branches finding an ornament. A round silver plate with a year engraved on it. Several years back.

Andrew stepped away. Those were the only ornaments on the tree. They were all the same, but different. All from different years. No balls, no tinsel, no garland. Just these little milestones that meant something.

'My mom passed away right after I graduated high school'. And there it was at the top… That year. Nothing before then and just a sea of sparkle for every year since.

There had to be a new plan; his old one had just been blown to shit. He didn't want to go back to the city. He wanted to stay right where he was. But how could he propose if the ring was in Manhattan? *Stupid, stupid, stupid*. It had to be sex depravity making him unable to think straight.

"Here you go. It's decaf I'm afraid." She handed him a plain blue mug.

He took the coffee in his hands and swallowed a sip. Ring or no ring, he was ready to ask her. "Gwen—"

"Andrew, I have something to tell you." She interrupted with words that pierced him like an arrow tip. Nothing good ever followed that sentence. But if she thinks she's breaking up with him, she could think again.

He drew a ragged breath and put the mug down. "Okay."

"I… Um. I know this is supposed to be some shining glorious moment for a couple."

He moved toward her, touching her arm. "Gwen, I messed up. I'm sorry. How could you think I didn't want to see you yesterday?"

"I can't read your mind, Andrew."

"Well, you should have!" He gritted his teeth. "I mean…you should have made that assumption. But I'm sorry I didn't make it clear."

"Me too," she said but her demeanor was cold and indifferent.

"Gwen how do we fix this, what can I do?"

She blew out a stream of air, puffing out her cheeks like she had no idea how to respond. This was going nowhere fast, except south.

He looked back at the bay window. "Your tree is great. I love these ornaments. But..." He held one of the plates in his hand from last year. "Where's one for this year?"

"I didn't hang it yet."

"It's Christmas Day. What were you waiting for?"

She swallowed and stepped to a small console table. There, she removed a square box from one of the drawers. "I guess I was waiting for the right moment. Here." She held the box in his direction.

Curiosity rippled threw him. He took the box from her and opened it. Silver glinted off the light coming from the window. The year was in block letters, all different sizes. Not very elegant compared to the rest. A charm hung from the numbers. A baby bottle. What an odd thing to... Andrew staggered back. His mind raced wildly to compute what was happening. His heart strangled with anticipation.

"Andrew?" Gwen called out to him softly.

His eyes shot to her. He didn't fully recognize her from the woman who stood before him a moment ago. "What does... what..."

"I'm pregnant, Andrew."

"Wha— What? Really?"

"Yes, really." She crossed her arms. "I didn't want to tell you over the phone or email. In fact, I didn't want to tell you at all."

"You didn't want to *tell* me?"

"I mean, I didn't want to *have* to tell you. This isn't where I wanted us to be...now." She turned around.

He sprang toward her and held on from behind. Relief pounded over him, feeling her soften against him. He whispered in her ear, "How could you think I wouldn't want to know?"

"I don't want to force your hand, Andrew." She turned to face him.

"*Force my hand?* Like I don't think I have a choice in the matter?"

She smirked. "I know you. That's not the man you are."

"So let me be the man already." He put the ornament on the tree. Next to the one of the year her mother died. Gwen's eyes watched him. He stepped toward her and seized the first *real* kiss from her. One of want and need. The feel of her lips brought his body back to life. He trembled, knees weakening, preparing to bend down. But he paused. If he proposed now with no ring, he'd be feeding into her fears that he was asking purely out of a sense of obligation. And she would probably say no.

No. He had to wait until he had his grandmother's ring in hand to show her, to *prove* to her that he'd planned this all along.

His proposal *and* his first 'I love you' would have to wait.

The kiss finished in a sweet swirl of her tongue, but Gwen stopped and lowered her head. "Andrew, I need to tell you something else."

Holding her face, he said, "I want you to tell me everything. Always."

Hearing she'd been pregnant once before…bothered him. But both he and Gwen had had lives before they met. The world had turned upside down to bring them together. He'd figured out in Milan, Gwen was *it* for him. And so far, nothing had made him even remotely waver from his desire to be with her. He just needed to recalibrate his plans to make sure they stayed together. Now, there was so much more at stake. He touched her hair. "It's okay. I'm glad you told me."

"What if…" She stopped and pressed her head into his chest. "What if something like that happens again?"

"*I* got you pregnant, Gwen." Andrew declared his virility, forcing her to look up. The expression on her face absorbing his confident-laced boast made him think a firestorm had rocketed between her legs. "Everything is going to be fine. And if it's not…"

Her finger tips pressed into his shoulder.

"Then we'll try again," he whispered smoothing her hair.

"Oh, Andrew." Her head settled back beneath his jaw. "I've missed you so much."

The words filled his body with adrenaline. He kissed her the way he'd wanted to last night. His long arms curled around her, tight. Too tightly, and he let go, worried he would hurt her. He knew what he was capable of doing to her. How would that work now if she were pregnant? "Gwen, I want you to be ready to make love to me again."

"I'm ready." She lifted up on her toes and kissed him, more passionately than he expected. With her arms tightly around his neck, she began a torturous trail along his jaw line with her lips and the edges of her teeth.

"Wait a second." Andrew feared he would get too crazy with her and get a police escort *back* to the Expressway. He clutched her hands and rested them against her thighs. "You know how much I want to put my hands and my mouth all over your body. I'm not so sure I can be gentle. Not after two weeks without you."

"I'm having a baby. I'm not going to break."

The words still shocked him, even though he had no real reason to be surprised. Finding that condom on the bed in Milan hadn't been the shocker he made it out to be. He'd known all along *something* had happened. It had turned scorching hot and very wet all of a sudden, but selfishly he hadn't wanted to stop.

He ran a hand through the gloriously long hair he also missed. "So, a baby, huh?" It was going to lead to this anyway. His stamina was back. And then some. They'd had so much sex in Milan, they exceeded the capacity of all those condoms in his nightstand. When faced with an empty drawer, the startled look on the conservative *farmacia's* face when he bought a second jumbo pack made him feel like a pervert.

"According to EPT."

He chuckled. There was no need for shame *or* blame. All he wanted to do right now was hold her. His hand brushed against her arm and her skin already felt different. Under his fingers, she felt firmer and he finally saw the glow he'd always heard about. A wild desire to yank her clothes off and be a part of what was inside her fueled his fire like kerosene. "Are you happy about the baby, Gwen?"

"I can think one thing that might *possibly* make me a little happier right now."

CHAPTER TWENTY-SEVEN

Gwen took Andrew's hand and led him up the stairs.

"I don't want to go into any lengthy explanations, but I don't really have any bedroom furniture at the moment."

"Okay." His smile drew to one side, as he followed her down the dark hallway. "Is there a bed?"

"Sort of." She stepped inside what was really the house's second bedroom, exposing where she'd been putting her head at night. "It's not much. But if it makes any difference, I've dreamt of you in this bed."

He stepped inside, keeping his eyes on her, their hands locked.

"I've even called out your name in this thing." Her body lowered on the mattress. "I'd love to scream it with you *in* it."

Andrew ripped his coat off and bent his knees. He was so tall; getting in and out of this thing was going to be a challenge. He wore the same dark-washed jeans he wore to the Cinque Terre and a simple V-neck sweater — charcoal, the same color of his eyes. "God, I've missed your body."

That morning her worn out yoga pants, a tank top and a boyfriend cardigan had been yanked on without a thought of Andrew peeling it all off later on. His fingernails teased her skin, as he skidded the sweater from her shoulders. Removing the thin tank top revealed how aroused she was, while he kissed her with a tongue that could drive her to madness.

He spread his large hands across her torso. His face dipped between the swells of her breasts, tucked inside a pale lavender bra.

Settling sideways into his lap she reached behind her. "Get this off me."

He pressed his hands against her back and unfastened the bra while he nipped at her neck and collarbone. His tongue flicked against rock-hard nipples. "I have to have you. All of you. Every part of you."

"I want this." She slid her hand down his chest to his belt buckle, but he grabbed her hand.

"No. Wait." He cupped her elbows. "Are you sure it'll be okay?"

She bit her lip. "What do you suggest we do until the baby is born?"

"Lie down and I'll show you." He slid next to her, cradling her head in the crook of his left arm, while his fingers danced down her body.

Andrew remained clothed while he pressed the outside of damp panties, and his lips brushed against her passionately. He wanted to kiss her and please her at the same time. How intimate and sensual. He'd never *just* touched her.

"I was so crazy for you last night," he whispered. "My body literally hurt."

Pulling her panties aside, he slid one long finger into her waiting flesh, her response a heated groan. Her grip on his shoulder tightened. She'd been aching for him as well.

With her legs spread wide, giving herself over to him, she rested her free hand on top of his. He slid his finger out and reinserted. The sensation combined with a rush of air on her skin, tightened her hard, throbbing clit.

"God, you feel so good," he said pressing his thumb against the swollen knot of nerves.

Her hips bucked from the pressure. She was so aroused, desire pulsed through her heavy beating heart. A spasm shot through her, making her whimper and her back arch.

"Oh God, Andrew, yes." Her tensions stormed up to the surface and hovered, warmth and tightening combining for the coming explosion, making her legs kick. She sucked in a breath and tilted her head back. "Yes. Yes. Andrew. Andrew."

Heat soared through her body. Andrew kept up the intensity and the deep thrusts from his finger in perfect rhythm, extended her orgasm, intensifying it.

He didn't stop. The sensitivity was overwhelming, her hands swatted at his to push him away for a small break of relief. It was too much. What felt like a drenched finger came out of her and now the pads of several fingers were rubbing her aching clit.

"Andrew," she panted in agony.

"That's me. I'm here, Gwen."

"I can't live with only that for the next eight months."
"Okay. But I have a request first."

* * * *

Gwen's warm breath spread over Andrew's skin and her hair tumbled across his lap.

His torso stretched up and his fingers gripped the bed covers. "Jesus, Gwen," he cried out as her tongue glided over his length. Every inch of his cock had fit perfectly inside her, like she was made for him. The same could be said for her mouth. He drew a ragged breath and braced himself against the edge of the bed.

Amidst frazzled thoughts, a cautious twinge shot through his heated body. Wrapping strands of her long hair around his fingers, he brought her head up to his. He roughly kissed her mouth and said, "I told you I wouldn't be gentle."

She stood and placed her hands on his shoulders while he gripped her waist. Her breasts were magnificent and the smell of her skin was an elixir to his need. He settled Gwen into his lap. Slick, moist skin, warm and tight brushed against his. A pair of heated moans were released from the same shock of desire as his body joined with hers.

No need for a condom now.

She remained on top, slowly rising her hips up and settling them back down. Her head was thrown back so far, her hair tickled his knees. Everything in the way she moved was different now, yet the same. Pregnancy makes a woman powerful, he'd heard. Has to be, to move another human through it. Her grip on his hands was firmer, and she took more control than she had the last time she rode him. In Milan...the night the baby was made.

She loosened her hands from his and leaned back, palms flat on the mattress. No longer on her knees but her feet, she rocked her hips up and down. He could see everything. He watched his entire length slide in and out at a pace only she controlled by her strong legs. She moaned wildly, taking what she needed from him. Using him almost, as he'd been doing very little at this point, except staring in amazement.

Gwen brought herself to a second orgasm, making small circles over her clit with her own hand.

Holy fuck! Who was this woman?

After a few more torturous moments listening to her stretch out her bliss, he took control and rolled her on to her back. Circling his hips, he kept his face close to hers. Every pulse and tingle brought him right up to the edge.

With a dark driving need to taste her, he pulled out, her skin not letting go so easily. She was so tight, even more so now that she'd come. He kissed his way down her body, stopping at her breasts, feasting on red hard nipples raging from her arousal. Her back arched and she gasped.

Oh, these next eight months were going to be fun.

Her skin smelled sweeter than ever, and when he got to her stomach, he stopped. His arm curled around her waist, bringing her even closer to him. He circled the area with his free hand and rested a palm over her belly button. "Mine," he whispered.

"There's no question about that," she groaned with lust in her voice.

He got to the spot he wanted most. The heat and warmth between her legs. She spread willingly and wide for him. Two of his fingers touched her first, so wet. From him. He loved licking where his dick had been, especially with Gwen. She was slick and tasty, and soon her hips rocking in rhythm with his tongue. "Oh God, Andrew. Yes," she cried, slapping the bed-sheet. As much as he wanted to lick her to another completion, he preferred to share the next one. He seductively licked his own lips and kissed her, holding her arms above her head.

Slowly, he entered her again. "Oh God," he groaned.

He wanted to be buried inside her and not stop until he got his fill. His rigid erection pressed deep, hitting her core. The skin inside her tingled with heat and need.

Despite his daily activities while they'd been apart, with the feeling of Gwen in his arms, her sweat soaked body against his, he found himself fighting for survival. The mixture of rapture and shame for releasing too soon powerfully combined to fill his body with tremors. He was ready to apologize for the preemptive explosion but mercifully Gwen shrieked, "Andrew, don't stop."

"Never, Gwen." He engaged in several forceful pumps while her contractions pulsed around him. "Ever."

Deeper and deeper Andrew plunged, until he too slipped into a powerful body rocking orgasm.

* * * *

Tangled and kissing, Gwen lay buried in Andrew's arms.

They were wound so tight around her, she couldn't tell which was right or left. It didn't matter though. His face skidded down her neck and he took deep breaths. "God, you smell so good."

"I think part of that scent is you at this point."

He moved some loose hairs out of her eyes. "Are you saying I sweat a lot?"

"That's not what I meant." She took his hand and put it on her stomach. "Here. It's you."

"You have no idea how this makes me feel. That inside you…" Emotion got the better of him. His lips found hers, sweet, and a wide tongue tousled with hers. Before it got heated again, he asked, "What time should we wake up tomorrow to drive back to the city?"

Gwen stretched, satiated and sore. "Four."

Andrew groaned and rolled over.

"Welcome to Darling Cove."

The next morning, traffic was light, and despite the snow piled up on the side of the Expressway, the Cadillac sailed into the city.

In front of Prada, Gwen turned to Andrew in the car. "When will you be in the office?"

He dipped a bushy brow over a tired eye. "I have to bring this car back. Pick up my suitcases…" He began counting on his hand. "Then I have to go home, drop off laundry, dry cleaning. I don't even remember if I paid my rent. I *have* to go to Flagship. My report is still due. And I have…other errands to take care of."

"So I'll see you tomorrow?"

"Nope. I'll be in before the day is over." He took her hand. "And when we get back to my place tonight, we'll…figure stuff out."

Figure stuff out. The words hung in the air. "Andrew, what's happened doesn't mean we have to automatically —"

"I know. Just trust me. By the end of the day, you'll see."

"I do trust you." She held his face to kiss him, while his hands gripped the leather bound steering wheel.

His tongue delicately swirled in her mouth. "Now, get out of the car."

The Cadillac drove off and Gwen stood in the middle of the street. The air smelled sweet and the sun had risen enough to sparkle against the glass of Prada's building. She touched her stomach. A wave of satisfaction swelled inside her. She had a job she loved, a man she loved and a baby on the way.

It was finally Gwen's turn to have it all.

She skipped to the curb and jumped over a pile of snow, sailing cleanly over the mound. "Good morning," she said to the guards. Her cell phone ringing stopped her from entering the elevator. The number on the screen sent a tiny chill through her — the breast surgeon's office. Her hands quivered. If it was Sylvie calling, then everything was all right. Surgeons don't make their receptionists deliver bad news.

Gwen swiped the call to answer. "Hello?"

"Ms. Foley?"

Gwen's shoulders relaxed. But she'd have to notify them of her name change. ASAP. "Hi Sylvie."

"Dr. Jesse is going to be on vacation for the rest of the year starting tomorrow. I'm just calling patients to let them know."

"Okay, thanks." Gwen, with her problems, was probably on speed dial. "Wait!" Getting an appointment to see Dr. Jesse could take months. This pregnancy was going to affect all the tests they love to do on her. "Um, Sylvie, is Dr. Jesse available to speak on the phone for a few minutes today? There's something I'd like to discuss with her."

Papers rustled. "She had a cancellation for eleven o'clock. Do you want to come in?" Phone calls were free. Visits were not.

Gwen sighed. "Sure. I'll see you in a bit."

The screen went dark. She brought up Andrew's number, ready to send a text telling him where she'd be, but paused. It wasn't fair to sneak off to her surgeon and not tell him. But... "I'll make that my New Year's resolution," she said to herself and dropped the phone in her bag.

Stepping into the Dr. Jesse's waiting room later that morning, Gwen grumbled. "I should have had some questions prepared."

Internet research on mammograms during pregnancy were so conflicting and confusing. It was best to get the doctor's opinion on the matter. Of course, judging by the age of most of the other women in the waiting room that morning—and all the other times Gwen had sat in those small wooden chairs, this probably wasn't a common consultation for Dr. Jesse.

"Any changes since the last visit?" Sylvie asked in a gentle voice.

Gwen opened her mouth, but closed it. Oh boy, how her life had changed since the last biopsy. But she'd rather discuss it with the doctor first. "No."

"Take a seat, Ms. Foley."

She sat down, grabbed a nearby *People* magazine and settled into the expected forty-minute wait.

What had been nagging at Gwen was that miscarriage she'd suffered. The fact she'd not missed even one period since had her worried that, perhaps, there was more going on in her body than breast calcifications.

"Ms. Foley, we're ready for you." Sylvie guided her to one of the small exam rooms. Inside, she pointed to the paper gown and said, "You know what to do."

After thirty-five more minutes, Dr. Jesse breezed in. Now, Greg would like *her*. Beautiful auburn hair sat on slender shoulders and around aquamarine eyes. Very serious about her patients and not very chatty, Dr. Jesse immediately picked at Gwen's thick stack of appointment notes and reports from Dr. Sage in radiology. The surgeon's fingers tabbed through a few pages, flipped the entire chart over and turned back to Gwen. "I don't see your latest report."

"I'm not scheduled for a follow up mammogram...yet."

Dr. Jesse's expression changed. In the past, Gwen had skipped a follow up here and there. The surgeon's hands were on her hips with a look that mirrored Skye's when she said: *Don't play games with this.*

"Well, you see..." Gwen raised her hands to quickly explain. Bringing her wrists to her nose, she smelled Andrew's scent out of nowhere. "I'm pregnant." Just saying the words now brought a rush of warmth tingling across her entire body.

"Congratulations," Dr. Jesse said with the look of a doctor who didn't hear those words too often from a patient sitting on her exam table. "That's wonderful." While patting her knee, the doctor shot a quick glance to admire the ring that wasn't there.

"Thanks." Gwen ran that hand through her hair. "It was a surprise."

"And, the father?"

"Um, a man I've been...seeing."

Dr. Jesse smiled and touched Gwen's cheek softly. "Congratulations. This is going to be one beautiful child."

"So, what are my options?"

"We'll start by doing this the old fashioned way," Dr. Jesse said. "Lie back."

The surgeon's fingers danced across the right breast—the troublemaker—like she was playing a piano concerto. Up and down the center and sweeping the sides, bearing down on scar tissue from years of Dr. Sage's biopsies.

"Ouch." It seemed only Andrew touching her there didn't hurt.

"It feels good, Gwen," Dr. Jesse said with her sunshine of a smile as she stepped around to the other side of the table. "I don't see a reason why we can't take a break for a few months."

At least the left breast wasn't filled with the same tender tissue. Gwen released the metal bar under the table, expecting to sail through the rest of the exam. While she kept her eyes closed, the same dance of Dr. Jesse's fingers tapped across her left breast. Up, down, right, left. *Sigh.* Right, left. Right, left; Left. Left. Press. Squeeze. Crunch. "Ow!"

When Dr. Jesse's warm hands left her body, Gwen opened her eyes. The surgeon had gone back to the counter and was feverishly swiping through all of the films. There were so many. How does she keep track? One X-ray after another flew in front of the surgeon's face.

"What is it?" Gwen asked.

With skilled precision, Dr. Jesse began stacking films against a back-lit X-ray illuminator. And then out of her pocket came a brass plated magnifying glass. In Dr. Sage's office, she had blown up X-ray images on a seventeen-inch monitor to show Gwen the initial set of suspicious cells. But here was Dr. Jesse using a seventeenth century trinket.

"Sylvia!" Dr. Jesse shouted through the closed door.

"Yes, Dr. Jesse?" Sylvie appeared after stomping up the narrow hallway between the reception desk and the exam rooms.

"I need the caliper," she answered looking at the films through the round glass. She swore and starting sorting films again. "When did you originate?"

At the near end of the pile, Dr. Jesse gripped another film, and held it up to the illuminator. "There you are."

From what Gwen could count, the next seven films or three and a half years' worth went back up one by one and Dr. Jesse circled the same spot with a red marker.

"Here." Sylvie handed the surgeon a metal tool with a clamp. Gwen had seen similar devices used to measure body fat.

"Thank you, Sylvia." She turned back to Gwen and gently shoved her down. Clicking and ticking, the device opened to allow the breast to fit inside. Dr. Jesse pressed and squeezed harder each time as tears cascaded out of the corner of Gwen's eyes, like when she was getting her lip waxed. Still, the surgeon's warm breath on her skin was oddly comforting as she compared the location to the small ticks of the caliper. Back at the desk, the measurement was transferred to a ruler and then the ruler was brought back to the films. "Yep, that was it. Damn it!"

"Dr. Jesse, you're really scaring—"

"Get dressed." She put her hand on Gwen's thigh. In a commanding tone, she said, "And meet me in my office."

Gwen swung her legs over the table and sat upright. "Dr. Jesse what did you feel?"

"A lump."

CHAPTER TWENTY-EIGHT

Gwen was alone in the cold room, shaking and confused.

She couldn't recall Dr. Jesse ever being so curt. In all these years, there had never been a look of worry on that beautiful face. But today? Dr. Jesse turned into a warrior. Even the shade of her skin changed. She seemed downright offended. It was like an enemy had crawled into her foxhole while she was sleeping.

In an office that looked more like a chic Manhattan living room, Dr. Jesse sat at her desk. Gwen took a seat and the surgeon spun the monitor around for her to have a look. Thank God, a computer! She was afraid leeches were next.

"Seven mammograms ago, Dr. Sage saw this." Dr. Jesse pointed to a miniscule dot. Like photos in a kaleidoscope, subsequent films slid by. "You see this here?"

Gwen squinted. "Sort of."

"It's a calcification. Your breasts are filled with them. They're more prevalent here." She tapped her pen against a spidery web of white lines in the lower right quadrant of Gwen's breast. "Calcifications turn into benign cysts."

Gwen draped her body forward; her head almost hitting the desk in relief. "So, all of that was just about a cyst?"

Dr. Jesse's eyes shot back at her. "Except when they become problematic masses. When they're in the calcification stage, see how unorganized the shape is?"

The group of cells resembled an amoeba. "Okay."

"It will usually enlarge and then take its new shape. That's why we missed it. It tricked us by keeping its unorganized shape right up until the critical moment of forming."

"What do I do now?"

"I'm calling Dr. Sage." The surgeon picked up the phone. "You're getting a biopsy *right now.*"

Slowing her usual brisk pace to a *Walking Dead* stagger, Gwen entered the hospital lobby full of anxiety and dread.

Even the Starbucks cart with its fresh coffee aroma and tasty looking treats barely registered. At the sign in desk, an extra twinge of venom was directed toward the clipboard and that pen

229

tethered by those damn dirty rubber bands. In the locker room, where the usual frigid temperature sent goose bumps over her body, Gwen robotically removed her dress.

The white and heather gray color-block shift dress had been the last in her size at Flagship, prompting the manager to discount it heavily, just to get it off the sales floor.

Dr. Sage appeared in the reception area moments later, to collect her. The leggy blonde must wear short skirts and high heels every day, because Gwen had never seen her in anything else. "Dr. Jesse said there's something in the left breast for us to look at."

"How could something that went undetected in my last mammogram grow into something Dr. Jesse actually felt?"

"The mass grew since the last test."

"But wait, when a mass grows *that* big in such a short time—" Gwen clutched Dr. Sage's white sleeve.

"Let's go have a look right now and see what we're dealing with." Dr. Sage set Gwen back under control.

"Wait!" The words Gwen had been stumbling over for two weeks easily spilled out of her mouth. "I'm pregnant."

"Yes, Dr. Jesse mentioned that." Dr. Sage pointed to the long cold hallway connecting the waiting lounge and the testing rooms. "We'll do an ultrasound before the biopsy. Both rooms are being prepped right now."

"I need a few minutes." Gwen snatched her phone out of her work bag and dialed Andrew's phone.

"Hey, can I call you back, I'm talking to the—"

"Andrew, I need you," Gwen choked out.

"Where are you?" he asked in a deep serious tone.

"I'm at the hospital." She'd hoped to find her 'It's no big deal' voice and be strong, but Gwen didn't possess anything but fear at the moment.

"Oh my God, what happened?"

"I was just at my breast surgeon's office. I made the appointment this morning. I didn't know…what being pregnant would mean for all of my…tests." Gwen exhaled. "She felt something, Andrew. They want me to do a biopsy, right now."

The silence meant she probably sent him into a tail spin. It took a full minute for him to respond. "Wait for me in the lobby, I'll walk up with you."

"I'm already up here." She cleared the crack in her voice that would only feed the fire of his fears.

"Okay, honey." There was rustling in the background. "I'm on my way. Gwen, wait!"

"I'm on the third floor."

"No. I... Gwendolyn. I—"

"No. You don't get to say those words to me *now*." Her clammy shaking fingers abruptly ended the call.

The sonogram was brief but painful, and Dr. Sage found the mass immediately. Gwen stepped into the biopsy procedure room and made eye contact with the dreaded table.

A piece of plywood with a comical hole cut in the upper portion masquerades as an exam table. The opening allows the breast to hang down so a vise can hold it in place. Then, several injections of lidocaine are administered, so when the tubes rummage through the breast tissue it only feels like pressure.

Of course, the lidocaine itself stings like hell, not to mention the enormous needle. All the while, the breast is clamped tighter and tighter. Dozens of images are taken while the technician guides a wire through the translucent marbled tissue. Once the suspicious cells are found, a microscopic clamp is threaded through and the tissue is removed.

Having gone through the procedure several times, Gwen answered the usual pre-procedure questions like a lifeless rag doll.

"How is this going to work if I'm pregnant?" she asked signing the consent form. And stalling.

"It's perfectly safe like this." Dr. Sage enunciated further in an effort to be empathetic. "In fact, the *board* creates a barrier. And we've put down a leaded apron."

Gwen's jaw trembled in lieu of a nod.

The door opened. Figuring it was Maya, Gwen turned away but the unmistakable shape of Andrew's body caught her attention. She raised her hands quickly to her face to hide the fear that had been pulsing through her.

Dr. Sage did a dramatic double take absorbing Andrew's features. But along with his beautiful face, he brought a surge of emotion into the room with him.

"I'll give you a few minutes," the doctor said tucking her hair against her neck.

Andrew was at Gwen's feet before she even stood up. She pressed her face into his chest and took deep successive breaths to force the tears away.

"I'm here." Andrew unfolded her and held her chin. "I'm here, honey."

"I'm so sorry."

"What *for?*"

"I feel like I made you some kind of promise that this wouldn't happen."

"You did no such thing and even if you had—" Andrew ran his hands up and down her ice-cold skin and could tell she was shaking. "It's going to be okay."

Their eyes locked. Longing and searching.

She nodded, but still felt afraid and confused.

* * * *

With a weak smile, Andrew exhaled. "I'm here Gwen."

The team returned wearing surgical masks; this was ready to happen.

"Maya, can he stay with me please?" Gwen asked.

"Sure, we'll get him an apron as well."

"Apron for what?" he asked.

"The mammogram machine," Gwen answered for the assistant.

"Hang on." Andrew faced the assistant holding Gwen protectively. "She's pregnant."

"I already told Dr. Sage that. I'm going to be lying on a wooden board." She pointed to an ominous looking table in the back of the room. "The machine is underneath and they put down a leaded apron."

Gwen had put her life into the hands of these people, but that didn't mean Andrew would automatically trust them on day one. Maya slipped the heavy plastic shield across his arms and he asked, "Gwen, where do you want me?"

"Do you think the table can hold both of us?"

Oh, how he missed her humor. "I'm guessing no. But that's because of me, not you."

She swung her right arm directing him to the space in between the table and the wall. "Can you stand over here, please?"

Andrew stepped around, took her right hand and placed his other hand across her back. As the table rose, the hydraulic moan stiffened his spine and he filled with fury. But the lift stopped at his chest, allowing his arm to completely engulf her waist.

She parted her lips to say something but she released a howling cry of agony; a sound he would expect to come from something that wasn't human.

"What happened?" he asked, frantic.

"The machine tightened. It's so painful."

"I'm sorry Ms. Foley." Maya's smothered apology from underneath the table was of little comfort.

"It's Mallory!" he barked. *And not for long.*

The procedure crept along. A few moments of being held in the same position, allowed the pain on her face to vanish ever so slightly. She relaxed her jaw and managed a small smile. Maya continued to ask her to either move up or move down, each time the loosening and then tightening changed Gwen's expression.

Andrew tried to keep her distracted, making encouraging small talk. But tears began to track down her cheeks and he lost it. *"Hurry up!"* he demanded through clenched teeth.

Touching his face, her fingers pressing into his eyebrows, she whispered, "Even furious, you're so damn handsome."

"It's not a look I'd like to wear often." He took her hand again and kissed her knuckles.

Gwen opened her mouth to respond, but instead she gasped in relief.

"Okay, we're all done here," said Dr. Sage who had slipped in quietly.

"Um, there's no graceful way for me to do this. Can you wait over there?" Gwen pushed up on her shoulders. "I can get down myself."

"I know you can. I want to help you."

She tugged her gown closed and climbed down with Andrew's hands gripping her waist. If she wanted him to carry her through the corridor, he would happily oblige. Instead she leaned against him as they walked to the dressing room. It was empty, and Gwen dragged him inside. Maya eventually came in and handed over films and ice packs. He placed himself between the assistant and Gwen's dressing stall to accept the package and instructions.

The artificial crystals that mimicked ice activated easily from his hard snap. Without asking, he opened the stall's door. She took the pack and hiding the pain, said, "Thanks."

In the taxi, Andrew held her so close that he could feel the frosty package tucked into her bra. He had given his apartment's address and leaned in to tell the driver, "But, make a right on 57th. I have a stop I need to make."

City traffic was light and the taxi made it from 77th to 57th in record time. Midtown however was more crowded, and the car crawled at a slower pace, heading toward the West Side of Manhattan.

"Pull over here please," Andrew said.

"Why are we stopping? What's—"

The creamy white cement building blended into the others around it.

But the name on the door, stood out in tall gothic letters and made Gwen dig her nails into his arm.

Tiffany's. A company actually older than Prada.

Staring at the two large windows and the flags flying overhead, her jaw dropped. "No."

Andrew jerked his head toward her in the car. "Is that your official answer?"

"I mean..." She shook her head. "Please don't bring me into Tiffany's. Not *now*."

"Why not now? What better way to turn this day around?"

Her hands rummaged through a tangled mess of hair, he couldn't care less about. "Andrew," she said softly swallowing. "Look at me. I don't want to walk in there like this."

"How much different do you think you would look if I brought you here one morning, the way you and I are going to be going at it every night?"

His bold and provocative statement made her cheeks flush. Okay, maybe bringing her into Tiffany's with sex hair wasn't what she wanted either. "Talk to me." He tugged at her arms.

"Can we just go to your apartment and talk about this first please?"

Andrew blew out an exhale and redirected the driver.

"Are you hungry at all?" he asked thumbing through the stack of takeout menus in his apartment. When she gently nodded, he smiled and said, "Udon?"

While they ate, his stare felt as if he'd laid an itchy blanket on her shoulders. With a steady breath, she said, "Let me get all this straightened out before we talk about *anything else*. And you're assuming I won't have to go off and live in Italy."

Andrew roughly wiped his mouth. "If you think I'm letting Enrico send you to Italy now, carrying my kid, you're out of your mind. There is no way in *hell* that is happening."

Gwen snickered. "Inferno—it does mean hell in Italian." She clarified it when he looked at her curiously. "*The Divine Comedy.* Maybe Dante was in a long-distance relationship."

Even after an emergency biopsy that may have a disastrous outcome, her humor was sharp and poignant.

"It won't come to that Gwen. I'm prepared to quit if it does. You'll be more valuable to Enrico in New York, if I'm not there."

"Do you see what a mess I've caused?" She threw her hands up. "Wait, when did you make *that* decision?"

"When you left Milan." A look passed between them. "I made a lot of decisions that week. And I didn't even know about…"

"I'm so sorry."

"Please stop apologizing."

"I can't eat any more of this." She got up from the small drop-leaf table and rummaged through the cabinets for a take-out container.

Andrew released a slow whirl of laughter. "You really know your way around here."

"It hasn't been fun staying here by myself," she said leaning against the counter with her back turned.

That burned. He'd been gone because of Marcello.

"I need to lie down." Without looking at him, she disappeared into the hallway leading to the bedroom.

He stepped into the bathroom to find her brushing her teeth with a toothbrush that wasn't his. A visual sweep of the counter revealed a few other things she'd purchased and kept there. All good signs. But something was going on in her head. Something darker.

"Gwen, I need to do some work. I lost a lot of time today."

With cold eyes, she said, "Sorry about that."

"Stop apologizing already!" *Good going. Yell at the mother of your child, because she's upset about her health.* "I'm… I'm sorry. I didn't mean to yell."

Gwen pushed past him and slammed the bedroom door. With him on the wrong side.

He woke up in the middle of the night, his head on his desk. A startled fear pulsed through him. He rushed to the bedroom and opened the door. Gwen's body under the covers settled his heartbeat. While it would have driven the sanity right out of him, he wouldn't have been surprised if she'd crept away while he was passed out.

How had so much gone so wrong in such a short amount of time?

He brushed his teeth and undressed using the light of the bathroom. Wearing only his boxers, he slipped in the bed. Waiting. He sensed she was awake and hoped she would roll into him. Let him apologize properly.

Nothing. Not a stir. Empty sheets between them.

This was not how he envisioned the first night in this bed with her. He wanted her panting and writhing beneath him.

Instead she was shattered and broken, clinging to the other side so she didn't fall off.

The hard and traumatic events of the day should have made him toss and turn, except he passed out and woke when the sun peeked through the bedroom curtains.

This time Gwen wasn't next to him.

Through what he was sure was one blood-shot eye, Andrew found her getting dressed.

CHAPTER TWENTY-NINE

"Where you do think you're going?" Andrew asked Gwen as she rolled on a pair of day-old stockings.

"Home."

"You are home." He pushed the covers away.

"This is an apartment. Not a home."

"And your empty house is a home?"

She stopped, and shot angry eyes at him.

Jesus! What was wrong with him? "I didn't mean it like that." He bent down in front of her. "Gwen, please just stay here."

"I have some serious thinking to do."

That jolted him. "Thinking about what?"

"Everything." She stood and grabbed her wrinkled dress. "Do you *want* to be a widower again?"

The question sent blood boiling beneath the surface. "This is different. Okay. You're going to be fine. We don't even know..." He couldn't finish due to the lack of breath in his lungs. What if she was right?

"Exactly. We don't know. And until we do, *this*..." She pointed to him. "Is officially on hold."

"On hold?" He got to his feet and grabbed her arm. "You're having my baby and I love you. I'm not putting *anything* on hold."

She blinked and said nothing. It took a moment for him to realize why she couldn't speak. He'd just told her loved her. Damn it. He wanted to do it with the ring in his hand, which he planned to pick up later that morning. But the fact that she didn't return the sentiment, made his heart beat wildly. "Please..." He was having trouble breathing. "Just...give me a few hours to get all of this straightened out. Okay, Cate please?"

Through heavy breathing that looked like it was going to lead to sobs, Gwen said through clenched teeth, "You just called me Cate."

"I... I did?" *Uh oh.*

"Yes." She yanked one boot on and grabbed the other, trying to balance and get that one on without sitting down.

He caught her wrist so she wouldn't fall. "I didn't mean for that to happen."

"I'm not going to wreck your life, too." She began angrily throwing everything she brought with her the night before into a pile.

"Whoa? Where did *that* come from?" He blocked her body from leaving the bedroom. "Stop. Let's talk about this. You have not wrecked my life. I'm right where I want to be, *Gwen*. With you."

"Oh yeah?" She spun on her heels and walked to his closet. From inside, she grabbed a golf club and jabbed at the hat box he'd tucked away. After two pokes it popped off the shelf, tumbled over and sent all its contents pouring down. "I don't want to be another woman you have to tuck away in a box."

Andrew's eyes blinked, looking at the mess.

But he said nothing. Shaking he bent down to pick up the pieces of his life she had just let spill onto the floor. The room began to spin. His ankles gave out and he sank slowly, his hand slapping the parquet floor. He wiped his mouth and caught Gwen staring at him. She was white.

"Oh my God. Andrew I'm so sorry. Please, let me clean this up." She grasped at his hands but he wrenched away from her.

Papers and photos crumpled in his shaking hands. But he threw them all down again. He stood and stomped out of the bedroom. In his living room, he tried to collect his frazzled thoughts, but she whirled in behind him.

"I'm so sorry. I don't know what I'm doing. I'm just confused. I saw pictures of the perfect life you had with Cate, and all I can think was..." She looked down. "I just don't understand."

"Don't understand what?" he asked through gritted teeth.

"Why you want to be with me." She sniffed. "It's why I didn't tell you about the baby right away. I knew you'd do the right thing. How will I ever know if you really want me? *Me?*"

"I'm trying to show you, but you're fighting me at every turn." He moved back toward the bedroom, but he stopped. His head dipped and with a hand on his mouth he turned back around. "Perfect, huh?"

"What?" she squeaked through tears.

"You thought my life with Cate was perfect."

Her breath escaped her. "What I meant was before. Before she got sick."

"And then she did. And the *perfect* life disappeared fast, Gwen."

"So why do you want to be with me?" she asked quietly.

"*Why?*" he looked around like she'd just accused of him something terrible.

"Yes, why? Why would you want a life with me when that terrible history could repeat itself?"

"Because I fucking *love* you!"

"Stop…" She slid to the floor and held her head. "Just stop saying that."

Andrew twisted his fingers in and out of fists. "I have to go to work. I have to make sure *neither* of us has to move to Italy." He'd been a few steps back toward the bedroom, when he turned back around and walked toward her.

She was frozen and silent.

He bent to press a soft kiss on her forehead and squeezed her hand. "I'll clean all that up when I get home. I *really* want you to be here when I get back."

Gwen stood and smoothed her dress. "I'm sorry. I have to leave." She didn't wait for an answer and fled out the door.

* * * *

The cold damp air outside made Andrew's lungs feel tight in his chest.

More snow, maybe. Hopefully another blizzard to ground all planes so no one could leave. As he made his way down the dank stairwell to the subway, his phone buzzed. He'd hoped it was Gwen. Had she even realized she left all her work stuff in the apartment? And where was she going?

But it wasn't a call. It was an email he'd been cc'd on. From Marcello. *To* Enrico. His year-end report. He'd sent it three days early. And without Andrew having one last look!

Jesus, no!

He climbed out of the stairwell and ran down the street for a taxi. He fumbled with his phone searching for a way to retract the message on behalf of Marcello. Even trying to sign in as him, using an old password he'd known about. It had been changed, though.

Damn it!

His hands were shaking. He had to get to the office right away and repair whatever damage that email may have already caused. But Gwen's ring was ready to be picked up. He had dropped off his grandmother's ring at Tiffany's the day before while running errands. He'd picked out a setting to complement the stone, and as a favor to his mother they'd set it right away. But Gwen's meltdown yesterday had prevented him from getting it. He certainly didn't want to force it on her.

Now, given all that's happened, he *had* to go get it. Tell her everything. That he'd been planning this all along. He wasn't asking her out of a sense of responsibility. He'd made these decisions weeks ago.

The baby was proof he'd made the right decision.

Standing in the street, Andrew was frozen. Go get the ring, find Gwen and propose. Or… go to the office and work some kind of miracle where Gwen doesn't have to move to Italy…then propose.

His body darted back and forth, deciding which was more important. If only he were two people. Wait, he already had another version of himself. He activated a call on his phone and murmured anxiously, "Pick up. Pick up."

"Yes, my handsome boy?"

An hour later, Andrew sat at his desk, staring at his monitor.

Every ding from incoming emails churned his gut. He'd been waiting for some kind of response from Enrico. The *no news is good news* proverb was bullshit at the moment. Besides, Andrew wouldn't be surprised if Enrico was putting Gwen's transfer to Milan in motion regardless. And the way she had looked at him that morning, he bet she'd go willingly. With his child! What she'd done that morning felt like small pruning knives hacked away chunks of his flesh.

He was ready to resign to keep her in New York. *There is no Goddamn way I'm letting her go.* He just didn't think he would have to quit *today*. Before he had a chance to propose. Who would want to marry someone who was unemployed? Hopefully his mother was on her way.

The body in his doorway broke him out of a trance.

"What do you want Salvatore, I'm busy."

The designer lunged over the desk and grabbed Andrew by the shirt collar.

* * * *

On the commuter train platform, Gwen held back tears.

Once she was in a seat, she could put her head down and cry. Not because this train would take almost two hours to get to Daring Cove, but if she continued to push Andrew away, eventually he would give into the slack and leave.

No, that's not what she wanted.

Dizziness had been coming and going, and the damn nausea that made her only able to take a few bites of every meal had been raging on.

She'd been on the train for almost twenty minutes before she tried to find a seat, preferring to stare into the darkness of the East River Tunnel to collect her thoughts.

Finally, the bright sunshine pierced through the door's window and she moved further inside the car. Warmth. Yes. She stepped toward the middle to be away from the door when it opened. This was a local train and there were plenty of stops. When she reached the center seats—a row of three that faced each other, she gasped. "Faith?"

The pretty redhead looked up. "Hello, Gwen."

She considered walking to the next row—heck the next car maybe, but that would be obvious. Not to mention rude. And that's not who Gwen was. She pulled her hair behind her ear and pointed. "Can I join you over here?"

"Of course." Faith tucked in her legs so Gwen could get to the window seat.

Maybe she could look out at all the snow the whole way home. "Thanks."

"No problem." Faith folded her hands and closed her eyes.

Snow it is. But she exhaled. "Did you have a nice Christmas?"

Faith opened her eyes and faced Gwen. "Sure. You?"

Best Christmas day ever. Worst day after Christmas ever. "Uh, huh." Gwen futzed with her phone. "Are you just getting off work?"

Faith blinked tired eyes. "Yeah. I work the overnight news shift."

Right. Word had made it back to Darling Cove that their own little Faith Copeland was a photo journalist turned executive producer, traveling all over the globe. She was beautiful enough to be in front of the camera, but her mind was razor sharp and she did CNN more justice producing news stories than reading cue cards. "So, work is good?"

"No. It's terrible. The world's a messed-up place Gwen." The way Faith looked down made Gwen think she wasn't just talking about the Middle East. Something else was going on with her.

"I get it. I do watch your network. And others."

"But it's easy to get lulled into a false sense that things are peachy, living in Darling Cove."

Amen Sister. "Um, are you living back in town…permanently?"

"Did Greg ask you to ask me that?"

There it was. At least they got through a few sentences until her brother entered the conversation. "No. He's not like that Faith."

Her head dropped and after a few moments, she exhaled. "I know, Gwen. I'm sorry." A few more seconds of silence stretched by before she spoke again. "And I only have myself to blame for what happened."

"What *did* happen Faith?" It flew from Gwen's lips so fast that she slapped her mouth. "Sorry. You don't have to answer that."

"It was bad enough Greg doesn't know why I really left. I can't tell you and leave you hanging with that information on your conscience."

"I understand. My brother *is* a cop with access to interrogation rooms and bright lights."

Faith released a soft laugh. "I'd almost forgotten your sense of humor."

"I'm here all week."

"Are you still with that lingerie designer?"

"No. I just started a new job a couple of months ago."

"Oh yeah? Where?"

"Prada." Damn, she liked saying that.

"That's amazing, Gwen. Good for you. Get your money's worth from that FIT education." Faith had changed the subject from Greg. But that was understandable.

"Thanks. It is kind of wonderful. I was just in Milan too." She squeezed her shoulders together. But the idea of Milan now made her queasy. There was no way she would take that job and try to raise a baby over there by herself. That meant Enrico would have to send Andrew. And what if he refused?

Gwen had put everyone's future in jeopardy.

"Gwen, are you okay?"

"I don't know."

Faith narrowed her eyes. "Man trouble? I heard you and Dan are getting a divorce."

"Yes. But I'm…seeing someone else."

"Been with him long?"

"No. That's part of the problem. Things sometimes just move so fast. First it's all great sex and then…"

Faith slammed her head back against the vinyl seat. "God. What I wouldn't give for great sex."

Now that Gwen's had a taste of how the other half lives, she'd never want to be sitting on a train not knowing when the next orgasm was coming. "I didn't mean to imply…"

Whatever had happened to make Faith run out on her wedding, it must have made sense to her, at the time. Or she felt she had no other options. She stared for a moment and looked down. "Don't make the same mistake I made, Gwen. Strong, deep emotions can cloud your judgment."

And *hormones*. Gwen dropped her head. This was stopping right now. These thoughts made no sense, yet they were driving her bad behavior. Her breathing became labored. She was about to make the biggest mistake of her life. She shot to her feet. "You're right. Happy New Year Faith!" Bending down, she kissed the girl she knew her brother was still in love with.

"You too, Gwen," Faith hollered, while she ran toward the doors.

The train lurched to a stop at a transfer station. She jumped out.

"Wait!" Gwen screamed to the conductor closing the doors to the Manhattan bound train across the platform.

CHAPTER THIRTY

"*You!*" Salvatore's garlic-laced spit flew in Andrew's face. "You had a hand in this, didn't you?"

"Hand in what?" Andrew briskly loosened himself from Salvatore's grip, sending the man stumbling back to the other side of the desk. "What the hell is wrong with you?"

"Don't play *sciocco* with me, Morgan."

"I'm not playing stupid. I have no idea what you're talking about."

The designer smoothed his dark blond hair in place. He caught a glimpse of himself in the reflective surface of one of Andrew's awards hanging on the wall. "I'm being transferred to Milan because of you."

"What?" Andrew shot to his feet.

Salvatore sent a derisive scowl up and down Andrew's height. "I'm not going to let some *ex-model* dictate my career." He said "ex-model" as if Andrew was a former prostitute.

Andrew held his tongue. So, Salvatore had known all along. *How* was the least important thing to him at the moment. Andrew rounded his desk. "I assure you, *I* had no idea you were being moved to Milan." As much as he despised the man at times, he wouldn't have let the top New York designer go willingly. Salvatore Corella was one of the keys to Prada-New York's *brand* success.

Salvatore puffed out his chest. "Enrico calls it a *favore*, of course. He needs a seasoned designer there to make Prada-Milan more productive. I have to clean up the mess *you* made with Marcello."

Andrew swallowed; he was losing control of his own office. Enrico was sending Salvatore to Milan to help *Gwen*. He began to shake. This wasn't happening. No. "Salvatore, you'll just have to live with Enrico's decision. I had no idea about any of this. I would love to stay and fight some more with you, but I need to speak to Enrico." Andrew was ready to quit. Right now.

His shoulder slammed into Salvatore as he stormed out of his office. The look that passed between them was pure rage and hate. Andrew needed to stop all this from happening. Now. Andrew's long legs were a few doors down from Enrico's office.

"Ei, stronzo!" Salvatore yelled. "I have one more thing to say to you."

Many heads in the office turned around; most of them knew *stronzo* meant 'asshole'.

Andrew spun around as well. The way Salvatore charged in his direction made Thalia look as nervous as a rodeo clown.

"What?" Andrew met Salvatore several feet away. "Don't do this in the office, Salvatore. This shit ends up on-line."

"Have it your way." Salvatore pulled him by the shirt collar into the copy room and closed the door.

Oh great!

Salvatore stepped right up to him, his chin raising to meet Andrew's eyes. In a low maniacal tone, he said, "I hope you and that little *cunt* will be very happy together."

The comment sent a shock through Andrew. He curled his fingers into a fist, and without thinking, executed a perfect jab into Salvatore's pudgy jaw. The designer flopped against the copier and hit the floor like a stone, blood and spit flying from his mouth.

Andrew shook his aching wrist, feeling nothing but panic. "Oh shit."

* * * *

Gwen feared Andrew really would quit to prevent her from having to go to Milan.

He may have said he wasn't looking for a princess, but she wanted to be the ultimate warrior princess — Wonder Woman — and save her man.

She was prepared to march into Enrico's office and turn the tables on them both by quitting first. Without Gwen to use as a pawn to move to Milan, Enrico would be forced to keep Marcello and let Andrew keep his job. His New York job. The job she knew he loved.

He'd been through so much. It was time Andrew got his life back.

Gwen just hoped he still wanted her to be a part of that life.

In Prada's lobby, Gwen approached the turnstiles with her access card in hand. At the guards' desk, she spotted a beautiful older woman bundled in an ivory wrap trimmed in brown leather looking quite annoyed while the guard made a call. Gwen's feet moved toward the woman as if she were being pulled by a magnet.

The woman turned in Gwen's direction and her carbon colored eyes lit up. "Gwendolyn?"

A bubbly feeling that had only happened whenever Andrew was near started again. Gwen absorbed the woman's features, particularly the nose and faint lines around the mouth. "Yes?"

She held out her hand. "I'm Sarah Morgan, Andrew's mother."

This was her baby's grandmother. The *only* grandmother the baby would have. Gwen choked up and thrust her hand out. "It's so nice to meet you."

"Oh, dear." Sarah's inky black bob, the same color as Andrew's dark hair swayed against her high cheekbones. "You look like you've seen a ghost."

"It's because you look…I mean Andrew looks so much like you." Except the height. His father must be tall.

"Gwen dear, this is my husband William, Andrew's dad."

The man stepped around a pillar putting a phone into his pocket. Jesus! Clearly, crippling good looks must be a dominant gene in the Morgan family. Gwen nervously tucked a hair behind her ear. "Hello Mr. Morgan."

"Call me Will." His handshake was firm and warm. "It's good to meet you."

Andrew's parents awkwardly stared at her for several seconds. How much did they know? They looked too chipper to know about her health scare and not ecstatic enough to know about the baby. Sarah looked at her watch and asked, "Working today, dear?"

"Yes. Does Andrew know you're here?"

"This new guard has been trying to reach him." Sarah folded her hands. "Don't let us keep you."

Gwen opened her mouth to ask if they wanted to come up with her, except her cell phone rang. "Excuse me."

She looked at the screen and her heart fluttered. *Dr. Jesse.* The flashing contact was calling with her fate. So soon. That can't be good. But she couldn't bear to have bad news sitting in her voicemail, there to listen to again and again. She tapped the green phone icon. "Hello?"

"Ms. Foley? This is Sylvie from Dr. Jesse's office."

Gwen clutched the edge of the guards' desk. It was Sylvie! "Yes?" Her heart was pounding in her ear. She missed most of the message, other than the lump was benign. She was fine. There was something about another surgery to clear out margins of the same tissue, but that could wait. "Thank you. Um, yes, okay. I'll call to make a follow up appointment in the New Year to discuss next steps."

"Dear, is everything all right?" Sarah was standing behind her, her hand on Gwen's shoulder.

"Yes. As a matter of fact." She dropped the phone back in her pocket and sniffed. "I'm great. And I want you to know…I am so in love with your son."

Sarah smiled, holding her heart. Will came up abreast of his wife, looking curious.

Gwen sniffed and approached him. "Mr. Morgan, you and Mrs. Morgan have raised such a wonderful man. I just hope that I…" She broke down and couldn't continue.

"Oh dear!" Sarah moved toward her and held her.

A *mother's* arms around Gwen shot a sensation through her she'd not felt in almost seventeen years. Not just warmth or love or safety. There had been plenty of that from her father and even Greg. But a mother's hold was different. A mother/daughter bond was…sacred. Gwen gently squirmed out of the embrace, but only because she was shaking. "Thank you."

"Excuse us for a minute, dear." Sarah touched her arm once more and then nudged Will away a few feet.

But Gwen was too anxious to wait anymore. She had to get to the office to be with Andrew. It was causing physical pain at this point to be away from him. She didn't want to be rude, but hopefully running off to be with their son, would be a good excuse to ditch them. She stepped toward them. "I *do* need to get upstairs to see Andrew. We have so many things we need to talk about it."

Sarah whispered into Will's ear one final time. He pursed his lips looking at his wife but nodded. "You should take this with you then." From her Prada purse, Sarah removed a box.

It was a perfect square. Light teal blue and was tied with a creamy white satin ribbon. Tiffany's.

Gwen stumbled back. "Wha—what's that?"

"Isn't it obvious?" Will looked like he had tears in his eyes.

"But how...when?"

"We're already ruining the surprise Andrew's had for you since Christmas Eve. And he'll probably kill us for this."

"Kill *you*." Will nudged his wife. "This was your idea."

"Christmas Eve?" Gwen took the box in her hand. "He wanted to give this to me on Christmas Eve?"

"It was still in its original setting," Sarah said, nodding, and she touched Gwen's cheek. "The stone was my mother's. It'd been in a Wall Street safe deposit box for *years*." Her emphasis on the time frame made Gwen step back. This ring would be hers and only hers. "My son didn't have to ask me twice if he could give it you. He went to Tiffany's yesterday morning and picked out a beautiful new setting. This ring is now yours, Gwendolyn."

"So...how do you have it?"

"They set it quickly as a favor to me, so he could pick it up the same day. But he never made it there for some reason and this morning he had some kind of emergency. He called me and asked me to pick it up for him and bring it here."

"This was at Tiffany's yesterday. Ready to be picked up." Gwen's voice was flat, unbelieving almost. That's why he wanted to stop there after the biopsy. That morning he had asked her to trust him and that she would know everything. She just never expected...something like this.

Sarah stepped closer, nodding, and closed Gwen's hand around the box. "Now go find my son already, and let him give this to you properly for Pete's sake."

Gwen hurled herself between Andrew's parents and hugged them both. "Thank you. Thank you."

Andrew had intended to propose all along! Before the baby. Before the biopsy. He wanted her, for her.

Just for *her*.

* * * *

"Andrew, Enrico wants to see you," Thalia said, standing by his office door.

"Okay, thanks." With a heavy groan, Andrew stood. "Does he know about Salvatore?"

"*Sì*. I'm jealous. I've wanted to hit that *stronzo* for years. You beat me to it."

Andrew needed a touch of humor at the moment, considering in the next few minutes his entire world was going to be blown apart. Marcello was going to be fired. Gwen was being transferred. And Andrew just laid out his head designer. He wondered if Enrico had ordered in lunch; this was probably going to take all day.

It took a lot of will power to not cast one more warning look in the direction of Salvatore. He was now in a chair with what looked like a harem of women tending to him.

Andrew stepped to his boss's office door and gently knocked.

"Ah, *suono*." Enrico was flipping over papers and removed his glasses. "Come in."

He walked right up to the desk with a hand on his heart and apologized in Italian out of respect. "Enrico, *Mi dispiace tanto per quello che è successo a Salvatore. Farò tutto ciò che è necessario dal punto di vista aziendale per far fronte a questo.*"

"For a scuffle?" Enrico waved his hand. "Salvatore is very passionate and he gets under my skin too. No need to apologize to him or file any report. And if *he* does, I will take care of it."

Andrew caught his breath. "Why didn't you tell me he was being moved to Milan?"

"I had planned to discuss it with you today." Enrico pressed his lips together. "He found out on his own. He has little spies all over the world. I'm sorry you had to find out this way."

Andrew's heartbeat was still wild in his chest. "*Va bene.*"

"*Siedeti, siedeti.*" Enrico pointed to his guest chair. "And how was Christmas with your family?"

His *family...*

Before Gwen, if asked that, Andrew would immediately think of his mother and father. Now his *famiglia* was Gwen and the baby. He now had a family of his own. But was everything all right? Andrew had no idea, but he nodded anyway.

"*Quello è buono.* And have you seen this?" Enrico pointed to Marcello's annual report on his desk.

"*Sì.*" He just couldn't stomach to read it.

"Andrew, I need you to be honest with me." The way Enrico put his glasses down made his reaction hard to read.

"Of course."

"Did you write this for Marcello?"

His eyes widened. "No. Not at all. I gave him the report I did last year to use as a guide."

His boss nodded and flipped over a few more sheets.

Before Enrico spoke again, Andrew leaned forward. "I think I've gotten through to him. I've been monitoring his performance almost daily. I think he's coming along. That report is hard to write." Andrew pinched the cover. "I can send it back to him to—"

"There is no need." Enrico closed the report and tapped the top sheet with the stem of his dark rimmed glasses. "*Suono,* I am disappointed in you."

Andrew hung is head low. He'd failed. Licking dry lips, he said, "Enrico...I think it's best if I—"

"I am troubled that you do not take enough credit for yourself."

"What's that?"

"Andrew, this report is *stellar!*" Enrico opened it again.

"Huh?"

"It is organized with a table of contents. And look at this." Enrico slid his glasses back on and pointed to his monitor. "The sections jump right to the page. He even embedded moving graphics!"

Okay, so he prettied it up. "But what do you think of his projections?"

Enrico took off his glasses and put them on his desk. "Don't worry about that. Marcello will be fine. And with Salvatore making beautiful clothes, the brand will market itself."

Andrew felt the world spin beneath him. It was done. He did it. Well *Gwen* did it really. "Gwen..." he grumbled under his breath.

"Oh yes, Gwendolyn." Enrico pursed his lips. "Do you think she will be disappointed not to move to Milan?"

Andrew stood and closed the office door. "Enrico, I have a lot to tell you."

CHAPTER THIRTY-ONE

Andrew Morgan tapped the toe of his left shoe...discretely, since it was not Prada.

Their shoes never fit his size thirteen feet very well.

Enrico Petrillo blinked his dark Italian eyes. He took a deep breath and said, "*Suono,* you are going to be a father. That is the best news a man can get. And with such a beautiful woman. *Amore* is a wonderful thing to have in this life. We specialize in love you know. Why else would we design such things of beauty? We want people to fall in love. *Vai.* Go. Go find your love, your *amore* and make things right."

"I don't know. She's pretty upset with me right now."

"It is just the hormones." He waved a lazy hand. "I could swear my wife wanted to poison me every time she was pregnant."

"That's amusing."

"Kiss Gwendolyn and make up." Enrico handed a manila folder to him. "These are the details of a last-minute showcase I need you *and* your *amore* to work on."

"Where will it be?"

Enrico smiled. "Where do you think? Marcello will never be as good as you and Gwendolyn *together.*"

Andrew propelled out of the seat and flew down the corridor. He barreled through the office without regard if he ran someone over. There was so much to do, including telling the neighbor in Milan who was taking care of Casper, that he'd be back in a few weeks. The cat was coming back to New York after that.

Inside his office, lost in his excited thoughts he tripped over his feet. "*Gwen!*"

She spun around and...smiled.

Next to her was a woman with warm dark eyes. Just like his own. "Ma?"

* * * *

Gwen stood shoulder to shoulder with Andrew's mother. This was going to be fun.

It was amusing to see Andrew look like he fell down a rabbit hole. He raised his hand to scratch his head, exposing a pair of bruised knuckles.

"What happened to your hand?" She rushed to look at his fingers.

"I'll tell you later." He closed his hand around hers. "Ma."

"Hello, dear." Sarah moved in his direction and kissed him on the cheek. She looked at his hand as well, but with it firmly in Gwen's comforting grasp, she nodded. Pleased.

"When did you get here?" Andrew asked his mother.

"Your father and I have been downstairs for thirty minutes. No one has been able to get a hold of you. He had to get back to the firm."

"I had an emergency meeting." Andrew raised his eyes to Gwen.

Sarah clasped her hands together. "It was a good thing we ran into Gwen in the lobby."

Still looking at her, he asked, "And what are you doing here?"

"I work here...don't I?"

Andrew nodded gently and touched her face. "How do you feel?"

Sarah moved closer. "Is something wrong?"

"No." Gwen bore into Andrew's eyes, hoping her answer cast a wide net that would let him know everything was almost *perfect*.

He squeezed her hand, completely befuddled looking. But Andrew leaned forward to discretely whisper something to his mother. He was probably trying to signal for the ring.

Gwen coughed. "I could use some water, though."

"Right." Andrew pointed. "I'll get it for you. Ma, why don't you come with me?"

A look passed between her and Sarah. "You need my help to get water?"

Andrew grunted.

Sarah waved her hands. "Tell you what…I'll get the water for her."

Andrew reached out to her wrap, hoping to stop her. But she was gone. "Let me make sure she doesn't get lost."

"Andrew, wait." Gwen moved like lightning to get into his arms.

It took a second before he responded to her, surprised by her need for him after what had happened a few hours earlier. He pulled her in and leaned his forehead against hers. "I am so sorry about this morning."

"No, Andrew. I'm sorry. For everything. I was out of line. But listen, it was a false alarm," she whispered through a jaw jammed up against his shoulder. "I'm fine. The lump is benign."

Andrew's grip on hers had bruising strength. "I knew it. I knew it would be okay."

"You were right. But it made me realize a lot of things. Life is short." She straightened her back. "I'm resigning today. I refuse to leave you to go work in Italy."

Andrew didn't say anything and looked as if he was stunned at her sacrifice. He smashed his body against hers.

The cottony scent of his shirt was the smell she missed most.

"Turns out Marcello isn't getting fired," he said. "I'm keeping my job here in New York. And you are not quitting. I need you. *Here* in New York with me." Without even looking to see if anyone was watching, he kissed her passionately. His mouth was warm and sensual.

A crushing weight dissolved away with his startling news. They would no longer be two people who rested their heads on pillows many miles and an ocean apart. And she could have a life where she worked with Andrew all day and made passionate love to him all night. *Every night,* would hopefully replace his *daily* routine.

The day had been a whirlwind. Gwen didn't even know what time it was. And now, with Andrew's lips on hers, days could slip by as well.

But they were in the office, so he stopped, but held on to her hands. "Oh, before I screw this up any further, what are you doing for New Year's Eve?"

She sneaked a look at his groin and smiled. "It's not like I can have any champagne."

"Oh right." He held her away and looked at her, his eyes moving protectively over her.

She touched his face, his eyelids. "After seeing your mother, I bet the baby will probably have those dark rich eyes."

"*Baby?*" Sarah cried out from the door way with a cup of water. It nearly spilled out of her hands as she pulled Andrew and Gwen into a three-way bear hug.

Gwen sank into the embrace, trying to figure out who was hugging who harder. It was a three-way tie. Sarah dabbed under her eyes when she stepped back, letting her and Andrew stay connected.

"Ma, can I take Gwen home now?"

"Mm-m," she answered warmly.

He cleared his throat. "Do you have that...*thing* for me?"

"What thing, dear?" She secured the strap of her purse against her shoulder.

"Huh? Ma, wait!"

"Call your father later, dear. I don't know how long I can keep this great news to myself." Sarah gave Gwen one final hug and kiss. After a wink, she left the office.

Without her there, it was quiet.

Andrew grunted. But his shoulders were broad. They stood in front of his desk, his hand in hers, much like the moment they met. He nodded, realizing it too. "I really want you to go back to the apartment. I want you to rest. I'll meet you there in a little while. I have something I need...to take care of."

Figuring out where the heck the ring was, she bet. "You know, let's just leave right from here and go out to my house. Tomorrow's Friday. We can start the weekend early."

"Anything you want, Gwen. From now on, we sleep where you want to sleep. But I have to stop someplace first."

"Why?" She stepped closer and whispered, "It's not like we need condoms anymore."

He choked and turned red. "True. But I need clothes. I can't wear this suit the rest of the week."

"So, I'm the only one who can walk around the office with the same clothes, hair messed up?" She ran her hand across his forehead.

He pressed his thick eye brows together. "Now that you're going to be the mother of my child, I'll have to rethink all of that. But seriously, I have to get my car anyway."

"I don't know." She tapped her chin. "Traffic at this time is brutal. Besides, the trains are empty."

"Gwen!" He held her shoulders and talked close to her face, as if he was spelling something out for an unwilling child. "I. Have. To. Pick. Something. Up. For *you*."

"Do you mean this?" From her pocket, she pulled out the blue box.

His head fell into her shoulder. "Ma!"

"Don't be mad at her."

"Did you open it?"

"Of course not."

"Were you surprised?"

"Everything about you has surprised me."

He sucked in a breath. "You have to let me do this right, this time. Gwendolyn Mallory, I—"

"Wait!" She placed her hands against the lush surface of his lips. "Andrew Morgan, I love you. You have changed my life and made it better. The moment you looked at me, I felt this pull. I didn't realize it at the time. But I know now it was my soul connecting to yours. It's not just your child inside me. *You* are inside me. Coursing through my veins. It draws me to you. I belong to you. I belong with you. I'm a better person because of you. And I want to spend the rest of my life with you."

Andrew stood, a slight tremor to his body, like he'd not been expecting such a declaration. "I...I can't say exactly when I realized I loved you. It didn't hit me like a thunderbolt. It was more of a wave building. The kind that starts far out from the shore, and builds slowly, and steadily."

Gwen smiled. "The kind that when it hits the beach, it knocks you over?"

"You have definitely knocked me over, Gwen." He took her in his arms and kissed her against the back of his office door. "Gwendolyn Mallory, I love you. I'm *crazy* in love with you. You've turned my world upside down from the moment I saw you." He lowered to one knee. It made sense to ask her right there. Where it all began. "Every breath I have taken since then has either been filled with your scent in my lungs or my longing for it to be there." He pulled her hands to his lips. "Let me into your life and let me light it up the way you have brightened mine. You've lead me out of the darkness, and I promise to be here for you. Forever."

There were warm tears rolling down her cheeks by the time he got to the question. "Gwendolyn Mallory, will you marry me?"

She straddled his bent knee so their lips were even. "Yes. Yes. Yes."

"Why three yeses?" He moved a bundle of hair away from her face.

"Just putting some answers in the bank for other questions you may have for me...later," she whispered in his ear.

"Okay, then." Andrew lifted her up so he could stand. "Can I have your ring please?"

She smiled and handed him the blue box.

He closed it in his fingers briefly. "This stone has been in my family a long time and...what?"

"Your mother kind of told me where it came from."

"Of course she did." But he smiled. "What's most important is that now, it's yours Gwen." He placed it back into her hand.

With shaking hands, she began unravelling everything, past each layer, the ribbon, the box, and inside...a red velvet cube.

"Open it," Andrew whispered, moving his body closer.

There was a gentle popping sound when the top flipped open. But for a moment she wasn't sure what she was looking at. "It's...a sapphire?"

"No. It's a diamond. A blue diamond. They're very rare. But the color...it matches your eyes." Andrew put the box in the center of his one hand and slid the ring out from the indentation.

Deborah Garland

"The shape is called a rose cut. Since the day I met you I couldn't get the smell of roses out of my system."

She held up his grandmother's stone set into a cluster of twelve smaller diamonds, creating a petal effect. "Andrew, this is overwhelming."

Sliding it on her finger, he said, "Appropriate, since you've completely overwhelmed me, Gwen."

With their fingers in a tangle, she noticed the bruises again. "What did happen to your hand?"

"I kind of punched Salvatore in the mouth."

Slapping his chest, she cried out, "And I missed that!"

He chuckled. "Trust me. It was intense. I'm glad you weren't here. I wouldn't have wanted you to see me act like that."

"What, all manly and protective?"

"Sounds like you're going someplace with that?"

"You've been acting that way since I met you. I'm surprised you haven't hit anyone sooner."

"Apparently, I've got a lot to lose now. I'll be keeping my hands to myself." He touched her stomach. "Not from you of course."

Gwen took a deep breath and clutched onto him.

"So, the riddle is supposed to go: Gwen and Andrew sitting in a tree. K-I-S-S-I-N-G. First comes love, then comes marriage, then comes—"

"Yeah, we got this a little out of order."

ONE MONTH LATER...

Gwen opened her eyes, and needed a minute to process where she was.

The feeling of cotton mouth and the searing pain under the flimsy gown reminded her she was in the hospital's ambulatory recovery room. The same place where she'd had mammograms since she turned twenty-five, many stereotactic biopsies she'd lost count of, and now her second surgery to remove questionable breast tissue.

"Oh, hello." A nurse was taking her vitals. "How do you feel?"

"Thirsty," Gwen answered, knowing they wouldn't give her anything to drink.

The nurse lowered her chin. "We'll get you some breakfast and something to drink in a little bit, okay honey?"

Gwen nodded and closed her eyes. She didn't want food. In fact, she knew she was going to eventually be sick.

"Oh and your husband is here." The nurse typed into a mobile records cart. "I'll send him in. You're a lucky girl."

"Okay," Gwen said, still foggy. "What? Um...no. My sister is picking me up."

"I think she's here too."

"No...wait," she said softly, but the nurse was gone. *Skye!* Why would she call Dan of all people? "And why am I lucky?"

"You're lucky, because the surgery went great." Skye streamed in with her dad behind her. He wasn't in uniform for a change. "Dr. Jesse came out and said the lump was definitely benign and she removed it cleanly. You'll have a smaller scar than she thought.

Lucky me.

"Hello, pumpkin." Martin pressed a kiss on her forehead and looked at Skye. "She's a little warm."

"That's just her body burning any infections off."

"Where..." Gwen was still in a post-anesthesia haze. She tried to sit up, but a shooting pain, made her think otherwise. "Who..."

"Why is she so confused?" Martin asked.

Skye touched her face. "Gwen what's wrong?"

"The nurse said my husband is here."

"He is. He's just getting your prescriptions all settled with the nurse."

"Why would...*Dan* be doing that?"

Martin and Skye sneaked a look at each other. "Gwen. You're not married to Dan anymore."

"Then who the hell *am* I married to?"

"I know our wedding was simple, Gwen." Andrew stepped into the room. "But I hoped you would at least remember *I* was there."

"Simple for now." Sarah strode in behind him. "We'll do something bigger soon."

It all flooded back to Gwen in a rush that made her start to cry.

"Why is she crying?" Greg asked squeezing into the space. "Andrew, what did you do to her?"

"Greg, stop it, already." Skye snapped at him.

"Honey, what's wrong?" Andrew was there, his body blocking everyone out.

"I just got so confused. I forgot where I was. And...when it is."

"It's just the anesthesia wearing off." He secured the paper hat on her head. "Do you really not remember our wedding?"

It was there in her memory. Certainly, the best day of her life. Only drugs could make her forget. It was very simple, but oh, so elegant. She wore a white organza empire dress, made for her by one of the Milan designers when they were there for the showcase last month. They brought the dress *and* Casper home.

He turned out to be the most expensive free cat in history, considering what it cost to bring him to the United States. But he was loving his new home in Darling Cove. At night, the cat curled between her and Andrew, purring against Gwen's stomach. And she often caught him sitting in front of the nursery, all handsome and formidable like one of the lions at the New York City Public Library.

When she and Andrew slept in the city, Skye and Casey would stay in her house to keep Casper company. The videos were hilarious.

Skye also convinced a judge to not only move Gwen's divorce papers to the top of the list to be signed, but to also perform the intimate marriage ceremony.

They exchanged vows behind her house, overlooking the Great Peconic Bay. Next to her beautiful engagement ring, Andrew slid a simple platinum band. His grandmother's diamond was more important to her. Looking at her bare fingers now, she asked, "Where are my wedding rings?"

"You don't trust me that we were actually married?" He flashed his band, a two-tone platinum and copper band. He kissed her on the nose. "Your rings are at home. Safe."

She reached up to touch his face but whimpered slightly from the pain. There was a stormy tension in his eyes. His anger engines were fired up whenever she was in any kind of discomfort. His hand closed around hers and he looked out at the room. Their families. All together. His dad and hers, talking. Will was helping with Martin's case. Sarah and Skye were chatting, politely. Even though those two were in a death battle to see who was going to spoil the baby more.

Greg sat in the corner by himself, looking out the window. With all the love around him, he'd find his way. Hopefully soon.

Dr. Jesse appeared and the room fell into a hush.

Martin began moving people out. "Come on, let's give them some privacy."

One by one, everyone slipped out. But Sarah stood next to the bed, opposite her son. It was clear, she wasn't going to be an ordinary mother-in-law, the kind that would take any kind of backseat, or be the first to leave the room. "Can I get you anything, dear?" She brushed her fingers against Gwen's cheek.

"No, Mom. I'm fine for now."

Sarah's face always lit up, ever since Gwen had starting calling her that. After the wedding, the original Mrs. Morgan had taken her aside and said, "You're my daughter now. It would be an honor if you called me Mom."

The invitation had come as a surprise, leaving Gwen weepy. "Okay. I'll give it a try, *Mom*," she had said with a baritone melody of the song: *You're a mean one, Mr. Grinch*.

Sarah had released a howl of laughter. "You'll have to practice. And I cannot wait to hear you call me Grandma, little one," she had said to Gwen's belly.

Andrew squeezed her hand, his emotion so evident. He'd given Gwen something he couldn't have realized would be so important...a mother. *His* mother. "Thanks Ma."

Sarah left the room, winking at her son, and the surgeon moved to take her place next to the bed.

"How do you feel?" Dr. Jesse asked pressing a stethoscope on Gwen's chest.

"Thirsty."

"Can we get her something, please?" Andrew asked.

"I'll have the nurse send in some ice chips." She put the device around her neck, and said, "I want to see if there's any more bleeding." She gently pulled the sides of the gown open.

Gwen caught her hand and looked at Andrew, who seemed tense. "You don't have to watch this."

"Of course I do."

"No, you really don't. Trust me, when this baby gets ripped out of me that will be traumatic enough."

He touched her face and moved to the other side of the bed, looking out the window with his arms crossed. His tall body cast a long shadow on the floor.

Her skin cooled from being exposed. It was tender under Dr. Jesse's touch. "Looks good. Just what I'd hoped."

Gwen tugged the gown closed.

"I'll have your discharge papers ready in about an hour." She tapped Gwen's shoulder and moved toward the door.

"Thank you, Dr. Jesse," Andrew said and turned back around, his face even.

"I didn't mean to imply you couldn't handle that, Andrew. It's bad enough I have to sit here with no makeup on, wearing this stupid hat..." Gwen pulled on it. "Meanwhile, you look all GQ as always."

"Honey, stop. You have to keep the hat on. If I write Prada on it with a Sharpie, will that make you feel better?"

"Ha ha." Her fingers kept the collar of her gown tightly closed but his fingers were sliding inside.

"Please let me look." Andrew's hands gently pried hers apart. "I want to see it."

She exhaled and released the corners. Having gone through this before, she knew he was looking at blood stained stitches, swollen tissue and the beginnings of yellow and purple blotches.

"Does it hurt?" he asked with a catch in his throat.

"A little." At the mention of pain, Andrew's body stiffened and his face hardened. But not from fear. From protective-based anger.

His hand hovered over her sensitive skin. "Is this what your other scar had looked like?"

"Yes." She looked down at his strong hands aching to touch her, like he wanted to make it better if he could. "I guess."

Andrew smiled, closing the gown. Over the fabric, he touched her lightly and said, "Now we know how this one will heal."

They were both healed. And now, Gwen really did have it all. "You know I plan to work even after the baby is born."

"I have no intention of keeping you barefoot and pregnant, Gwen."

"Barefoot no. But pregnant..." Her eyes fluttered. "The way you and I *go at it*, I have a feeling this isn't going to be our only kid."

And the way she'd been enjoying sex while pregnant, she didn't see a downside in getting knocked-up again soon after this baby was born.

"Tell me the truth, Andrew. Are you upset we're not having a boy?" They'd learned it was a girl at her last doctor's appointment, where they watched in amazement the little opaque image floating against the dark charcoal background.

"I know I said I'd been picturing a boy before we found out." He'd made a heart filled confession, saying he'd heard having a son was like getting to live his life over again. She'd give him a boy if she could. Give him anything he wanted. "Now, I can't wait to watch our little girl blossom into someone smart and beautiful like you. How can I possibly, ever, thank you for that gift?"

"I can show you when we get out of here." She responded with a kiss that was way too heated for their situation. She'd already been ravenous for sex, thinking it was her surging hormones. But another chemical reaction coursed through her body — the attraction to a man who was so masculine he had the power to alter her own body.

Yep, there will be another kid.

THE END

ACKNOWLEDGEMENTS:

No author can write a manuscript without sharing it with someone before submitting it. There are always people in our corner who take the time to read our stories and go further to make comments, trying to help.

I first want to thank author, Jessica Verdi, who helped me when all I had was a proposed synopsis of Must Love Fashion. Her comments were invaluable in shaping the story. Through RWA (Romance Writers of America) I found an amazing critique partner, author Alana Lindsay, who provided page by page notes to bring this novel to life. Thank you also to author Patty Blount, who read MLF's predecessor and provided great feedback that I was able to use in this novel.

And to all my beta readers, Lisa S, Debra L, Dawn G, Nancy P, Janine R, Dennis B, Uncle Jack and of course… Mom.

Finally, I have to give a special thank you to my husband who allowed me to leave my full-time job to pursue this dream.

*Update - An additional thank you to Sal Puglia for his spirited input and more accurate Italian translations.

ABOUT THE AUTHOR:

Deborah Garland is a former computer and sports journalist, turned romance and women's fiction author. She likes to write about love and the struggles of complicated relationships. Her heroines are strong, and the heroes fall hard for them. She lives on the North Shore of Long Island with her husband and when she's not writing, she's either in the gym, or reading, cuddled up with their two pugs, Zoe and Harley.

www.DeborahGarlandAuthor.com

MUST HAVE FAITH
DARLING COVE BOOK 2
COMING JUNE 2018

CPSIA information can be obtained
at www.ICGtesting.com
Printed in the USA
LVOW13s2128200218
567275LV00013B/844/P